2

ISBN: 978-0-9561591-0-6

3

FORKS OF THE OHIO

BY MARTIN CLAYTON

Cruedo Books

Holmfirth

ONE

"That'll be five dollars."

No 'please' then?

I handed the money over to her, and almost got a smile in response.

Almost.

What is it about stewardesses on US owned airlines?

Some old housewife must have won a law suit against a big company which dictated that, from that moment on, airlines could not hire young, smiley, happy, friendly – you get the picture… If you've ever flown on one of these airlines you will know exactly what I'm talking about.

And when exactly did they start charging for alcohol? And five dollars? For a screwdriver! They must be raking it in. They certainly don't charge those fees to discourage drinking on airplanes - that was the seventh that I'd ordered and we still had 3, or 4 hours to go.

Wait… this could be a problem! I was planning to rent a car in Philly.

Shit!

I forgot that minor technicality.

Oh well, I didn't NEED to rent a car. As a matter of fact I didn't need to do anything anymore. I was practically in charge of my own destiny. Unless you wanted to debate structure versus agency, but that could get a little long winded.

So … for the record, and to aid your understanding of this drivel, my name is Michael Huntingden. At 35 years of age I'd had enough of the boredom and rigidity of everyday life and sacked it. I'd packed in my job of 12 years, which paid very nicely thank you. I'd left my girlfriend of 5 years, who obviously thought I'd gone insane. And all my family and friends, who were also mystified, were currently waiting for the other shoe to drop. I was currently on a plane to Philadelphia.

That's the abridged version. I'll probably go into things a bit deeper when required, but maybe not.

I know most people in mid life crises head to India or South America. Some sleep with one of their daughter's college friends… but I don't have a daughter so that's out. I don't have any children actually – which is going into things that I promised not to. And I didn't want to go to India or South America because frankly I'm a bit of a wuss, and I like the convenience of the US, and more importantly, the standard of hotel bathrooms, compared to the horror stories that you hear about the other alternatives.

I know that the US only allows travellers 90 days, and I don't really know what I'll do when that's up, but I am not concerned with that just yet. My girlfriend – or is it ex-girlfriend? I'm not really sure yet – kept on telling me that I was just going on a long holiday and I should stop being selfish, and stupid. A couple of my friends did mention that she had a point and that I wasn't exactly going to discover myself or reach enlightenment in Orlando or Palm Springs… which obviously shows just how much they understood. They all came across as being a bit smug and condescending for my liking and to be honest that's probably why I was on my 7th screwdriver… to drown them all out. I knew that they'd all be ringing each other now saying things like, "Don't worry, he'll be back soon," or "wait till his savings are gone then we'll see."

I'm sure that you can understand how desperate I was to prove them all wrong.

Another problem was that I didn't really know what I WAS searching for. I just knew I didn't have it and wasn't likely to find it in customer service, or spending two hours driving to work and back every day. The other things in my life, my family, friends, and my girlfriend were all very supportive and essential to my day to day existence but… just not enough… do you know what I mean?

I hope so.

The food cart was on the way now, with the second meal – if you can honestly call it that – the second offering is probably more descriptive.

We'd already been served a choice between chicken, and beef. I'd plumped for the chicken, and been given what I can only describe as elastic band-like noodles with a little of what was presumably – hopefully – chicken and some sauce with a vague taste of hoi sin. It was vile! Of course I also got the obligatory 'salad package' which looked 3 days old and came with a dressing guaranteed to mask the taste. Oh, and a dessert that you would have turned your nose up at in school.

So the upcoming meal was presumably the 'snack' that we were promised. I was thinking of waiting till we arrived and just ordering more alcohol in the meantime. I'd been through Philly a few times and now that I was obviously going to be looking to transit to somewhere I would have access to the food market in the airport, which was actually very good.

"I hope this one's better than the last one," said the girl in the aisle opposite.

I wasn't sure if she was talking to me at first and whilst I pondered this she continued.

"Are you planning on drinking all the vodka they have on board?"

I turned to look at her and realised that I hadn't noticed her up until this point. Clearly I'd been completely lost in my own little world for the past four hours.

I'd nodded a polite hello to the guy who was in the window seat next to me when I'd got on board, but thankfully he'd been asleep since we set off, thus avoiding the embarrassment of trying to avoid speaking to someone that you really don't want to speak to. I mean, he could be a nice guy and all, but he was wearing a shirt and tie in economy on a transatlantic flight. That, to me, signifies someone who may be a little bit tightly wrapped and God knows I was trying to escape all of that.

My over the aisle female travelling companion, in contrast, was wearing some dark grey cargo pants with Skechers and a loose fitting black sweater, which would suggest a certain amount of relaxation. I realised I'd probably better reply before she pushed the stewardess button and asked to be moved.

"Why, should I save you some?"

Looking back I'd say that was a fairly decent response and it did bring forth a smile. She was actually quite pretty – not a stunner, kind of approachable and interesting looking. Long blondish hair in a bit of an unkempt ringlet sort of way. Blue, maybe green eyes.

"Well I should probably get into the spirit of things, so why not."

She was obviously from the States and I was frantically trying to place the accent from my half decent US accent log – if such a thing exists? In my experience it's a very dangerous thing to try and guess where someone is from within the US from a couple of sentences. It's a very big mass of land and lots of accents really do sound similar. It's not like the UK with the vast differences within a sixty mile radius, from say, Barnsley through Manchester to Liverpool. Indianapolis sounds quite similar to Chicago, Milwaukee and St.Louis if you ask me. You could strike out and find out that the person is from Canada and that really would end the conversation. Still I didn't gamble with money so I thought it was worth the excitement.

"Cleveland?" I ventured.

"Actually that's very close," she replied, expressing quite obvious astonishment, "I'm from Akron."

"Rubber town!"

I was on a roll here.

"Yep, that's right, do you know Akron?"

"Not really. I drove through there once".

Her look turned to confusion. "You drove through? From where, to where?"

Oh boy, it was too late to turn back. She'd either think I was extremely sad, or quite cool. "From Pittsburgh, to Canton."

"Canton? Why would you be in Canton?"

Here it came…

"The Pro Football Hall of Fame."

Silence.

Blank look.

Then maybe, was it intrigue?

"But you're English… why would you go there?"

It looked like I had the chance to turn this around. "I love American Football, always have."

She smiled, a nice friendly, hey how ya doin' smile.

Yey… I wasn't a total dork!

"I'm Carrie-Ann Novitski," she said, holding out her hand. I took it and shook it twice, then let go.

"And I'm Mike, or Michael. Whichever."

"Can I buy you a screwdriver, Mike?"

Now this WAS promising.

"That would be lovely, thanks."

Lovely indeed. Particularly since I was worried about having to ask for another drink. So far I'd had no problems but then I'd only gone off-piste once, so to speak, pushing the attendant button. The rest of the purchases had been purely from the trolley during normal service. I'd just been asking for two drinks instead of one. For all they knew the other drink could have been for Geoff or whatever his name was, in the seat next to me.

It's a difficult thing to do when you're English. I may have paid three hundred and fifty quid for this seat but I still didn't want to trouble somebody into actually doing their job. You can push it too far you know. They weren't exactly friendly to begin with. I didn't want to make an enemy of one of them. I guess it's because they don't get tips. Thinking about it, it must be the only occupation in the US service industry where the employee doesn't get tips for serving food and drinks to the public. Boy that must really suck. I'm not surprised they weren't smiling.

I was about to share this revelation with Carrie-Ann when I realised that I was seven screwdrivers ahead of her and I'd best just listen for a while, agreeing and adding to the conversation only when I'd made a proper analysis of the situation.

The cart was here now and I made a quick judgement to accept the 'snack'. This was also because I was English, and hadn't got it in me to refuse something that this woman obviously thought I should have. Also I realised that I should probably soak up a little vodka. At least so I was capable of chatting.

Carrie-Ann, because she wasn't brought up with the same values of simply accepting things because they were offered, refused her snack, and asked for two screwdrivers. I was looking away at the time but I could be certain that the stewardess looked in my direction before answering, "You'll have to wait until we've finished with the food service, Miss."

"That's fine," sang Carrie-Ann.

She really did sing it – trust me.

Now I realise that with my newfound spirit of abandoning life as we know it and casting off shackles, I should have refused the snack. I didn't want it after all. But, as I pointed out, I'm a bit of a wuss. It was purely one step at a time for me at this juncture.

Geoff was stirring next to me now.

Oh God no! Please don't let him wake up, and want to go to the bathroom!

Is that not just the worst thing on a plane? When you have your tray thing down with food and drinks on it and the person in the window seat wants to get out? And when the trolley is in the aisle at the same time it just spells disaster. Who was I kidding? If it was going to happen it was going to happen here. I was trying not to look but Geoff had his eyes open now and was shaking his head, apparently trying to come round properly, but it was most disconcerting I can tell you.

I suddenly had another panic. I hoped that Carrie-Ann didn't think that Geoff was with me. I looked around, but the stewardess was still in the aisle next to me, talking to some lady behind. So it was just me and my buddy, Geoff at the moment.

"Excuse me, I don't suppose I could get out and go pay a call could I?"

Marvellous!

"No problem mate, but I think we'll have to wait for the stewardess to get out of the way first," I suggested.

"Of course," said Geoff. "Have I been asleep long?" he asked.

I could see that we were going to be fast friends here.

"Erm, yes. You've been out like a light since we took off," I told him.

"Really!" he seemed quite chuffed, "that is good news. Normally I can never sleep on aeroplanes".

He actually said 'aeroplanes'.

I thought it was 'airplanes'? I made a mental note to look up this information before I travelled by this means of transport again. 'Aeroplane' sounds a bit like something that you learn when you are four years old, as in 'A is for aeroplane'. Surely it is 'airplane'? I tried to think of a song with the word in it. What was the John Denver song? 'I'm leaving…' no that was 'jetplane'. I could see that this was going to drive me insane.

"My name is Richard by the way."

Not Geoff then… similar though. I could see that Richard was also going to drive me insane.

"I'm from Denton, and I'm going to Detroit to see a man about a motor car."

I couldn't decide whether I was supposed to laugh at this remark. He didn't seem to be laughing. I didn't want to cause offence but I could feel myself smiling. Was he for real?

"Hi Richard, I'm Mike," I replied cordially, "nice to meet you."

"Where are you headed then?"

Shit this was not good! I looked around and was relieved to see that the cart had gone.

"Oh look," I remarked, "the aisle is clear, you'd better take advantage."

I then looked at my tray table, full as it was with… stuff. Think… Quick!

"Here, pass them to me," said Carrie-Ann, noticing my predicament.

"Really? That would be a big help. Thank you," I said, trying not to sound too desperate.

"No problem."

I passed the 'snack' tray over and then the beaker with the remnants of my screwdriver. Carrie-Ann put them on her tray with a minimum of fuss.

I quickly stored my tray away – as they say in the safety message – and unclipped the seat buckle by pulling on the silver tag. Childs play! I eased myself into the aisle, and stood on the foot of the bloke behind me.

"Oww!" he screamed.

"Sorry mate, I didn't see you there," I quickly said.

He just looked at me.

Well bollocks to him! He was only five stone, wet through, but looked like he was trying to put on his 'Mr.T' face.

I felt like growling "UURGHH" at him, in my best Mr.T impression. You know how you feel when you've got a bit of liquor in your veins?

But instead I just smiled at him. I could see that pissed him off.

Richard was almost out. I backed up a bit to give him a bit more room and he eventually made it into the aisle, then steadied himself, standing on Mr.T's foot in the process.

"Bloody Hell!" said Mr.T, incredulously.

This was pure Keystone Cops now.

"I'm very sorry," said Richard, "but you've got your foot out in the aisle, young man. You should tuck it away."

Go Geoff! Sorry, I mean 'Go Richard!' He was starting to grow on me. I wondered whether he'd done it on purpose. I hoped so. Excellent entertainment!

I sat back down, well aware that Mr.T was sitting behind me now, probably plotting my downfall.

"It's a regular Abbott and Costello routine you two got going there," ventured Carrie-Ann.

"Yes, it's coming on," I replied, "we just need a bit of inspiration in the closing, but it'll come."

She laughed. Or was it giggled?

"Do you want to pass me the tray?" I asked.

"No," she replied, handing me the last of my screwdriver, "Costello will be back soon so

I may as well keep it until then."

"He could be some time, he's practising the next routine back there," I said.

Where was this coming from?

My new travelling companion was having a bit of a chuckle next to me. It was definitely infectious.

It sounded like she was having fun.

'Fun' – that's the actual word that sprang into my mind. And I found myself wondering when I last had fun.

I didn't dwell on it though. I thought I'd come back to it later when I was alone. The important thing was, fun had now arrived, and it was here to be enjoyed until someone came along, and took it away.

"Ten dollars!"

That'll do it.

TWO

In the next couple of hours we had a great deal of fun despite the stewardesses, and Mr.T, who kept 'adjusting' his tray table.

I did a little listening and a little digging and found out that Carrie-Ann Novitski was on her way home to Akron for a family funeral – an aunt on her mother's side. Apparently she'd been in the UK for 'some time' living in North London. She never said exactly what profession she was in and after three subtle attempts to discover it, to no avail, I gave up. Perhaps she was a lap dancer? Anyway she seemed to have a full social life, and clearly enjoyed every moment. She hadn't really got out of London though so I extolled the virtues of the Yorkshire countryside, and the friendly nature of people further north than Watford. I also went out of the way to explain that they had two rather large international airports in London, which would have been easier to use, instead of heading up to Manchester, but she had confused me with some tale of departure times and connections. She was getting a connecting flight in Philly onto Canton/Akron, or was it Akron/Canton airport? Well anyway she had three hours to kill in Philadelphia. I partly explained my predicament to her, leaving out the part about me going through a mid-life crisis and abandoning everything that I had spent 35 years building up. In fact I think that I simply told her that I wouldn't be very safe driving a rental car at this stage and that I was going to get a connecting flight also. Mercifully for some reason she didn't enquire, or wasn't interested, as to where I was headed. This was probably good as I still had no idea either. But we did make a loose arrangement to meet up for a drink and something to eat in the airport, which was kind of exciting, almost like a date! She had written her cell phone number on the back of an old envelope which she had found in the bottom of her bag and I had stashed it in my rucksack, which meant I would probably never find it again, amongst all the crap that was in there.

We also spent time discussing the subtle differences between English and American people, and our common language. This is one of my specialist subjects, and evidently hers too. The vodka was a great aid in this department and more than once we got stern stares from stewardesses for enjoying ourselves too much. But they kept bringing liquor so we can't have upset them too much.

I was beginning to think that I'd made a pretty good friend here and was wondering if my trip could pass through Akron before Carrie-Ann returned to London? Maybe I'd broach that subject in the bar at the airport.

We endured a bit of a bumpy landing in Philadelphia. One of those where only one side of the plane seems to touch down and you sit there for an eternity waiting for the other bump. Then when it finally happens the captain pulls the brakes on straight away and the plane feels like it's going to flip over.

Did I mention how much I hate flying? Well not flying in itself, just the taking off and landing. Some people enjoy those parts the most but I figure if something is going to happen, that's when it's going to happen!

The important part is, we were down, which is when relief floods over me. I always try to read something while we are in the stages of taking off or approaching landing to take my mind off of things but, when you think about it, that's a little bit stupid. I end up reading the same paragraph about twelve times cos I'm not really concentrating. And coming into land the book generally makes no sense to me anyway as I've not picked it up since the take off and I've had enough vodka in the meantime to make anything seem confusing by then. But I still persist with this strange ritual.

Odd, huh?

After the usual fight with the overhead bins and the jostling for starting positions on the race to leave the plane, I was now headed along the labyrinth of hallways, moving walkway, and escalators, to immigration.

This part is always a personal favourite when I arrive in the US.

Why is it there are twice as many desks open to US citizens as there are to overseas visitors? This results in there being twenty desks with nobody at them and a very long snake of overseas visitors, who are doomed to pass each other every five minutes for the next hour whilst going backwards and forwards in the snake. I can only assume that somebody is getting kicks out of watching from a TV, in a comfortable room to, see if any prospective terrorist will get so nervous at the prospect of seeing the same family from Dudley once again, that he will start to sweat and eventually give himself up.

The only result that I notice each and every time is that, when you finally get to the front you are so fed up with the United States and its petty bureaucracies that you really can't be bothered whether you are granted admission or not. This is generally the moment that you are called forward from your designated area behind the yellow line to face either a fifty year old who looks like a particularly surly walrus or an African American woman who is the size of a Chevy Silverado.

However, despite previous experiences, I walked into the immigration area to find that there were probably only twelve people there and as I headed for the tiniest of tiny snakes I was directed into another queue, which consisted of a German couple, and me. What a turn up for the books! Totally unprecedented!

Either this new life had been waiting for me or this is how everything was destined to be from now on, ie no waiting and endless fun conversations with laid back blondes from Ohio, or… any moment now something terrible was going to happen.

I was seriously leaning towards the first option at the moment, but that could have been the vodka again.

The German couple were already talking to the walrus in glass booth number 23 and I was anxiously waiting for Aretha Franklin to shout me over.

"Next please!"

I turned to my left to see an open booth but there had obviously been a change in official procedure here as I was being beckoned over by an attractive young lady. Any moment now I was going to wake up back on the plane two hours west of Manchester.

"Good afternoon, sir," she smiled.

"Good afternoon," I managed, thoroughly gob smacked.

Her name badge said Ripley, and she must have been in her mid to late twenties, very pretty with blonde hair tied up at the back and happy smiley features, or a pleasant countenance, as my grandmother used to say. Most importantly though, she seemed to be very happy in her employment. I believe that people in this profession are taken to one side, as a rule, and forced to do menial tasks for fifteen years until they become unpleasant enough to be able to deal with tourists. Ripley had obviously slipped under the wire; either that or her dad was the governor of Pennsylvania.

"What is the purpose of your trip to the United States, sir?"

"Vacation," I replied.

I was thinking about saying something about how pleasant it was to meet a US customs official who is pretty and seems to be enjoying her job, but there was no point in risking ruining the day when it was going so well. The last thing I wanted was to be hauled off into some room by a linebacker with Vaseline and rubber gloves.

"And how long will you be staying with us, sir?" she asked.

"Approximately one month, depending on how fast I get through my pocket money," I smiled, thinking 'pocket money.'?

I was getting increasingly concerned about the selection of phrases that seemed to be presenting themselves to me today. Perhaps this was another of the ways in which my new life was manifesting itself?

Ripley seemed happy with the answer though and she was now flicking through the pages of my passport. She finally came to rest on a clean page and placed a stamp on it, writing 'WT' on the dotted line.

Should I ask? Nah… one day somebody would tell me what 'WT' was, I was sure of it.

"Thank you, sir. Have a great trip!"

"Thank you, Ripley. Have a good day."

I smiled at her, and strolled away.

Restraint! That was the key. You had to know when to quit while you were ahead.

I followed the signs to the baggage retrieval area and checked the screen to see that I needed to be at carousel number four, which was stationary when I located it, with several people hovering at its perimeter. I had a look to see if Carrie-Ann was among them but was disappointed to see that she wasn't. I had got through immigration in record time so perhaps I had even beaten the US citizens through? She was bound to turn up while I was waiting. I kept my eye out for her while willing the conveyor belt to start turning.

Wasn't this just so ironic? You get ahead of yourself and end up waiting anyway. There is just no quick way to get through an airport!

I still had to give some thought as to where I was headed. Should I go somewhere that I had already been before or a completely new city? I could see pro's and con's for both choices. Familiarity was good, especially arriving somewhere at night, needing a good sleep. But new was exciting and part of the reason for the trip. I decided to wait until I got through and then I'd check out the departures board to see what tickled my fancy.

The conveyor was fighting inertia now and people were edging closer to the belt as if their lives depended on being able to see the bags at the earliest possible moment.

My bag was black, which wasn't too good, as eighty per cent of the bags that come around are black. I always dreaded the scenario that somebody else grabs my bag in their haste to escape the airport and get to fresh air in order to smoke a cigarette. This must actually happen a lot. Although, saying that, I've never heard of it happening. But you'd think it would, wouldn't you?

As luck would have it, and I realised that I was still getting the rub of the green here, my bag was about the fourth one out. I had tied a blue headscarf around the handles so that it was more noticeable. As I lugged it off the belt, avoiding my old mate, Mr.T, I took another look around to see if I could spot Carrie-Ann but she still didn't seem to be here so I headed out into the airport in search of inspiration as to my destination.

Once out in the arrivals lounge I followed the signs up to the departure area and ticketing, and found myself at the desk smiling at an Indian looking gentleman, who was smiling back very enthusiastically.

"Hello sir. How can I help you?" he asked.

"Well…" I began…

It was at this point that I noticed the desk calendar in front of me and the page that was open had a picture of that skyscraper in Pittsburgh that looks kind of like a castle. It's called the PPG Building and if you haven't seen it then I suggest you look for pictures of Pittsburgh's cityscape and you will immediately see what I mean. It's a very beautiful looking building.

I'd been to Pittsburgh once with a friend on an ill-fated trip during which I was sick the whole time. In fact this was the same trip when I had driven through Akron, as I had mentioned to Carrie-Ann. I'd woken up with a hangover after a night out in Fell's Point, Baltimore and as I sobered up I came down with a fever and a hideous sore throat that turned out to be laryngitis AND pharyngitis. I ended up visiting pharmacies in five different states and by the time we reached Chicago I could have probably hawked all the drugs out of the back of the car in Cabrini Green. As it was I tried to put a brave face on it but my buddy, Graham must have been well and truly fed up with me. He didn't get another night out after Baltimore. We drove for hours every day then spent the evenings in the room watching movies. Him drinking a couple of sociable beers and me wearing eight layers, shivering under the bed clothes. Looking back it probably wasn't as bad as I remembered it but Graham would maybe tell you a different story.

We had stayed in Pittsburgh for one night and had tickets to see the Penguins against the Canadians. Unfortunately the Penguins got soundly thrashed but we had good seats as I remember. Anyway, the point is we never really saw any of the city itself and I'd always had it at the back of my mind that I'd like to go back. So here was the chance beckoning…

"… Could I possibly have a one way flight to Pittsburgh please?" I asked.

"Certainly, Sir, we have a flight departing in just over one hour, at 16:10hrs. Would that be ok?"

"Perfect," I answered.

It would give me time to have a quick beer with Carrie-Ann, and find my gate.

I handed over my credit card, and waited while the ticket printed out.

The clerk was extremely efficient. I found myself wondering if he worked in a formula-one pit crew for a hobby. I know it's his job and everything but he seemed to be effortlessly using both hands, not wasting any time or energy, handing me the credit card slip to sign with one hand whilst pulling the tickets out of the printer with the other. I'm sure that he does this all day but it's like checkouts at supermarkets, sometimes you can get a tiller who is operating so slow that it defies logic. The time and motion people would be major impressed with this operation. Before I knew what was happening I was being pointed in the direction of departures and being encouraged to enjoy my trip to Pittsburgh. Excellent!

After temporarily removing my belt and shoes, and going through security, I was allowed into departures and headed for the food hall, where I had loosely arranged to meet Miss Novitski.

I wondered if it was Miss?

Maybe it was Mrs … the conversation had never wandered into the marital section and I had not even thought of looking for a ring.

Oh well, what did it matter anyhow? I was going to Pittsburgh.

There was a bar in the food hall that I'd been in a couple of times and we'd mentioned it on the flight, so I was hoping to meet up with her there.

The 'Britishness' in me refused to let me simply turn up though, I just had to confirm the arrangement, so I stopped at a rocking chair and sat down.

Philadelphia airport has a thing for white rocking chairs, as you'll know if you've been there. They are very comfortable on the whole, but I suspect they are there to make the place look more homely, less 'awayly' – obviously not a real word. They do brighten up the place and it's always good for the soul to have a rock. It takes you back to being a baby I guess.

I had found my mobile phone and switched it on. Whilst I waited for the airwaves to catch up and send me six hundred welcome messages I hunted for the envelope, which Carrie-Ann had written her number on. I found several items that I couldn't remember packing in my hand luggage including a CD by Izzy Stradlin, which would come in useful if I ever sobered up enough to drive a car. The envelope was bigger than I remembered when I finally found it, A5 size I think it's called. It was addressed to Carrie-Ann Novitski, 26 Highbury Grove, Islington, London, England (the world?), and another address was written on the back: somebody else's name: a Mr. Lewis Pine, who lived in Akron. I wasn't sure that Carrie-Ann knew that she'd thrown all of this out? I'd make sure and give it back to her when I met up with her.

My mobile phone was obviously upset after its eight hours of down time and was beeping away like crazy.

Two messages from Rachel, that's my girlfriend / ex-girlfriend / whatever, both saying that I was an asshole and don't bother coming back, and three others from an assortment of friends, all hoping that I'd had a safe flight, and imploring me to get in touch. Oh, and a message from some network provider welcoming me to the area and offering me lots of premium services which I couldn't afford to miss.

I skipped to the main menu, intending to go back to them later, and dialled Carrie-Ann's number.

The phone rang twice and then picked up.

"Hello?" an oddly quiet sounding woman's voice answered.

"Carrie-Ann?" I asked, uncertainly.

"Who's calling?"

This immediately seemed a bit strange and I started to think she'd given me a bogus number to get rid of me. It was like somebody was intentionally trying to sound like an older woman. But I thought I'd give whoever it was a chance before I hung up.

"Hi, my name is Mike. I've been given this number, and I'm trying…"

"Mike, hi, it's me," came the sudden change of voice.

Odd maybe? Hmm… Keep reading…

"Mike? Are you still there?" This was definitely Carrie-Ann now.

"Yes. You just had me fooled there for a minute. Are you screening calls?" I asked.

"Well you never know who's gonna be at the end of the line," she replied. "It could have been a crank call."

"I've been accused of worse in my time," I admitted.

"Oh dear," she said sounding all sympathetic, and very Marilyn Monroe all of a sudden; "well I'd better buy you a beer to make up for upsetting you then."

Happy… birthday… Mr… Pres – i – dent… Sing along now!

"That sounds like a plan," I said. "Where are you?"

"I'm just finishing up eating, out in the food court, and can be in the bar we were talking about in two minutes."

"Sounds good, I'll see you in there."

"Great," she said, and hung up.

Maybe she fancied a trip to Pittsburgh after the funeral to loosen up?

I gathered up my belongings, and headed towards the bar, which was about fifty yards in front of me on the right. As I approached I saw Carrie-Ann appear from the food court on the left and was just about to wave when somebody stepped out about ten yards in front of me, blocking my view.

He was a big guy, certainly over six feet tall, with long black hair tied up in a pony-tail, wearing blue jeans and boots and a red and black checked jacket / shirt type of thing. He was facing away from me and headed directly for Carrie-Ann with obvious intent. Instinctively I ducked to the right behind a pillar and as I did so I caught sight of Carrie-Ann's face.

She was wearing a look of absolute shock!

It was clear that she knew this guy, and didn't exactly look pleased to see him.

I was behind the pillar now though, not able to see anything and wondering what my next move was.

Did my new persona include saving damsels in distress? Or was this a good time to turn and head for the city on three rivers?

One thing I did realise though was that I was standing with my back to the pillar looking a bit like James Bond and that I'd better revert to a natural look quickly before airport security pulled people off of watching the snakes at immigration and sent them out looking for John McClane.

Yippee kai yay!

THREE

Amazingly, nobody seemed interested in my quick feint behind a pillar.

Everybody was filing past, intent on their own thoughts and destinations.

This was a bit of a dilemma I was in here.

I didn't know the girl really. I'd spent a maximum of three hours in her company, and didn't have a clue what secrets she could be hiding. For a start, I never saw any ID; she could have been lying about everything. Her name could be Martha for all I knew.

Well, probably not Martha.

The guy could be Lewis Pine?

Or Mr.Novitski? Hell of a welcome if it was, she had looked terrified.

Perhaps I should go find Richard, and Mr.T from the flight? We could do an A-Team style rescue? This thought made me smile, which actually helped, and cleared my head for a second.

I decided to go back to the rocking chair, and have a mull. It couldn't hurt. I needed a time out to consider my next move.

I headed back towards the same chair that I'd just sat in moments earlier, in a direction away from the bar. I still hadn't looked back, and they hadn't passed me, so I had no way of knowing what was going on.

When I reached the chair I sat down, as unassumingly as possible, and made an exaggerated effort of opening my bag, whilst turning to my right in an attempt to see what was happening.

When I could eventually see where Carrie-Ann and her friend had been stood, they weren't. They'd gone. Where to was anybody's guess.

At this point I should say that part of me was imploring – ok Mike, rule a line underneath this, and get on with the trip. Go catch the flight to Pittsburgh, and forget about everything that just happened.

But you know that I didn't listen to this part don't you? For a start, things are just starting to get interesting aren't they? Perhaps you wanted to hear more about life back home? And the reasons for my mid-life crisis?

Well that's not why we're here kids.

Not totally anyway.

And besides, I wouldn't be a very good, Good Samaritan if I simply walked away, would I now?

I must be honest and say that I'm not the bravest warrior that you ever met. In fact, up until that point I had never hit another person in my life! I'd only ever been hit myself once, and that was deserved! I was seeing the guy's girlfriend... and he had warned me off – which, if you think about it, was pretty nice of him. Despite that, I carried on seeing her, so it was only fair that he clocked me full on in the jaw in the middle of the town centre on a Saturday afternoon. It was still a bit of a shock, and I was a bit disappointed when it didn't bruise. I told everyone about it nevertheless, and traded on the macho image for a while –

even though it was me who got hit. I have to say though… all in all, I didn't particularly enjoy the experience, and it wasn't something that I ever wanted to happen again.

So I sat there, in the rocking chair, and considered the start to my new life. I mulled away for a good five minutes, and finally decided that, even if I wasn't the last samurai in Philadelphia airport, I should still at least have a quick wander about to see if I could see Carrie-Ann, and if I did find her, maybe I could ask her if she was ok. If the guy still looked a bit scary I would revise my tactics, make my excuses, and walk away. Standing up, I began to walk back towards the food court, and the bar, convincing myself that I was doing the right thing. If I walked away, I would only lie awake tonight anyway, wishing I had the balls to get involved in situations like this.

I was about level with the bar when I decided that Dutch courage wouldn't hurt, so I walked straight in, fully intending to sit at the window, and keep a watch out. I wouldn't be needing to though, as it turned out.

They were both seated at the bar!

I had been in this bar, the 'Independence Brew Pub' on several occasions. Despite there being no actual doors, just a large opening at either side of the barroom, which was about twenty five to thirty foot long, smoking is allowed, and I had spent many a post transatlantic flight hour in here catching up on my nicotine, back in the day.

The bar itself almost spanned one entire wall, and there were bar stools all the way down it, with more at the window facing out into the airport at the opposite side of the room. For an airport bar it was pretty cool, and was all glass, and wood. You could almost get away with not feeling like you were actually in an airport. There were the obligatory four or five TV sets on the walls tuned to different sports channels, and the seats at the bar opened up at regular intervals as you would expect in a place where people are arriving and leaving with regularity.

Carrie-Ann had her back to me as I entered, and was certainly unaware of my presence at this point. Her pony-tailed friend was facing in my direction, but not looking at me. His eyes were firmly on Carrie-Ann. Something was definitely not right. It was in the air, like an aroma, and unmistakeable. I was astonished that other people in the bar weren't aware of it.

I made the decision to walk right by them both, and take a seat behind them at the bar. That way, if this simply was an old friend of Carrie-Ann's that she'd run into, then she'd see me, and at least acknowledge my presence, and say hi. If she ignored me, it could be a husband, or jealous ex husband, or boyfriend, or maybe something else.

As I walked past him I couldn't help but notice just how powerful he looked. I mean, I knew he was a tall fellow, but he had a chiselled jaw, and 'looked' strong, with big, wide shoulders. I really did not want to be messing with this dude! I was sure that he could snap me in half without thinking about it.

I apologised as I brushed past him but got no response from either of them so I sat down at the stool, putting my bag on the floor next to me, and stared straight ahead. Carrie-Ann had said nothing! What was this about?

Right in front of me, behind the bar was a mirror that ran totally across the back of the bar, and behind that a glass window, which gave views out over the runways. I guessed that there must be a moving walkway between the bar, and the windows though, as people were intermittently surfing past.

There was no way that this guy could see me without turning his head right around. Carrie-Ann, however, could see me, and must have recognised me by now. I was less than three feet away from them, and could have heard everything that they were saying. But they weren't saying a thing. He was still just staring at her, and she was sat in silence. Spooky! I noticed that they both had drinks in front of them; Coke by the look of it, but neither of them appeared to be very thirsty.

"How are you today, sir?" the bartender called in my general direction, whilst serving somebody to my left.

'How are you today, sir?' I love rhetorical comments like this. It's totally contrary to the way we are schooled in England. You can go into a restaurant and the waitress will come over, she won't look at you either, and she'll say "Hey, how ya doin?" It's just an opening gambit. Like 'Now then', or 'How's it goin?' He was asking what I wanted to drink. He didn't really give a shit how I was, but if he had to just stand and ask people what they wanted to drink all day, he'd run out of different vocabulary pretty quickly. There should be a thesaurus for the catering industry. Maybe there is? Perhaps it's a bestseller?

The funny thing was that still the urge was in me to say that I was very well thanks.

Well not today buster!

"A bottle of Corona with lime please," I replied, feeling very happy with myself.

"Sure!"

As Tom Cruise busied himself, I turned my head to the right and looked right at Carrie-Ann through the mirror. Now you know what that's like. When somebody is looking at you, even at your reflection, you can feel it, and you are compelled to turn and look. But she didn't. It was like she was under a spell. She looked – not frightened – maybe timid was the word, no, not timid... resigned, defeated. All of the joy that I'd seen in her before, and heard on the phone just minutes earlier, was gone. She was a different person. A shadow of the one that I had met just hours before. Something weird was afoot that's for sure.

I didn't like it. It felt uncomfortable. And at that moment, even before I got my beer, I decided that I wanted to get as far away as possible. I could do no more here. I wasn't wanted.

The barman had returned now, placed the Corona in front of me, without a word, and departed.

I pushed the lime in the neck of the bottle, took a large swig of my beer, and picked my bag up. I left five dollars on the bar, and walked out without looking back.

I wonder if Carrie-Ann noticed?

I grabbed a Philly steak sandwich in the food court, and walked to my gate whilst eating it. I hadn't realised just how hungry I was after my flight, and had to stop myself from walking back to buy another!

I decided that it was best to push the whole Carrie-Ann incident out of my head. There was no sense in thinking about it any longer. I had a new life to get on with now, and I couldn't see it involving Akron. I knew that I would probably wonder about it all at a later date, simply because it was a strange old episode, but for now I was moving on. I hadn't left one set of women dilemmas in England, simply to come to a new continent, and open up a whole new set with a different woman within 24hours. Surely I could wait at least a week before I did this?

The plane that I boarded for Pittsburgh was one of those cool ones. The description is definitely a bit ropey here, as I have no idea about different models of planes. I couldn't tell you what a 757 is, or the difference between that and a 737. All I knew is that I had been on one of these a few times before, and they are cool. They have about twenty-five rows, maybe a few more. At one side of the aisle there is one seat, whilst at the other, two. The seats are leather, and you feel like you're on a private jet or something. Like you're in a rock band. Are you with me now? Unfortunately you still get the same standard of stewardess, and the one who greeted me when I got on board reminded me of the woman who played Cliff

Clavin's mom on Cheers.

There only seemed to be about ten of us flying all the way across the state of Pennsylvania, so it wasn't long before we were airborne.

I had managed to read about five pages of my James Patterson novel – which you will know, if you read his books, is about four chapters – when my mind wandered back to what had just occurred. I couldn't help thinking about it, and the change in her character. She didn't seem the sort to be so deferential to somebody. She had appeared confident, and outgoing. No, it must have been something else. He certainly had a hold over her. And how had he known that she was going to be there? I hadn't thought of that until this moment. He must have been waiting for her, looking out for her!

Why?

This was tiring me out. I was shattered. I closed my eyes for a moment, and the next thing I knew we were descending.

I must have been asleep, or at least dozing. I could tell that, because I now felt shocking. I'm not one of those people who can catch forty winks. I could never have been in the armed forces, or a fireman working shifts, and getting sleep wherever possible. I need a good sleep pattern otherwise it throws me totally out, and I can't operate properly. I felt nauseous, dizzy, and had a headache coming on.

Besides that I had a raging thirst, and needed water desperately.

I pushed the stewardess button, without feeling guilty, and watched out for Cliff's mom. She arrived, and I fought hard to resist the urge to apologise.

"Could I have a glass of water please?" I asked politely.

"We're coming in to land, sir," was the response.

Huh? I wasn't putting up with that kind of crap anymore. I was a changed man!

"That's lovely, but could I have some water please?" I said, somewhat sarcastically.

"As I said sir, we are making our approach. The captain has switched on the fasten seatbelts sign."

Now, this is when the English person in me wants to cave in, and say sorry for daring to request a drink that will cost the airline next to nothing. But I was working hard at this attitude.

"Ok, I don't want to get up, and go anywhere. I'm just really thirsty. I'm sorry to trouble you, but I don't feel very well, and really need some water. If there's no water, then Coke will do, Sprite, or 7-up, whatever you have."

"I'll see what I can do," she muttered, and walked away. How unbelievably helpful!

I was amazed at myself though. I really did say all of that. Normally I would have agreed with her, and behaved like an English version of Marty McFly, but I stood up to the old dragon, and it would have felt good if my stomach wasn't churning so much.

If she'd had room in that little cubby hole area that they call the galley on these things, I'm sure she'd have hitched up her skirt and pissed in my water, but she didn't look to have been that agile for a few decades. She was on her way back now with my drink, and I hoped someone would see it, and get the same idea, just to piss her off.

"There you go," she said, handing me the drink, with a fake smile, that seemed to have a warning behind it.

Well I didn't care what it was, I needed it, and I downed it before she'd gone. Not even close to hitting the spot!

I looked out of the window; we were pretty low down now. I reached for my Patterson, and re-read the last four chapters while we came in to land.

FOUR

"Welcome to Pittsburgh International Airport," read the sign.

Home of the most user-friendly international airport in the USA, apparently… according to my guide book anyway.

And as airports go, it was ok. User friendly… mmm. The jury's out on that one, but then again I didn't really need to make much use of it.

All ten of us seemed to go away with our own bags, and the exit was clearly marked, so I guess it did all that could be asked.

I jumped in a cab, and asked the driver to take me to the Marriott hotel, next to the Mellon arena, as it was the only hotel that I knew in this city. It was where I had stayed on my previous visit with Graham, and to be honest at that stage I wasn't really up to discussing tourism, and my options with a guy who listened to Maria Carey. Very loud!

I checked in relatively smoothly and headed up to the comfort of my room on the seventeenth floor. I can not accurately describe the feeling of relief that I felt when the little green light flashed on the key card box, and the door opened when I turned the handle. Walking into the room I could have just flung myself on the bed and lay face down for a week.

Slight exaggeration maybe, but I am sure that you are aware of the sensation that you get after a long journey, when it finally ends, and you have reached your destination.

The fact that I had had no idea of my destination when I had left home nearly fourteen hours ago now, and the intervening mini-adventure had only made it an even more energy-sapping trip. I was determined to get everything necessary accomplished though before I laid my weary body down for the night.

It was still early evening, not even six pm, but I had decided that I was not going to venture out again. I was drained mentally, and physically, and previous trips in a westerly direction through time zones had taught me that an early start was on the cards tomorrow.

I looked around the room, and got my bearings. For a single room it was remarkable, and well furnished. Thinking about it though, I had never had a single room before. Previously I'd always visited the US with Rachel, in double rooms, or with friends, staying in twin rooms. Here I had a large double bed, with a bedside table at either side. Then there was a desk against the wall near the window, with an upright chair. The desk had an ornate lamp on it, 'various' stationery equipment, and a fax machine. The window was the width of the room, approximately fifteen feet, and in front of it at the other side of the room there was an easy chair, and a footstool.

The TV was in the usual generic large cabinet, hidden by doors. It was sitting on a small shelf that could be pulled out and turned at angles, in case I had company I presume, or wanted to watch TV whilst writing to my bank manager at the desk. In the doors below the TV were the mini bar and the room safe. Next to the TV was a small piece of furniture designed to put your luggage on. I have no idea what this piece of furniture is called and so added it to the list of things that I needed to find out, along with airplane vs aeroplane, CantonAkron, or AkronCanton airport, and the meaning of WT.

As I'm doing a hotel room review, I may as well continue with the bathroom, which was also larger than necessary for one visitor. It contained the usual things that you would expect to find, plus a nice array of freebies, in a wicker basket. I should also point out that the bath was actually long enough to have a bath in. This is more important than regular hotels seem to realise.

Basically if I was in Europe I had a deluxe double room. Here in the US, this was the standard single, and I could continue here, to rant about the standards in my country, and how American tourists must weep when they are shown to their rooms in tired old English hotels, which charge double the amount that they would expect to pay in a US city. And the ice machines... don't get me started...

I placed my large black bag (with blue headscarf), on the aforementioned piece of furniture, and unzipped it. I am not the kind of person who can fling his clothes aside in carefree nature across a bedroom floor, much as I long to be. I would inevitably find myself tossing and turning in bed until I gave in and got up to fold everything up in neat piles on a chair.

So to avoid this intrusion into my sleep I set about getting settled. This included arranging my toiletries in the bathroom, taking a shower, cleaning my teeth (very important), depositing dirty underwear in a plastic carrier bag (which I always bring along with me) and stowing it away in a separate pocket in my bag, throwing on a clean t-shirt and clean boxers, closing the curtains, switching on the TV and grabbing a beer from the mini bar before collapsing on the bed.

Anal... moi?

The headache that I was promised hadn't yet materialised, but it was still hanging there, like dark clouds sitting over the hillside opposite. You are never sure whether they might blow off in another direction, or head towards you. I had brought some Advils, but was determined not to use them except in dire emergency, preferring to use will power where possible. I popped the top on my Heineken – the only decent beer in the mini-bar/fridge, and lay back against the pillows that I had propped up against the wall at the top of the bed. I had found ESPN on the TV and was being regaled with the story behind the season of some college basketball team. I wasn't capable of taking anything in at this stage of the proceedings though.

I half entertained getting dressed and heading down to the hotel bar, after my shower, but just didn't have the oomph left in me, and I knew that jet lag was ticking away at my body clock. I was guessing at a five am alarm call, so I reasoned that I might as well just relax.

I decided to check the messages that were on my mobile phone, as I hadn't really paid attention earlier, in my haste to get hold of Carrie-Ann.

Carrie-Ann… she seemed like a distant memory now. It honestly did feel like it was a couple of days since I had seen her in that bar. Amazing! But for some reason I felt some kind of an attachment, and was a bit hurt, and also angry about what had happened. Maybe I was starting to sober up?

I located my phone, and turned it on.

ESPN was now advertising tonight's games. The 76ers at Minnesota was on at 7, and after that the Mavericks at the Lakers. That seemed like quite a good evening. Shame there was only one more Heineken. Then it was onto Bud, and Bud Light. Good god, who drinks this stuff? There was a shop in the hotel reception, maybe I would have to go down, and pick up a six-pack at some stage.

The phone was beeping for my attention now.

Two more messages: one from some network provider who wanted to give me information at the touch of a button, and another from Rachel. This one seemed friendlier than the others.

"Please ring or txt me to let me know you are safe. Rachel".

I looked back at the others... they hadn't been so good...

"You selfish bastard I can't believe you have actually done it!"

And...

"Don't think you can just walk back in here after this you arsehole!"

On the whole she seemed to be mellowing with time.

She had a right to be mad, don't get me wrong, but she hadn't exactly gone out of her way to listen to me, and try to understand what I was going through. In fact she'd basically ridiculed me, whenever I'd mentioned 'taking off'.

We'd been with each other for just over five years, and spent nearly all of that living together. Looking at it now, through the haze of alcohol, I think we'd just outgrown it.

Or she'd outgrown me?

We'd originally met whilst working in the same office building, and whilst we'd never gone out, or even flirted with each other, we'd always said 'Hi', and it had been very easy being around one another. We'd both had other partners at the time, and I suppose the timing just wasn't right. She'd moved away, gone to work at another firm, where she still was now, working for some solicitors, at the other side of town and we didn't see each other for maybe two years. Then one night, out of the blue she turned up at my sister's birthday party, with a friend, who had been invited by my sister. Complete coincidence! We got chatting, had both become single in the meantime, and within the space of a few hours ended up in bed together.

We got into this infatuation period, and within three months we'd rented a house together; the same house that we ended up buying off of the landlord a year later. It literally all happened that quickly! We never had time to sit down, look around, and take stock of what was happening.

In the last three years or so, Rachel got very career minded. When we had started seeing each other she was basically an office secretary. The company she worked for must have identified her as a bit of an asset, and capable of more, and so they began to throw training at her. To begin with it was all very exciting, and we were both thrilled that they thought so much of Rachel. But slowly over time the we, became just Rachel. As she became more confident in her abilities, and started taking courses in her spare time, and doing day release towards legal qualifications, I didn't feel like I was the person that she was sharing her excitement with anymore. Maybe she thought (probably quite correctly) that I wouldn't begin to understand the complexities of the new things that she was coming across. Maybe she wasn't talking to anyone about it all, perhaps she was doing this all by herself. But the point here was, 'we' weren't doing it together anymore.

You might be reading this, and thinking that I'm childish.

You could be right.

But what I was most of all was jealous. All of this self-improvement forced me to take a hard look at myself, plodding along in my comfortable job. Why didn't I have the same drive, ambition, and thirst for more? And when I started thinking in this vein, that's when I began to get a bit restless too. Maybe I needed to find that 'something' in my life too. Maybe I owed it to myself to find it?

I'm overjoyed for Rachel, I really am. She deserves all of the success that she will undoubtedly get. I'm glad that she's found something so obviously important in her life. But it has been at the expense of 'us'.

I'd tried talking to her about it all, but she didn't, or couldn't understand what I was saying. That is when the piss-taking usually started. She was bettering herself. I had heard her say it on many occasions. She was striving for more.

But during all of this, she had left me behind. And the important thing was that she must have known this. She must have looked over her shoulder at some stage, and thought, 'well I could wait for him', or 'I could encourage him to catch up', but she hadn't. Instead she'd kept on going. Because, at the end of the day, as I said, she'd outgrown me.

And I knew that, after she got done with being pissed off, and hurt, she'd know that too.

Perhaps I should leave it another couple of days before answering... Or should I really be answering at all? I was supposed to be casting off all the old shackles, and launching forth into a new life. Not being dragged back into the usual, I wonder if I'm supposed to answer this text message, or not, life. That was behind me now surely?

I decided that I couldn't be expected to answer this question definitively today. It had been a long day. If every day for the rest of my life was going to be this long then I was gonna be old real quick.

I quickly scanned the other three messages. One was from Graham. I knew that I could trust him to keep quiet, so I would text him back tomorrow, whatever happened. The other two were from people who required more thought. I wasn't particularly sure as to motives here. Tony had always had a bit of a thing for Rachel, and this could be him testing the water as to whether he was free to go around and play the sympathetic friend, with two bottles of wine, who was only there because he was feeling it too. I could just see it. I decided not to bother replying to him, and deleted his message. He could decide on his own whether or not he was an arsehole.

The last message was from Richard, and I'd not really held him in high regard since the last time he got extremely drunk, and started asking me what the fuck was wrong with me, and why couldn't I cheer up for fucks sake, as I was depressing the lot of them. I deleted that message too.

Bollocks to them all tonight I thought. There was a double header on the TV and I was in Pittsburgh! This was exciting, this was what I was searching for wasn't it? I'd left them all behind.

I dropped the phone on the bed next to me, lay back into the pillows, and before you could say Andrew Carnegie I was fast asleep.

I awoke with a jolt, feeling the sense of panic that you get when you wake up in a strange room, and you've had a lot to drink the day before.

Something wasn't right.

In fact there was quite a lot that wasn't right.

Starting with the TV that was blaring away.

The lights were still on too.

I worked out that I was in the hotel, in Pittsburgh, and that I must have fallen asleep whilst watching the TV.

I was still wearing my glasses, albeit at an Eric Morecambesque angle. But something else wasn't right … what was that ringing?

My phone…

My phone was ringing… where was it?

I sat up, and felt all around the bedclothes. It wasn't here! It sounded further away.

It must have dropped off of the bed. I dropped forward onto my chest, and looked over the edge of the bed. It was face down on the floor.

I picked it up, and looked… number withheld.

Shit! Should I answer it? Well I might as well now it has woken me up, I thought.

Maybe, in hindsight, I shouldn't have answered it.

Maybe I started things in motion there, and then.

Perhaps the person would have kept ringing until I eventually gave in and answered it anyway.

But I didn't usually answer the phone if I couldn't see who was ringing me, so maybe they just got lucky that I was half asleep.

I pushed the little green phone button, and the ringing ceased. Hesitantly I put the phone to my ear.

Now, bear in mind that I wasn't really compos mentis here.

"Who's that?" the voice demanded.

"Huh?" your genius-like narrator answered.

"Who are you?" the voice persisted.

"What?" I replied… getting better. At least it was a real word!

"WHO am I speaking to?" the person at the other end of the phone was male, American, and sounded like he was running low on patience.

I was about to begin my next startling reply with an apology, then suddenly came to my senses, and checked my watch. 4:32 am!

4:32!!!!!! Watch out!

"Who are YOU speaking to? Who am I speaking to? Do you have any idea what the time is? Don't ring me up at four thirty in the morning to do a census. Who the fuck are you?"

I took a deep breath, and mentally I cupped my hand with my finger nails towards me, blew on them, and rubbed them on my shirt. Now who's in charge?

"Lieutenant Saxton, Homicide," came the answer.

Hmm… Obviously not me then.

FIVE

So far, I couldn't complain that my new life was boring.

I had enjoyed a transatlantic flight in the presence of a charming beautiful girl, who then turned out to be under the spell of a six foot pony-tailed hoodlum in Philadelphia, and after flying away at high speed, I was now in my hotel room in Pittsburgh at four thirty in the morning being interrogated by a Lieutenant from homicide!

Exciting? You betcha!

Not exactly what I signed up for though.

Now again, I must remind you that this was all happening right after I had woken up, and there were questions that even I wished that I had asked afterwards.

It could have been anybody ringing me at that time of day, and I would have struggled, but the fact that it was a member of the police force, just made things ten times worse.

I'm not afraid of authority, or authority figures, don't get me wrong. But I was brought up to respect those in uniform. I always feel a little like I'm in front of the headmistress back in junior school, or the scary deputy head at high school, when confronted by a cop today. I automatically feel like it is up to me to prove that I aren't a criminal, and I begin the conversation feeling that I am clearly in trouble otherwise they wouldn't be talking to me. I know that cops are aware that they often begin conversations from this lofty position. They obviously teach them psychology in training school.

All of this went through my head at 4:32am whilst the phone sat in the palm of my hand, and I tried to think of an answer, to what palpably was not a question. Though it hung in the air like one.

Silence.

"Hello?" the receiver, or probably Lieutenant Saxton said.

"Err, yes," I managed, composing myself, "sorry officer, I mean Lieutenant…"

I wasn't doing very well here. Quite honestly though I had visions of them hauling me off down to the cells below some police station in Pittsburgh, and me spending the night being buggered by someone who looked like Warren Sapp, before they threw my (now sensitive) ass back on a plane to the UK, where I would have to go begging to Rachel for crumbs of forgiveness.

But… hang on… I'd done nothing wrong here… what was wrong with me?

"… You'll have to excuse me, but I'm very tired, I just got into town last night, and I…"

"I'm sorry to wake you at this time, sir," he interrupted, "but we're investigating a homicide here, and it's very important that we follow up on any leads immediately. I'm sure that you understand?"

The way he worded it, I just had to, didn't I?

"Yes, of course," I replied, "but how on earth can I be of assistance?" I asked. "After all I only arrived in the country last night."

It struck me at that point that I was volunteering information that had not been asked for, and whilst I knew that the police would quite easily be able to find out such simple things, as:

a) when I had arrived in the country, and: b) what flights I had been on, so there seemed to be no point in my giving them these details if they didn't specifically request them. I'd read enough crime novels in my time to know that fools who babble on, coming up with alibis, and excuses before they have to, usually end up being earmarked for further investigation. Change of tack then.

"I'm sure that's true sir, but we have to follow everything up, so if I could have your name?"

"Michael Huntingden," I replied.

Doing well so far…very covert!

"And your current address, sir?" he asked.

"May I ask why you need this information, Lieutenant?"

"Because it would be better if we could come and have a chat to you in person, rather than over the telephone, sir," he answered.

It made sense, unfortunately.

He had a very calm manner, one that made me feel like I could drop my defensive guard actually. It neither conveyed a suspicion of guilt, nor an inquisitive manner, despite his questioning. It was simply very neutral. Again, this is something that is obviously taught, and I could see how it could be very useful in certain situations.

I gave him my current address, and room number, and he said that somebody would be in touch in due course to arrange for an officer to come around to see me, for what, he assured me, would be a simple fact finding exercise, and nothing to be worried about. He apologised again for waking me, and ended on a "Good day, sir."

I bade him a "Good day" in return, and pushed the end call button on my phone, silently berating myself for not switching the damn thing off the night before.

I had no new messages listed at the moment, and decided to switch it off. At the same time I made a mental note that I needed to recharge the battery at some stage, especially as it had been on standby all night.

It was almost 4:45am now, and it was clear that I was not going to get any further sleep. For some reason I was still sat in the same position on the bed as when I had answered the phone, and was unable to move.

I knew that my bladder was screaming out to be emptied, and I also needed some water to drink, desperately. Sounds pretty crazy when you put the two together. In one end, and out the other. But it's a common feeling first thing in the morning, and I'm sure that I'm not the only one feeling it.

I made the effort to stand, and headed for the bathroom, turning around before I got there, to head back, and grab a bottle of water from the mini bar/fridge.

I know, I know, it's outrageously expensive, and I could get water for a fraction of the price at a local deli, but … come on! It's still only five bucks at the most. I'd spend that in tips just trying to get out of the hotel.

This is just part of the argument that I have with myself whenever I take water from a hotel mini bar. It's my mother inside me, trying her best to stop me from being extravagant. It happens a lot. And it's good. But it was too early to have the full argument, so I unscrewed the top, and drained it all whilst treating myself to a sit-down piss.

While I was in the bathroom I did the full pentathlon in the end. Toilet, teeth, shower, shave, and hair. I've not mentioned my hair yet have I? It's getting a little long. My fringe just about reaches my mouth now, if I pull it forward, but I don't wear it like that generally. It makes me look like one of the muppets. For fun sometimes I pull it all forward with my hands, and put sunglasses on over it. That always goes down a treat with small children.

I wear it all back, kind of like… I don't know… Johnny Depp.

(Did you see how I did that? I made it look like I wasn't actually trying to wear my hair like Johnny Depp, by pretending to search for his name.)

Anyway it's getting longer, and it sometimes needs a little encouragement from mousse to stay where I want it, and not over my face. I know guys don't like to talk about mousse, because it's considered a bit effeminate, but I don't go around discussing its merits with people, it just serves a purpose.

Bathroom pentathlon over, I returned to the main living space of my new home, and debated clothing, and where the hell I was headed at this time of day.

I threw a pair of jeans on, and an old Harvard t-shirt that I had bought on a holiday in Massachusetts. As opposed to buying whilst studying there, which I hadn't done... well not yet anyway.

Then all of a sudden question number one hit me like a brick in the face!

WHO THE HELL HAD DIED?

For a moment everything went quiet, and the world just seemed to stand still.

If the Lieutenant was ringing about a homicide, then by definition somebody had died.

But who? And why the hell did I not think to ask?

I sat back on the bed – in a state of total bewilderment, staring at the wall in front of me.

Question number two arrived, and again it hit me with some force.

HOW HAD THE POLICE GOT MY NUMBER?

I jumped up, and reached into my bag for my phone. I know that the caller withheld their number, but I just wanted to double check that the phone hadn't held a number in the register. Stupid thought I know, but it really did seem to make sense having a second look to be sure.

I switched my phone on, and waited.

Why would the police think that I was involved? Was I being set up? I'd just got here for Christ's sake!

How could I get back in touch with them, and ask these questions?

It then occurred to me that I had no idea where they were ringing from! There was surely a homicide division on every force. They could have rung from North Dakota for all I knew. Why in hell didn't I ask where I could get hold of them? Was I supposed to simply sit here in my hotel room until they got in touch to tell me when they were coming to see me?

And why couldn't they ask me what they needed to know over the phone?

Was it serious?

Was I a suspect?

I was getting carried away now, and I knew that, but at the same time I was pissed off with myself for not asking simple questions. The police lieutenant had gotten away with doing exactly what I myself had thought about. He'd not told me anything that he didn't need to in order to get what he wanted. And now he'd got it.

My phone was on, so I checked in the call register.

Nothing! Excellent!

Think Mike…

How long had it been since I put the phone down? I looked at my watch… it was now just after 5:20am.

Quick mental arithmetic – a little more than half an hour since the call ended. If I was wanted for homicide they would have been here by now, that was for sure.

Wouldn't they?

They definitely had police in downtown Pittsburgh. So yes, if I was a prospective danger then they would have been banging on my door while I was stood in the shower.

This was a good sign.

They also hadn't told me not to leave town. But then again maybe they didn't actually do that. Perhaps that was just in the movies?

Who had my number here in the US? Nobody. I didn't give it to Carrie-Ann yesterday, and I hadn't even had to give it at check in.

I had rung Carrie-Ann's phone from my phone. Perhaps that left my number in her call register?

But it shouldn't do, because normally if you are calling from abroad, or from a foreign phone it won't register, I'd experienced this several times.

Wait a minute… was this a wind up?

The person who called didn't have to be ringing from the US did they? It could have been somebody back home. They could easily ring from a number that I didn't have in my phone, so it wouldn't show up anyway, because I was out of the country!

That had to be it; especially with the time difference. It was after 10am in the UK on a Friday. Anybody could have rung and put on a phoney accent. The accent was good though. I couldn't place it, but then I hadn't had much chance, Lieutenant Saxton – or whoever it was – hadn't said a lot. And after all, I was half asleep at the time.

Yes, that had to be it.

But who could have made the call? It wasn't really Rachel's style to do this. No, I couldn't believe that she'd even be in on something like this. Graham certainly wouldn't – it wasn't in his nature.

Both Tony and Richard were definite maybes.

They could even be in on this together?

Yes. I could see them thinking this was a brilliant idea, and getting very excited about it. But neither of them would have been able to get away with the accent without giving it away, no matter how tired I was. They must have got somebody else in on it. A third party. That was it! Although I couldn't think who. Oh well, not to worry, at least I'd sussed them out.

But now I was even more pissed off at myself, because I'd fallen for it, and they'd succeeded, and they would be having a great laugh at my expense.

They'd both be holding court at the Cat n Feathers this evening reciting the conversation, word for word, and laughing like two little girls.

I knew them though; they wouldn't be able to resist trying it again. And they'd given themselves the perfect opportunity by saying that they'd be in touch, to arrange the time for us to meet.

Well I'd be ready for them! Bastards!

Maybe I should send them a text message? Something along the lines of, 'Hope you are all well back in the UU. Just going out now to find another victim!'

That could work. But I was desperate to avoid them thinking that I was worrying about this, and that it was ruining my day. They'd get even more of a kick out of that. So in the end I decided that, no, I'd just ignore them both. Eventually that would get to them even more.

I was claiming the high moral ground here people.

And with that, I switched my phone off, once again, vowing not to turn it on again that day. I gathered up my wallet, and jacket, slid into my trainers, and headed out to see what Pittsburgh had to offer me.

SIX

Pittsburgh, named after the former British prime minister, William Pitt the elder, settled in 1758, population a little over a third of a million inhabitants, sitting at 760 feet above sea level, but nestled below the Allegheny Mountains, at the confluence of three rivers, Allegheny, Monongahela, and Ohio.

I could give you the full Rough Guide treatment here if I had time. I could also tell you the story behind the great George Washington's visit here as a young man, when this whole area was still but a wilderness. I had learnt all about the history of the Carnegies, and the Fricks, and the Mellons.

Suffice to say that, given the wake up call, and hence my early introduction onto the streets of Pittsburgh, I did it justice.

I had heard, and read quite a lot over the past couple of years about Pittsburgh going through a renaissance period. Enlightened political leaders and a dynamic local community were driving most of it. I have to say that I was impressed with the results of the hard work, which was there for all to see in the clean streets, and parks, and bright modern buildings. There seemed to be a lot of local pride, which is something that we don't seem to have much of in the UK, sadly. I keep up to date on US cities, and affairs. I've always been very interested in the topic, heaven knows why. Maybe in preparation for what was to come? Perhaps my whole life to this point had been geared around what was to come? Or maybe I was just a sad case, who clinged to the promise that the grass is greener.

I'd spent the better part of the day walking the length and breadth of the city and found that I had been right in my conviction in wanting to come back. The feel of the place was right up my street. I know that it sounds like a cliché, but the people really couldn't have been friendlier. Twice, whilst simply stood admiring something, and thinking about which way to head next, I was approached by somebody offering their assistance, in case I was lost.

On four occasions somebody remarked upon my being English with such amazement that I can only assume that there aren't many of us in town. This only added to my appetite for the place, as I can be a bit of a snob in this department.

The one thing that I can't stand when I am out of the country is to be in the presence of English people. In fact, most of the time I am simply embarrassed by them.

I am sure that Americans must think the same when they are in Rome, and can hear some Texan exclaiming how he can't believe that he came all the way here to see the Coliseum, and 'Would you look at the state of it! You should see the Reliant back home! Now that's a stadium.'

But being in the presence of English people over here makes me feel as if I'm a teenager, and my parents are in the same room. You know the feeling, when all you are trying to do is enjoy yourself, but you know that your folks are going to keep saying dumb things, and there is nothing that you can do to stop them. Do you understand?

Really?

Maybe it's just me, I don't know. But I can feel myself cringing as I overhear their stupid comments like, 'the weather is so much better here than it is back home'. Again, I'm sure there are probably psychology degree papers written on subjects similar to this.

Luckily, though, I seemed to be the only Brit in town at present, which made me feel like some kind of frontiersman, like a young Washington, searching for signs of the French. Yes, a pioneer, maybe that was the feeling that I was searching for? The feeling that I was stepping out for mankind, but at the same time being able to stop at Starbucks for a tall Americano, and a cinnamon twist.

The same people who had remarked on my Englishness had also all, to a man (and one woman) mentioned a local bar, which went by the name of Harry's Pub, and apparently had an English theme, and a dartboard. And the irony was I now totally planned on going there that night. It was a little out from the centre, on Liberty Ave., so I'd not passed it on my hike, but I planned to catch a cab there anyhow.

Why was I going?

Probably for the same reasons that I was in Pittsburgh and not Nepal, a little familiar ground. It seemed like it could be a good place to meet a few folks, either ex-pats who were in town, and knew the ropes around here, or Brit friendly US citizens who were anxious to cultivate a little diplomacy. Either way, it would be a good excuse to relax, have a couple of beers, and maybe have a decent chat with somebody.

After the exertions of the day, I had managed to find my way back to the hotel, and stopped at the shop in the ground floor lobby to pick up a six pack of beer, which I had made room for in my mini-bar/fridge by ditching the light beers and leaving them out on the table to get warm. Maybe the person who was restocking would take the hint?

When I had got back, I had followed up on my intention of the evening before, and I had sent a text message to Graham. I had thought a little about this also during the day, and decided that I would feel happy if I had at least touched base (awful phrase – sorry!) with somebody back home.

I was planning on getting in touch with Graham anyway, and had thoughts that I may invite him out to wherever I was when I got settled. I knew that he'd be good for a trip or two each year. He was a good bloke like that.

But I had also been wondering if I should get in contact with somebody else. Dunno why really? I had discounted Rachel, and the two jerks who were having fun at my expense, but had thought a little about checking in with my mother. This was something that I knew I was going to have to do at some stage as it was only fair to her that she knew I was ok. It was also only fair that, as my mother, she get to have a rant and a rave at me, and question her methods of upbringing over the phone. These were her unwritten rights, and could not be denied in any court of law. But before I rang her I at least wanted to be able to tell her something positive. Exactly what straw I was clutching for there I could not possibly imagine at the moment, but I was quite sure that the moment would come and I would know when it was. Until that moment there would be radio silence with my family. My sister would not be particularly bothered whether I rang her or not, in fact she probably hadn't noticed that I'd gone. If I rang her she'd only sound pissed off, and turn up Eastenders in the background as a hint that she had something more important to do.

When I turned my phone on, I had been happy to discover that there were no more messages for me, and no missed calls either. This was gratifying, as I was almost expecting a prank message from Interpol, or the FBI.

My message to Graham was short, and to the point – "All ok here mate, will be in touch soon. Keep this quiet for the mom tho pls."

I knew he'd be happy with that, and I fully intended to send him another message in the next day or so.

I made sure that this time I switched the phone OFF after using it.

And following these chores around the house, I was now lying in a hot bath, reading my Patterson, with an open beer close at hand. You really can't beat a relaxing hot bath you know! It's very underrated in my opinion, especially with my generation, and gender, where the quick shower seems to be the runaway choice. My feet were certainly happy with the feeling, after pounding mile upon mile of hard pavement.

I'd left the room around 5:30am, and, apart from a breakfast snack in a Starbucks, and a lunchtime visit to the Hard Rock, I had been on my feet until walking back into the hotel room around 3pm. So I had earned this bath, and didn't plan leaving the room until nine, unless hunger got the better of me.

I had already decided that I would flick around the TV channels for a while, maybe watch a new movie and then try to get a good two to three hours of sleep. None of this nap business, a proper sleep, which would give me the energy to get back out there again.

Then there was a knock at the door.

To begin with I wasn't sure that it was my door that was being knocked on. I was in the bath, and it was kind of hard to tell. I mean, from where I was laying, the door to next doors room was probably as close. I know there was a wall between us, but the way sound travels in these buildings, who knew? Anyway I said nothing, and after a short period there was another knock.

This one was certainly on my door. It was a little more definite than the first, which had maybe been a little 'tentative?' I know what I mean here, bear with me, I know it reads a bit oddly, but the knock on the second occasion was clearly louder than the first, giving me no doubt at all on which door the person was knocking.

So, why the first 'unsure' knock? What was that about? As if somebody wasn't wanting to draw too much attention?

Now all of this may seem like twaddle to you, but immediately gave me a feeling of dread in my stomach. It just didn't feel right; like something was going on that I didn't want to know too much about.

Thankfully I had not volunteered a sound at the first knock, and I repeated this silence now. I just lay very quietly in the bath, book in hand listening as hard as I could, bearing in mind that I wasn't Steve Austin.

The only things that I could hear were the bathroom fan, and my breathing, which always seems to be deafening at moments like this. I tried to hold my breath for a few seconds, but realised that this was just stupid.

The bathroom fan wasn't too loud, but I did start to wonder whether I would hear somebody trying to enter the room over the top of it, and decided that I should get out of the bath to investigate.

Surely nobody would try to enter the room? Except housekeeping, but they always hollered 'housekeeping' as they were knocking, and opening. All at the same time, so that you were in absolutely NO doubt at all as to what was going on.

I had not ordered any room service, or asked for a maintenance man, and they were the only people who I could think of that would make room visits.

I had placed my Patterson on the bathroom floor, being careful not to get it wet – cos that was REAL important to me at the moment – and I was now out of the bath, and grabbing a large white bath towel.

I tried to quickly dab away excess water (as you do), and opened the door to the little hallway that connected the main room, and the bedroom door. The door to the corridor was on my right, and nothing seemed out of the ordinary. Nobody had pushed anything underneath it, and it was closed firmly, with the deadlock turned, as I had done when I got back to the room, as a matter of course.

I stood for a second, in contemplation. Why was I freaked out? What was there to worry about? Probably somebody just knocked on the wrong hotel room door. It happens.

Then why didn't I think that that was what had happened?

Strange things were starting to happen a little too regularly for my liking.

First the whole Carrie-Ann incident, then the early morning homicide call, now this.

Or were they just three easily explained isolated incidents?

I was undecided. But there hadn't been a third knock so I could only assume that whoever had been at the door, had now gone on his, or her merry way.

I decided to check the spyhole just in case.

Now this was a whole new area to think about. I'd love to take a poll of a hundred people to see how many of them think that if somebody is looking out of their spyhole, the person at the other side of the door can see them. I'm not talking about being able to see back through the spyhole to the extent that you can tell whether the person in the room is wearing red, or say, holding three fingers up, but can you actually see the shadow of the person, so that you know that they are looking at you?

I'm willing to bet that, in my position, at least two thirds of the people would vote that, yes, the person on the other side of the door can tell that they are being stared at.

Now, sensibly, I don't know, I honestly don't. I'm gonna have to file it with airplane vs aeroplane, akron/canton vs canton/akron, WT, and the piece of furniture to rest luggage on. BUT… what I am willing to bet on is that, irrelevant to whether the person can see a shadow, they know that somebody is looking at them, watching. As I said earlier, you can just feel it.

Slowly, like a big girl's blouse I edged closer to the spyhole, or is it peephole? I wonder why I never picked up on that until this point. Jeez my list is just getting bigger!

I got so that I was right up to the door, and looked through, my eye slowly adjusting to the new doll's house view of the world.

There was nobody there… just a regular hotel corridor.

I waited maybe thirty seconds, just to be sure, then realised that I was wet, and getting a little cold, so I headed back into the bathroom, dropped my towel, and climbed back into the hot bath.

I reached for my beer, and took a swig, and a new thought entered my head. And this was a beauty!

I had not switched my phone back on until I got back to the room… what if the call this morning WAS from a real Lieutenant Saxton, who really DID want to speak to me regarding a homicide, and he had tried to ring me on my phone, found it switched off, and therefore decided to come to my hotel room, as I had given him that information.

How about that then?

I realise now why I have never gone away on my own before!

I mean it's nice being able to do things whenever you want, and not have to worry about whether other people really want to be doing them, and not have to wait for people to finish in the bathroom, or on the phone, but travelling, or I guess just being alone really gives you entirely too much time to think. This was not a problem that I'd ever come across before.

Obviously I think, we all do, but not in depth, at least, not about everything, to the nth degree.

With another person you just talk it over, and sometimes one of you will disagree, or maybe one will play devils advocate for a while, but generally, especially when you are friends, by the end of the conversation, you have sorted it out.

It was odd to be in this position, and I realised that I needed to go out, meet some people, and if I really was going to be able to make a success of my trip I needed to be able to deal with situations like this, and not go through a coronary every time the phone rang, or somebody knocked at the door.

"It's all part of it…" I said aloud, to nobody in particular. But it was. I had to get on, and go forward.

I was going to go out to Harry's and have too much to drink, make some friends and wake up tomorrow with direction.

Little did I know which direction tomorrow would take me in!

SEVEN

The sleep did me good. I felt great and was now heading towards Harry's in a cab. I checked my watch; it was 9:15pm. Excellent!

The area we were driving through wasn't quite city centre, but it wasn't suburbs either. Both sides of the street seemed to consist of businesses, and stores, with the occasional bar here and there. People really worked in this part of town, it wasn't for show. Not to impress the tourists or visiting businessmen, like the areas I'd been walking through this morning. This was the engine room, where the real work went on, and it showed.

We were approaching the area known as 'the Strip', which is where Harry's is located. It's apparently a good place to have a night out. 'The Strip', and 'the Southside', according to one of the people I had spoken to this morning.

The cab pulled over, and the driver, who could quite possibly have been mute, as he hadn't said a word since I got in, pointed at the meter, which read eight dollars seventy five cents, and nodded in the general direction of the other side of the street. He couldn't even muster a grunt! I gave him ten bucks, and got out without saying anything in reply.

Harry's looked immediately inviting, so I crossed the street without getting killed by passing cars, and walked right in.

It was busy, but not crazy. If I could have picked a perfect amount of people for the size of bar without feeling intimidated, then this would have been it.

The bar was directly in front of me, but because of the clever use of separating walls, there were three distinct areas, and the bar served them all by being in a long u-shape which ran through them. The room to the right seemed to be populated by college types, young trendy looking kids, playing pool, and sitting around one very large table in front of a big old fireplace. I spotted the toilets through there too. Always a good idea to know where they are!

Directly in front of me, between me and the bar were a few people propped on bar stools, with a cigarette machine and a large coatstand / hatstand (there's another) on the left. These people all seemed to know each other, and by the looks of them had come directly from work, and were doing their best to drink away the pressures of the day. It was Friday after all! There were about ten or twelve of them, and a couple of the ones, propped on bar stools facing me, looked a bit worse for wear, like maybe they would be on the floor if somebody removed their bar stools.

I headed straight through to the room on the left as if I'd been there many times before, and was very happy to discover a cosy room with a few scattered tables, and a couple of empty places up at the bar. Not exactly an English tavern, I thought, but a pleasant place to spend the evening. I knew I'd do well here.

The lighting throughout was just perfect too, 'dimly lit' is how I'd describe it. Not dark, but not bright. Easy on the eyes.

There were a couple of staff behind the bar, a guy in his mid to late twenties with a grungy black haircut, and a ring through his eyebrow, who was serving a similarly coiffed guy at the other side of the bar, and a girl who looked to be in her late teens, early twenties, with long blond straight hair, who looked remarkably like the character, Donna, from the 'West Wing' TV show. She was heading my way with a big smile and I just knew that I'd be telling her that she looked like Donna, from the West Wing before I left.

"Hey, what can I get for you?" she asked in a very happy voice that just reinforced my happiness at the choice of watering hole.

Anyway...

"Good question," standard breathing space answer. "What imported beers do you have?"

"Oh, we have... erm..." she looked to her right into the fridges below, and called out, "Becks, Corona, Heineken, Dos Equis..."

"Oh Dos Equis please," I interrupted. "Is it the amber?"

"Yeah, is that ok?"

"That's brilliant," I replied enthusiastically. "Just what I wanted, even though I didn't realise it until this moment."

She laughed at this, as did the guy next to me, who was listening in, and I wondered if he was being protective of my new friend. He seemed a bit older than her though. I stole a quick glance, and he appeared to be about my age, with hair a little longer than mine, dark brown, and he was reading the sports pages.

"So where are you from?" she was asking over her shoulder, as she grabbed a beer from the fridge.

"The north of England," I always put the north in. You have to do, otherwise everyone, from all over the planet always follows it up with the inevitable, 'London?' and that really annoys me.

"Cool, like whereabouts? Would I know any cities near where you live?"

"Sure, maybe you've heard of Leeds, or Manchester, or Liverpool?"

"Yeah, I've heard of Manchester, they have that soccer team right?"

She opened my beer, and put it in front of me, with a smile chaser.

"Oh god, yes, let's NOT talk about them though," I said, making my distaste clear.

Donna laughed again, and asked, "You wanna open up a tab?"

"Sure, that's probably a great idea. I'm Mike by the way," and I stretched out my hand.

"Hey Mike, I'm Beth. Nice to meet you."

I was just pondering over my follow up line when the guy next to me proffered his hand, "And I'm Stevie. Sorry to butt in, but I have to ask, if you hate Manchester United that much then you have to be either a Liverpool, Arsenal, or Leeds fan, right?"

Now it was my turn to laugh. Two new friends for the price of one! What a good do!

"You got me – Liverpool. Good to meet you Stevie," I said, and shook his hand. "Can I get you a beer?"

"That'd be great. I'll have a Dos Equis with you. I've not had one for absolutely years, and had forgotten they existed till I heard you ask for one."

I got a good feeling from this guy immediately. He was dressed in the same relaxed manner that I adopt, and seemed quite laid back in his attitude. He also seemed to be quite amazed that a complete stranger was buying him a beer.

Beth was already pulling another Dos Equis from the fridge. "And one for you Beth, if you're thirsty?" I offered.

She smiled, opening Stevie's beer. "Gee thanks, but I'm ok for now. I'll maybe take you up on that later tho."

"No probs."

She put the beer in front of Stevie, who was just draining his draught. He put the empty glass on the bar, ran one hand through his hair, and picked up the bottle of Dos Equis.

"Cheers Mike," he said, raising the bottle in my direction.

"Cheers," I returned, and clinked bottlenecks with him. We both took a good mouthful.

I love Dos Equis, especially the amber version. It really is refreshing. I always feel like I could drink it all night. Most beers blow me up, but not this. I took another large swig from the bottle.

I was seated sideways now, facing a little towards my new buddy Stevie, expecting conversation, and I could see that there were quite a few people sat at the tables behind us. They all seemed to be reading, newspapers, and novels. Maybe it was a little English? Nobody was talking that was for sure. Perhaps it was a literary tavern? I should have brought my Patterson!

I also noticed that there was some music on in the other room, but not where I was. It sounded like there could have been a jukebox in there. Despite the reading room in here, it seemed to work quite well, and added a little something to the atmosphere.

The work crowd was getting a little rowdy now, and the grungy guy behind the bar was heading over, looking like he was going to give them the hard word. I put my beer down on the bar, and sighed a big old sigh. I really felt relaxed.

"Heavy day, huh?" asked Stevie to my right.

I looked at him, and smiled my best ironic smile. "It's been a bit of a strange old couple of days, let's put it that way," I said.

"Why are you in town? Business?" he asked.

"No. Purely pleasure," I said, taking another large gulp of my beer. I'd nearly drunk it all already! God I had needed it. I hadn't realised how much.

Stevie noticed, and made a signal towards Beth, who sauntered over, keeping one eye on the rabble, who seemed to have elected a spokesperson to discuss the situation with the grunger.

"Can we get two more please?" he asked.

"Sure. You guys thirsty?" she said with a smirk.

"I am," I answered on our behalf. "I've spent all day pounding the streets of Pittsburgh in search of your city's soul. It's thirsty work."

"Did you find it?" asked Beth, reaching into the fridge, and hauling out two more bottles of Dos Equis.

I thought about this for a second.

"I'm not really sure to tell the truth. I feel like it's there, and it's all around, but maybe it has to be earned, like you have to put the time in."

"That's excellent," said Stevie, staring over the top of his beer into space, nodding, "and well put."

It was. I couldn't have put it better if I'd thought about it for a few days. The truth was, I'd thought a lot about this whilst walking around with nobody to talk to. I'd been lost in my own thoughts and had many of them.

I decided to continue… "Thanks, I'm glad you know what I mean, cos it's hard to explain. It's a different type of city, Pittsburgh."

I stopped suddenly because they were both staring at me now. I'd heard that the locals could be quite defensive of their home, 'da burgh' as they called it. I didn't want to upset someone before I'd started.

"No, go on, you have the floor," Stevie encouraged. He seemed genuinely interested, they both did. Okay. Here goes.

"Okay, the way I see it is this… Pittsburgh seems to be a city in transition at the moment, you know, a bit of a work in progress? It's got very strong working roots, but it's taking on a new identity, and it's trying to do it without losing the old one. The people I've met so far have all been very real, and very proud. I can see that you guys are more protective about your city and its image than citizens of say, Miami, or Los Angeles. That's a big thing that I get from being here. That this city is alive through its citizens. How about that?"

I took a deep breath, and grabbed my beer.

They were both still looking at me, and neither of them seemed to be blinking. It was like the ending sequence of Police Squad, where Leslie Neilson, OJ Simpson, and everybody else just stand still while everything continues around them.

"And…" I added, "I'm only on my second beer! Wait until I've had another three or four, I'll be running for mayor!"

That seemed to cut through the still air between us, and now we were all laughing.

Phew! Where did that come from? I really did need to get out, and be with people. It was obviously dangerous being by myself for long periods of time.

"And you've been here how long?" asked Stevie, breaking my thoughts.

"This is my second day here." I answered.

He shook his head, "You should come along to one of my classes, and talk with some of my students."

"Oh, you're a teacher?" I asked.

"Lecturer… at Pitt. The university."

"Sure I know it; they have a basketball team called the Panthers." I watch a lot of US sport. I'm a bit of an anorak when it comes to basketball, baseball, football, etc. I'm held in quite high ridicule with my friends, especially the ones who like rugby. Stupid game!

"That's right!" he looked quite shocked. "You know your sports, huh?"

"Yes," I answered, "but to be fair, so do you. I bet there aren't many people in this town who could name four English soccer teams."

"Yes, he seems to be as bad as you are," interjected Beth, "you should get on like a house on fire. I'll leave you to it." And she departed with a smile to see how her colleague was getting on with the folks at the end of the bar.

There were quite a few raised voices now, and one of the guys was jabbing a pointed finger in the direction of the grunger.

"Should we be helping out here?" I asked Stevie, nodding my head towards the action.

"Nah, don't worry yourself. Ray is a lot meaner than he looks, and he has a bunch of friends in the next room who are on the wrestling team if it kicks up a gear."

Ray was obviously the grunger. Funny… I never would have predicted that one.

Over the next couple of hours we drained more than a few beers, and talked a lot. It turned out that Stevie was a part time lecturer, in what seemed like a whole host of different subjects, all relating to social sciences. We discussed the merits of the US versus UK, and the grass is greener syndrome. I felt like I could be totally open with him, and gave him the whole story of why I was here. He seemed to be very impressed to go by what he said, and offered a lot of encouragement. He'd done a similar thing several years before, leaving a job in manual labour, and heading off to the far east for a couple of years, then coming back to Pittsburgh, and training in teaching, before staying on at the university, where he was studying for a Phd whilst lecturing. He said that he had needed to get away so that he could come back to do something else. Otherwise he would have still been a mechanic. Maybe that was what I was doing? But Stevie said that he always knew that he would go home, whereas I was totally adamant that I never wanted to.

He had introduced me to a group of students, who were hanging out in the next room, including two girls, both of whom were very pretty. I'd left him with them in the end, as I wasn't really sure what was going on, but I knew I didn't want to chat anybody up. I was enjoying myself too much to want to bother with anything as difficult as that. God I was getting old! You know when you are getting old when you would rather sit at the bar, nursing a beer, than chatting to two pretty college girls. D'oh!

"Penny for them," asked Beth leaning on the bar.

"I was just thinking how much I've enjoyed tonight," I said. It wasn't a lie. I had. "I mean, it's great to be travelling about on my own, but you can't beat a bit of company, and a good chat, you know?"

I looked at her. She really was lovely. I had to remind myself that I had drunk a lot, and needed to be careful. Remember the last time I got talking to a girl while I was drinking?

"Well I haven't really travelled, but I've spent time on my own, and there's a lot to be said for it, sure. But you can't beat interaction with people. Take tonight. I've met a real English guy!"

We both laughed.

"You never had that beer I promised you," I said.

"That's right I forgot!" she said. "I'll get it now if that's ok?"

"Sure, and I'll have another while you're at it."

"You got it," she said, and headed over to the fridge.

"Do you ever watch the W…" I began, but was interrupted by a hand on my shoulder, and turned to find Stevie staring at me with a big goofy smile on his face.

"Hey you, I've seen it. Keep your eyes off my sister!"

Stevie was back.

"Hey dude, welcome back. Another beer?"

"Sure. Why not," he said, and called out, "One more over here, please."

"Which one's your sister?" I asked him. I didn't remember either of their names.

"Beth," he replied, quite matter of factly.

Huh? Beth was his sister? I looked at him with a quizzical expression, if such a thing exists? He just smiled back at me.

"Fancy a nightcap back at mine?" he asked, "There are a bunch of people coming. Beth will be there."

He arched one eyebrow.

Sounded like a plan.

EIGHT

"Here we are," yelled Stevie, climbing out of the cab.

"Ok," I answered, "but where is here?"

His place was 'just over the river', and now here we were. Place was a euphemism though. It was quite clearly a hotel, or an inn of some kind.

It wasn't small either. It looked to be three storeys high, from the front, with huge heavy looking iron gates, and a small front yard from which wide stone steps led up to the doorway. The building itself was probably older than most in the city, I'm guessing at one hundred to one hundred and fifty years old, built of big old blocks of stone which looked weathered even in this light. The top floor windows were set into the tiled roof, giving it a bit of a 'Scooby Doo' haunted house look. It was certainly no Holiday Inn, and it didn't look to have a gym, or a car park for that matter, but it looked cool, in a kind of rambling old place tucked away in the corner of a city way. "You never told me I was drinking with Donald Trump," I remarked, with a smirk on my face.

Stevie laughed, and threw an arm round me as we followed the laughing from one of the students that he'd invited, who were already heading in through the colossal wooden front doors.

"It's a family heirloom," he said, with more than a hint of stories to be told in his voice.

"So you run this place and do your studies and lecture part time... and have time to go out socialising?" I asked.

"Whoa there..." he said stopping dead in his tracks. "I know you've been hitting on my sister, but surely she's not got you on her side on this already?"

I just looked at him, puzzled as to what my response should be to this.

We were stood in a tall ornate archway, which covered the front steps. There was a bit of a chill in the September air, and I realised that this was the first time I'd been outdoors on a night since I'd arrived. Maybe this drop in temperature was normal. Perhaps it was just a warning that the cold, cold winter was just around the corner. I hoped that I wouldn't be trying to find my way back to the hotel in it.

Stevie looked at me with a serious expression. Then he seemed to lighten up, as if reconsidering his thoughts.

"Beth worries about me," he said, "she worries about everything man, but jeez she gets on my back morning, noon, and night. She thinks I have too much on my plate, and I'm gonna end up getting ill, or killing myself, or something." He stopped, and sighed.

I just looked at him. I liked this guy, and was hoping that we were becoming friends, but no way was I about to start analysing him. I was quite happy to listen thought.

"Sorry man," he said, after what seemed like an age, and he tucked hair behind his ears with his fingers.

"Don't worry about it," I said, "you've sat and listened to me ramble on tonight."

"True. Fairs fair I supposed. I'll shut up now. Anyway, you never told me what it was that made the last couple of days strange," he headed in through the doorway, still talking as he walked. "Surely simply coming here wasn't what you had in mind?"

I pondered briefly. Was I ready to unload the weirdness of the whole trip up until this point onto him?

I'm the sort of person who doesn't have much of a problem being open, but maybe I should retain a bit of mystery. I didn't want my new friend to think I was without depth.

I realised that I was standing in a hallway, which was used as a reception come parlour. The ceiling seemed incredibly high, and an antique looking chandelier hung from it. The floors were wooden with tasteful rugs thrown here and there, and the walls hung with black and white prints of city scenes, of buildings and bridges, which I knew I could spend hours looking at. To the left was the reception desk with a large railway station clock on the wall behind it. To the right was an open door, and inside I could see a long table, with high backed chairs set around it, like some kind of royal dining hall. On the table was a glass vase, of what looked like tropical flowers. I was speechless whilst trying to take all of it in.

"That's our posh dining room," said Stevie, pointing inside. "Never gets used though. Shame really. But we all use the kitchen. It's big enough, and that's where the food is anyway. I guess times just change, huh?"

Stevie shook his head, and walked around the back of the reception area, and into a little room, where there was somebody else talking on a phone. I heard him mumble a couple of things, and he returned, standing behind reception, where a flat screen computer terminal was humming away to itself.

"Sorry, just wanted to check everything was ticking ok. That's Gerry back there. He works most nights here. He's an absolute hero. I don't know where I'd find anyone who could replace the guy."

"Do you have a lot of staff here?" I asked.

"Nah, thankfully I don't need them. I have a couple of people who come in to clean and that's about it. When Gerry's not around at night, I make sure I'm here in case anyone needs anything, and during the day Beth helps out when I'm lecturing. We could probably do with someone full time, but we get by. Why, you want a job?"

"You never know… I might need one to pay my bar bill if I carry on every night like tonight."

Stevie laughed.

I was still scanning the room, open-mouthed. This place was so cool. "Did the place always look like this, or is this décor yours?" I asked.

"I'd like to take the credit, but truth is it's a bit of both." He was leaning on reception, and looking around at the walls as if he was seeing the place for the first time himself. "This place is awesome when it's stripped down, and empty. It doesn't need any decoration to make it look good. It lends itself well to almost anything, so I guess the trick is, not to overdo things, and you're fine."

"Well it's fantastic. It really is."

"I'm glad you like it Mike. Come on, let's grab a couple of beers, and I'll show you around properly."

"Sounds like a plan."

We spent the next thirty minutes or so walking around the building. I gathered that there were eight guest rooms, plus Mike's own quarters on the top floor in the roof, which I'd seen from outside. You got to the upstairs rooms from a sweeping stone staircase, which headed off reception at a right angle. Halfway up it cut back on itself at a big landing then led up again onto an upstairs corridor, which was carpeted. Doors were at intervals down the corridor, and at the moment apparently six of these opened onto rooms which were taken by students from outside the area, on a long term basis. It sounded like the prices weren't cheap, and students could certainly find a lot better prices elsewhere, but Stevie knew that he could attract a more well heeled student, and didn't seem to have problems keeping the rooms occupied. Word of mouth from the university was his only form of advertising that I could ascertain. The accommodation was good from what I saw. He showed me a room, which had just been made vacant by a student who had got homesick, and headed back to the heat of Arizona once the cold evenings began. It was large, with the same high ceilings, lots of closet space for storage, and a bathroom with a deep bath. Did I mention that I like baths? Right up my street. Lucky students. Maybe I should enrol?

Stevie's pad was an open plan floor, with strategically placed furniture to divide up what was once the old attic. We helped ourselves to a cold beer from his personal stock, and he pointed out what was his pride and joy, a large stack of records, and several boxes besides. He had a great system, he promised me, but didn't want to crank it up whilst he had guests sleeping below. The room felt a lot warmer, and cosier than the rest of the building as the roof was lower, and at crazy angles in places, which made ducking a bit of a sport.

There were some back stairs from the top floor into the kitchen downstairs, which was vast, with the ubiquitous high ceilings. This area was clearly shared by all with extra refrigerator space which Stevie had had installed, so that the students could all store their own food. Then there were the usual amenities, cooker, microwave, and a mammoth farmhouse kitchen table, with about ten chairs around it.

This was where the party was happening, and the crew had all arrived by now from Harry's. I recognised Ray, the barman formerly known as the grunger, and was formally introduced, and I said 'Hi' to another couple of guys that I had seen at the bar. I was trying to be sociable, and chat with everyone, but seemed to find myself being drawn towards Beth, who was stood over by an island, talking to another girl, that I hadn't met before. This girl turned out to be one of the paying guests; she was called Angie, and was just heading off to bed, which conveniently left me alone with Beth.

"So… do you come here often?" I ventured, with a smile. It was meant as a comic opening, but Beth seemed happy with it.

"Too often I fear," she replied, "I could be at home right now catching up on my beauty sleep."

"I'm torn here between saying 'you don't need beauty sleep' and 'you don't live here then?' so if you could just acknowledge the first part with a polite nod, and move right onto the second part I would appreciate it."

If I was chatting Beth up here, I was doing it without concentrating, and if she minded, then she didn't show it.

"Ok, here's your polite nod," she nodded – quite politely, "and the answer to your second part is, no, I live right around the corner. I don't know how much Stevie told you, but this place used to belong to our grandparents, and I live in the home that we grew up in."

"With your parents?" I prodded.

"No, they passed on a few years back."

Oh god. Keep talking. "I'm sorry to hear that, and feel like a jerk for bringing it up."

"Don't, and you're not. It's something that happened, and we live with it. They were in an auto wreck while on vacation on the west coast. It was very hard at the time, as you can imagine, but a lot of water has flowed under the bridge since then."

She went on, with very little help from me, to tell me about how this had happened whilst Stevie was in the Far East, and it had taken several days to get hold of him. There were only the two of them siblings wise, and it sounded like a whole lotta emotion had been stirred up by these events.

Stevie had returned to the US, and stayed. It seemed that both grandparents had relied on Stevie and Beth's parents quite a bit for help with the running of the hotel, and following their deaths, they had decided to call it a day, and retire to the sun in Florida. Stevie had managed to convince them that he was the man to keep the old place going, and they had worked out some kind of deal.

Beth had remained in the family home, and had finished high school, before going on to Pitt Uni, where Stevie lectured. It hadn't been her first choice, and she had been accepted at Stanford, but had not wanted to either leave her hometown, or take up residence in California, with all of its lasting memories of being the place where her parents had died.

Beth seemed to be enjoying getting this off of her chest, and I got the feeling that it wasn't something that she mentioned very often. At the same time I was conscious that I had drunk a lot, and was trying very hard to think of the right things to say. As I said, I wasn't really chatting Beth up, but we seemed to be in that situation that you occasionally get into with a member of the opposite sex, or your own sex, depending on your preference, where you feel like you are heading that way without trying. I was acutely aware that I had grown very fond of my new friends, and didn't want to do anything dumb that I would regret later. I needed to regroup, and think things through. I was starting to think about maybe quitting whilst ahead, and heading off back to the hotel. However, a very large part of me wanted to be here, chatting to Beth and that part was winning, whilst acknowledging the concerns of the little angel on the other shoulder.

I noticed that Beth was running low on drink, and thought that it could be a good natural pause.

"You fancy a refill?" I asked.

"Thanks, I really would love to, but I think that I should be going, I have a lecture tomorrow at ten, and already know that it will be a struggle."

I looked at my watch. SHIT – it was 3:45 am!!!!!

"Oh my god I can't believe the time," I said, "I'm sorry to keep you up till this time."

"Are you crazy? I've really enjoyed talking to you. Thanks. You're a good listener…" she paused… "I hope you're gonna be sticking around for a while."

I put my hand on her arm. "I've made some great new friends tonight, and am starting to love this place, so don't count on me leaving town too soon."

"What did I say about hitting on my sister," said the voice from right behind me.

I turned around. "Will you stop creeping up on me!" I said with mock annoyance. "Anyway, I've bored her to death now, and she's going home."

"Well this party is about over anyway," he said, and I realised that everybody had disappeared except Ray, who was fastening up his jacket.

"You want me to walk you round home Beth?" asked Ray.

"That would be great, I'll just get my coat," replied Beth.

I decided that this was as good a time as any to make my exit. "Can I trouble somebody for a telephone number for a cab?" I asked.

"Are you kidding me, why don't you grab a room upstairs man and walk home in the am?" asked Stevie.

As soon as he said it, it was a done deal. All of a sudden I had become overcome with tiredness so heavy it was squashing me. "That would actually be great. I would appreciate it." I said.

"Yeah well, if you liked the room you were in earlier, take that one. I'll grab you the key from Gerry. And hey, while I'm thinking about it, you should check out of that expensive corporate monster that you're staying in tomorrow morning, and haul your gear over here. We're a heck of a lot cheaper."

"That would be superb! I would really love to do that!" I said. "And I could help out with the front desk."

"You've already recruited Mike for the front desk?" said Beth, returning and catching the end of the sentence.

Stevie had a big grin on his face. "It was my master plan all along," he said, "and it worked a treat."

He headed off towards the reception area with Ray, and I walked behind them with Beth.

"So I guess we really will be seeing more of you then," she said.

"Yes. Do you think you can put up with me?"

"I'm already looking forward to it," she said. And with that she leaned forward, gave me a peck on the cheek, stepped back with a smile, turned, and walked out of the front door with Ray. I felt a warm glow all over. Big smile inside my chest trying to get out!

"Seeya later Mike," called Ray over his shoulder, interrupting the moment.

"Night, Ray," I shouted after him.

Stevie walked over still smiling, shaking his head. He didn't say a word, and didn't need to. He led me back upstairs, and showed me where everything was, then bade me a goodnight, and we agreed to chat everything over in the morning.

I lay down on the bed for a minute to try to get the strength back in order to get undressed, but I need not have bothered, as I was asleep before my head hit the pillow.

I kid you not!

NINE

Waking up with a jolt; then wondering where the hell I was, seemed to be becoming de rigueur this week.

The light flooding in from the windows and the bulb above the bed soon had me alert enough to decipher the puzzle though.

It was almost eight thirty by my watch and my opening thought was that I had not cleaned my teeth for a long time. This was troublesome to me, and was all the incentive that I needed to get me out of bed. That, and the bright light shining in my eyes.

Stopping only to turn out the light, I paid a quick call and by then had decided to head back to the hotel straight away to pack up my things for my move over the river. And to clean my teeth. That was important!

There was nobody around downstairs. After examining the lock on the front door and establishing that I would not need it, I left the bedroom key behind the reception desk and hit the street.

Fortunately there was no alarm, or if there was, it wasn't set, so I pulled the front door shut, hearing it lock, realising that I wouldn't be able to get back in with my stuff until people were up and about.

Perhaps I shouldn't have been worrying about all of this, but it's strange how your mind works, when all of a sudden you don't have the normal day to day worries, like should I stop for fuel on the way to work, or on the way home? When would I most like to have more time? You fall into a routine, which seems to suit you fine, and pretty soon start to worry about which parts of your routine aren't quite right. Maybe we should all just avoid routines? Maybe, but it seems that we simply replace all worries with other, unforeseen worries. As a race, certainly in the Western world, if we don't have something in our lives to fret about then we aren't normal. That's when we actively go out looking for trouble.

Anyway, aside from all the concerns, it was certainly a beautiful morning, just perfect for moving home. There was a crisp feeling in the air. The sun was out, but it didn't seem to be warming anything up just yet. There was a 'new day' feel in the air. The feeling that you get right after a storm, like the cycle has ended and a new one is just beginning. It all pointed to good omens.

As I walked out onto the street, I noticed that the hotel had a sign, which I hadn't seen the night before. 'Forks of the Ohio Inn' it read. So it wasn't a hotel, it was an inn. I wondered what the difference was. Maybe a couple of thousand in tax, I thought sceptically. I made a mental note to ask, and also to ask about the name itself, 'Forks of the Ohio', it must mean something. Or maybe it was just the position?

The streets of this part of Pittsburgh were bustling. I suppose that's the most descriptive way of putting it. It wasn't mad, with people rushing about, like you see in most cities during rush hour. Instead people seemed to be going about their business in a leisurely way, with a healthy portion of bustle. Rush hour didn't seem to be too much of a rush. There was traffic on the freeway going over the river, which I could see up ahead, of me, but it wasn't madness. It was flowing. Back in the UK at this time on the M1, or M62, I would be bumper to bumper, getting more and more frustrated. I was liking this city a lot.

I could see the football stadium to my right literally five blocks or so from me. Heinz field I think it's called now. Used to be Three Rivers Stadium, the home of the Pittsburgh Steelers and their Terrible Towels. Shame corporations had to insist on their name being used. Three Rivers Stadium was a great name, almost native American.

I walked all the way back into the hotel, feeling almost like an eighteen year old kid sneaking into his paren'ts house after a night out on the tiles. The doorman who held the door open for me said "Good Morning" in a way that I read as "A-ha, you've been up to no good," with almost a wink in his eye. I probably imagined it, as I'm sure I imagined all of the girls behind the reception desks looking at me with expressions of disapproval.

I grabbed a bottle of Gatorade from the shop, being careful not to breathe on the lady behind the till, even though the smell of beer must have been oozing from every pore. By the time I reached the room I was longing for a shower.

I kicked off my shoes, and flung off my clothes with abandon, walking naked into the bathroom. I started the shower running, and squeezed toothpaste onto my brush, climbing into the shower whilst brushing my teeth. I could almost feel the plaque, and fur falling off of my teeth. Marvellous!

I stood under the shower for some time, enjoying the warm jets on my neck and shoulders. I could have stood there for hours, but finally I gave in, climbed out, and dried myself off.

I then attended to the crumpled up clothes on the bed, and repacked my case, selecting jeans, and a long sleeved t-shirt as my uniform of the day.

This was exciting! My trip was already turning into an adventure. I was moving in with a new friend, and it looked like there was a possibility of some part time work also. Not to mention the possibilities with Beth. Things were decidedly better than twenty four hours ago.

I made a mental note to check my phone for messages when I got installed in my new room, and maybe give my mother a call, as I now had a contact address where I could be reached in case of crisis. I'm not sure what crisis I was expecting, but you know what I'm talking about. Maybe this was a portent of doom?

The front desk did not appeal to me, so I checked out using the television express checkout system, which is THE most tremendous addition to hotel travel, and did a final sweep of the room for stray items before leaving.

There was a complementary copy of USA Today left outside the door, so I took it with me, even though I knew that I would end up only reading the Sports section.

While waiting for the elevator I began to read the leading sports article which was about two new players that Bill Cowher had brought in for the new football season. Apparently they had both performed very well in pre-season, but the rushing back in particular, who had had personality problems with his last team, Carolina, that had affected his performances, was being tipped for greatness this season. The article was predicting Cowher to be the man, with his straight talking no nonsense attitude, to get the potential out of this kid that everybody knew he had. I'd not heard of him personally, but made a mental note to enquire about Steelers tickets with Stevie. I really wanted to get to a game.

The elevator doors opened, and I busied myself bending down to pick up my suitcase, and rucksack as somebody else got out. I performed a shuffle into the empty elevator car, managing to keep hold of the newspaper as well as the luggage, then stood up as the doors began to close. As this was all happening, the person who had just exited the elevator halted in his tracks, and turned to face me.

It was one of those moments that happen in slow motion. Even before the guy turned round I knew exactly who I was going to be looking at.

Tall figure, with long black hair tied up in a ponytail, red and black checked jacket.

It was the guy from the airport in Philadelphia!!

The guy that had spooked Carrie-Ann!

And he was looking at me. He knew who I was, there was no doubt about it.

And it was obviously me that he was coming to see!

In that never ending moment all of the thoughts that were going through my head made it sound like a rock concert was going on, then all at once, the elevator doors closed leaving me standing in total silence. I dropped the newspaper.

The ride down to the reception was trancelike. I don't even remember pushing the button to go down.

Somehow though my body had it within itself to go into automatic pilot; I honestly believe this. Because looking back, the actions that I took in the next ninety seconds seemed to be happening around me, as if I had no control over them at all.

The elevator doors opened and without a moment of delay I found myself walking towards the front entrance of the hotel. Not running, or moving quickly attracting attention, just walking, like it was every day that some nutcase, who I don't know follows me from one city to another, and stakes out my hotel room.

Perhaps I am like the guy out of the Bourne Identity? Maybe really I am a secret agent, and I've been 'sleeping' until this moment. Everything that I previously thought to be real was in fact a created illusion, masking my real identity?

Errm… no.

Anyway, the hotel doors were standing open as I reached them, which was mighty fortuitous. A couple had just climbed out of a cab and were retrieving their luggage from the driver who had collected it from the boot. Things were all happening in time with my needs. I wasn't about to start questioning why, I simply passed the driver my black bag, and jumped in the back with my rucksack.

As the driver got in, I told him I was heading over the river towards the football stadium. I decided not to give him the full address as it may delay us. Sometimes a driver will want to know every possible detail, so I figured that naming something large and recognisable like the stadium would at least get us close by before he started asking where I wanted to be dropped. Then I could direct him to Stevie's place.

It seemed to work, as with no fuss whatsoever, he pulled away from the hotel, and we were on our way.

At this point I don't think that I had breathed for about four minutes! I caught up with a few quick breaths to try and encourage oxygen to my brain.

As the driver pulled into the flow of traffic I was able to look out of the right hand side window without being obvious about it. I saw a flash of red and black, which I guessed was my friend, coming out of the hotel.

I suspected that, even if there wasn't a cab out front at this moment, which there probably was, it would only be a matter of time before he was able to get one, and he would be on my heels.

I exhaled…

"You in trouble buddy?" asked the driver, staring at me through the rear view mirror.

I ignored him for the moment, as my thought processes were starting to kick in.

Maybe the guy was a cop?

Maybe he was Saxton?

Either way he found me, in Pittsburgh, so it must have been him who rang me claiming to be Saxton? Unless he had managed to get hold of the information from Saxton?

This all related to that telephone call.

And if that was the case, then the homicide was for real.

Which meant that this all tied into Carrie-Ann.

Which meant that Carrie-Ann was the homicide victim!

Which is how he got my telephone number, because somehow it has registered on Carrie-Ann's cell phone.

So… I was certainly being pursued by somebody who was not stupid.

And maybe he killed Carrie-Ann?

"I changed my mind," I said to the driver who was just in the process of switching lanes at an intersection, "I want to go to Pittsburgh International Airport. Departures, please."

He swerved back into the lane that he'd previously been in, muttering under his breath, and I decided to level with the guy, as it could just buy me some time.

He was eyeing me, suspiciously now. I'm not surprised. In his job he must get pretty good at reading people, and despite my best actions I didn't exactly look like James Bond.

I guessed that the driver was in his late thirties. He was a white, heavy-set guy with stubble, and an oversized Steelers baseball cap perched on his head at an angle. I don't like to stereotype, and hate making assumptions, but this guy didn't look like a live wire. Maybe a bit of action might be what he needed?

"I'm being followed by someone," I started. "I have no idea who he is, but he's clever, and I don't get the feeling he wants to buy me lunch. I'm guessing that he's finding out as we speak, where we are heading, so I'm asking you to please get me to the airport as soon as you can, and I'll throw in an extra twenty bucks."

He smiled. I couldn't see his mouth, but his eyes said it all. "You got it buddy. I'll get you there in no time."

And with that he floored it.

I have no idea how long it took me to get to the hotel from the airport when I had first arrived, but I'm guessing we broke that time on this journey. I never felt in any danger, and I never heard a wheel squeal, but then, my mind was working overtime, and I don't think I would have registered if we'd been in a three-car pile up. I spent the whole journey deep in thought. I needed to be clear on what I was going to do here. If this guy was a cop then I was clearly evading him, and that could be considered as an action suggesting I had something to hide. I didn't. So why was I running?

I was running because something didn't sit right. My instincts were telling me that this guy was bad. Don't ask me why. I certainly don't claim to be an expert judge of character.

"Here we are pal," he said, as I saw the signs for different airlines coming up in front of us.

"That's great, how much do I owe you?" I asked, dragging my wallet out of my pocket.

"It'll be around sixteen dollars, but we haven't stopped yet so I can't be sure."

I passed him two twenties as he pulled up to the kerb.

"Gee thanks buddy. I hope that everything goes ok," he said as he got out, and headed for the boot, to get my bag.

I got out, and joined him at the back of the car, not daring to look around for fear that I might see something that might actually be there.

"Do you want me to call the cops?" the driver asked me, as he handed me the suitcase. He looked genuinely concerned for my welfare.

"No, don't worry. You've done more than enough to help me. Thanks again."

And with that I walked through the revolving door, rucksack over my shoulder, wheeling my bag along side me.

"Welcome to Pittsburgh International Airport" read the sign.

Wasn't I just here?

TEN

I had a plan.

In my head it seemed like a good plan. I had formulated it on the way to the airport with Jimmie Johnson at the wheel.

I entered the terminal and scanned around for the sign of an elevator or an escalator.

I saw an escalator and took it to the arrivals floor.

Next I found a sign that read 'Rental Cars' and followed that.

Before I knew it I was stood facing a Mexican looking guy wearing a white, short-sleeved shirt and a blue tank top. His nametag read 'Jaime'.

I handed over my driver's licence and credit card and told him that I was going out of state on a trip and planned to rent a car for approximately three days. I told him that I would be bringing the car back to this depot, as I knew that I'd get the third degree if I told him the truth. Which was I didn't have a clue where I was going; that I was using the force at the moment.

I decided that safety could be a concern so went for the SUV, which would give me a bit of protection and make me feel more secure.

I soon found myself sat in the driver's seat of a fairly new looking dark blue Dodge Durango.

I was keen to get a few miles under my belt before I did anything else and so, after making sure that I still had everything that I had come with, I pulled out of the parking lot and followed the airport directions to the exit.

I kept one eye in my rear view mirror for any sign that I was being followed but I seemed to be leaving the airport in a quiet period and there were no other vehicles in sight.

My plan seemed to have worked and it looked like I'd given my new friend the slip.

Once I reached the signs for the highways I was faced with two clear choices: 'Pittsburgh' or 'not'. I plumped for 'not' and found myself heading for New Castle and Youngstown.

I looked at the clock: it was 10:45am. I had only been awake for just over two hours and my trip had taken a decidedly different turn to my earlier expectations.

I was still in that dreamlike state where I wasn't thinking about anything in particular but my brain was obviously trying to piece things together. Kind of like a computer when it shuts down to sleep, to save energy, or like when a normal human falls asleep. I have this theory, which probably won't sound revolutionary to you, but I think that while you are asleep your brain is still working and spends the downtime working out the problems and dilemmas in your life. This is why people grind their teeth in their sleep, and toss and turn. And dreams, if you know how to read them, are your body's way of telling you how to solve the problem. I think I may have read that last bit somewhere. I seem to remember that each dream has four distinct parts to it, I can't remember what each part is so I probably shouldn't have started this, but I do recall that the last part of the dream is the solution to the problem and if you can make it out then you should probably follow it. But then again, who's to say that your mind is going to be right in its assumption of the answer? This is probably something else that I should save for another time. When I've read up on things...

Anyway... the reason for me going into everything about dreams is that I was now driving up the highway, heading to god knows where, with no radio on and for all intents and purposes driving whilst on shut down mode. I have no exact way of knowing how long this went on, but I do know when I woke from this trance.

It was when I saw the sign that read 'Youngstown, AKRON, Cleveland'!

Suddenly I was alert and ready to make a decision that turned me from defence into offence in the blink of an eye.

I indicated and lined my car up with the section of the highway that put me on the '76', the Pennsylvania turnpike, heading northwest into Ohio.

I think I may have actually smiled when I did this.

I decided that I needed to take a pit-stop. I hadn't eaten or drank anything except Gatorade so far that day and needed a toilet visit too.

I planned to take the next exit that had a sign for some kind of food outlet. I was in luck almost straightaway as there was a Cracker Barrel in just over three miles. I would be able to get OJ, coffee and some kind of food inside of me.

I still wasn't totally clear what my plans were but I knew that I was headed in the direction of Akron and I certainly hadn't planned it that way. I also knew that I was going to be stopping when I got to Akron, but didn't exactly know why, or what I would do when I stopped.

I also knew that I needed to get in touch with Stevie or Beth and try to explain to them why I had done a runner without telling them what was going on.

I had made a mental note to get in touch with my mother only a few hours before but I would put that off for now. What I did also need to do was switch my phone on to see if I had any new messages on it or at least check if anybody had tried to call me. The guy who rang on Friday with the wake up call had promised that somebody would get in touch with me and an officer would call round to see me. So if this was all legit then surely somebody would have tried to get in touch with me before simply showing up at my hotel bedroom door. I hadn't noticed my room phone flashing, which would have indicated a message at reception and surely a hotel like that would have let me know if somebody, especially the police, had come looking for me. I decided that a call to the hotel to ask them if they had any messages left for me would be a good idea.

Another point here was that Lieutenant Saxton had said that an officer would be coming to see me and not a plain clothed assassin looking type person.

I thought back to the previous evening when I had been in the bath and thought that I'd heard a knock at the door. That must have been the same guy! He must have thought that I wasn't in the room and left. Maybe he'd hung around in the hotel for a while afterwards, waiting to see if I showed up. But I'd had a nap and anybody would have got fed up with waiting, so perhaps he thought he'd try again first thing in the morning? Certainly if he'd seen me leaving the hotel then he would have followed me to Harry's bar, but he never showed up there. This meant that he didn't know about Stevie's place. So at least he wouldn't try looking for me there. I logged that in my memory banks.

I was at the exit now and could see the huge yellow and brown sign, on the top of a 100ft pole, to the left of the highway. I took the exit ramp and followed it down to the junction, then turned left back underneath the '76' and pulled into the parking lot of the Cracker Barrel. I had eaten at these places before. They always had a smokey smell to them inside which was quite relaxing and appetite inducing.

I locked the Durango and headed inside, where three people said good morning to me before I even got to the bathroom.

When I had finished powdering my nose and got sat down, a lady called Alice came over and took my order. She made me feel settled straight away with her soothing tones and I decided on an omelette with a side of toast. The place was almost empty and had some country music piped in, mixing very well with the smokey smell, which I decided was the aroma of burning wood... hickory?

I didn't have long to wait for my food. It came pretty quickly and was exactly what I was looking for. The coffee was hot and strong, and Alice kept coming back to fill it up. Bless her!

My thoughts were becoming clearer with the addition of food to my system so I turned my phone on and buttered the last piece of toast while the phone searched for a signal.

I had intended to use the phone only in case of emergency, as I had no way of paying the bill which would be delivered to Rachel at some stage. This could be considered an emergency situation in anybody's book, but I still felt guilty about it, so I made an executive decision to use a payphone. In addition, my phone had got me into trouble once already by leaving a tell tale number on somebody else's phone.

Carrie-Ann's phone!

Of course... I had her cell phone number stored in my phone! If she was dead then this could be a waste of time, but I had to try the number didn't I?

If I didn't then I'd always wonder...

I had no messages on my phone at all. Not even from Rachel – which I didn't have time to analyse at the moment.

Alice brought me the check. "There you go honey," she said leaving it on the table in front of me. "You just go ahead and holler if you need any change."

She was a lovely woman, probably in her early fifties, with curly brown hair and glasses, like a favourite aunt. She had a very happy look to her. Why couldn't the airlines take their staff from the Cracker Barrel chain? It should be their training ground.

I overpaid by about ten dollars on purpose. You can't overestimate the value of staff like Alice. It's good to leave a place feeling well fed and happy. It's worth far more than twenty four dollars that's for sure.

I had already spotted the payphone when I came in and headed back there now.

I decided that first of all I would ring Stevie. However I didn't have his number, so I stuck a few quarters in the phone and dialled '4 1 1' then asked for the number for the Forks of the Ohio Inn, in Pittsburgh. I decided to take the number down into my mobile phone as the automated voice read it out, rather than shovel in eight hundred quarters to be put through on some expensive tariff.

I then rang the number through. It rang two, maybe three times and was answered by a female voice.

"Hello, Forks of the Ohio."

"Hi... is that Beth?" I asked. It didn't sound like her.

"No, this is Angie, who's that?"

Ah, Angie. The student that I had met last night.

"Hi Angie, this is Mike Huntingden. I met you last night."

"Oh hi, sure I remember you. You're the English guy that Beth introduced me to."

This was going well. "That's me. I don't suppose Stevie or Beth are in, are they?"

"No, neither of them are here at the moment, I'm kinda helping out. I think Stevie's looking to get somebody in to cover days, but until then we all get involved when we can," she explained.

Great… I really didn't want to leave a message with this girl. It would sound stupid explained to somebody that I knew, never mind to an acquaintance to pass on as a message that would be bound to alter while being passed on. Before I could come up with a thought, she continued…

"I have Beth's cell phone number here if you want to get hold of her now?"

Awesome! This was one helpful girl.

"You are a saint, thank you Angie, I owe you one," I said, as I grabbed my mobile again to input the number.

I started to type 'Beth' into the address book on the phone.

"You ready?" she asked.

"Fire away."

I took Beth's number and saved it, then thanked Angie profusely, promising to buy her a drink, and hung up.

I then threw another quarter into the phone and keyed in Beth's number. I wondered why I was nervous. I had more important things to be worried about than some silly crush on a girl almost half my age for fuck's sake. Get a hold of yourself Mike!

It rang for quite a while then Beth answered tentatively, "Hello?"

"Hi Beth, it's me… Mike."

"Oh… Hi Mike. I'm sorry I was in a lecture, that's why it took me so long to answer. I had to leave the hall."

Oops!

"Oh god, I'm sorry!" I said.

I felt like a jerk. She had told me that she was going into a lecture.

"No, don't worry it's nearly over and it was boring anyway. I'd rather talk to you."

Was she flirting?

Could I get on with things and stop thinking like this?

"How did you get my number?"

"Oh, I rang the hotel... I mean 'Inn', sorry."

She laughed.

"Angie was kind enough to give it to me. I had to ring Beth, because I lied to you last night."

I found myself pausing for dramatic effect. Don't ask me why. I was doing a lot of strange things at the moment.

"You lied to me?"

Oh shit, now I'd scared her. I was no good at this bluffing business.

"Yes... I said I that I wouldn't leave town and I'm currently heading for Akron."

"Ohio?"

"Unfortunately, yes. It's a very strange story and one that I really can not explain at the moment. But I just wanted to let you know that I haven't run away and that, as soon as I've sorted everything out, I will be back... and I'll bring you a present from rubber town."

I have no idea why I threw the last comment in but it was in keeping with the last three days.

"Ok... so are you in trouble?" she asked.

"To be honest Beth, I really don't know," I said. "I hope not, but some very weird things are happening around me and I want to try to get to the bottom of it all."

She was silent for a moment.

"Did you ring Stevie?"

"Well I rang to speak to whichever one of you I could get a hold of and you drew the short straw unfortunately."

She forced a laugh. And it was forced. I was aware that I may have soured this relationship already and didn't really know how to rescue it without sounding like an escaped convict running from the law. Maybe Tommy Lee Jones would be listening in?

"How long will it take... to sort whatever it is out?"

Bless her. I liked this girl. I may have already said that?

"I don't know," I said. "Hopefully I will find out whatever I need to find out today. But to be truthful Beth I don't know what I'm looking for, or where to find it. I just know that it's in Akron."

"Maybe I could help? Or Stevie?"

"Maybe... but I don't want to get you guys wrapped up in something that could get you into trouble. It's probably best if I try to figure a bit more out first."

I could tell that this was not making her feel any better so I continued... "I promise that when I know what is going on I will tell you."

"I hope so Mike. We... I... don't want to see you get into trouble. If there's anything that we can do..."

"Beth, you guys have done enough already. I will ring you later when I find a place to stay. Ok?"

"Ok. Hey... do you have a cell phone that I can reach you on?"

I thought for a second. "Yes... but it's an English one and it'll cost you a fortune to ring me on it. I was thinking of getting a cell phone here when I got chance."

Which wasn't technically true but actually sounded like a good idea.

"Great. Promise me that the first thing you do in Akron is go get a cell phone and ring me with the number," she said.

How could I turn the lady down?

"Ok. I will do, it's a promise. But I have no idea how to go about getting one."

"Mike … it's a doddle. A child could do it."

She was playing again. Good!

"Just go into a phone shop and sign up."

"Roger. Understood."

With that I bade farewell, and after promising again to ring later, I asked her to tell Stevie to keep my room free and hung up.

I felt MUCH better as I walked out into the parking lot. I had eaten, visited the bathroom and spoken to a wonderful girl who cared about my safety. And I best not forget about Alice.

She was lovely as well!

ELEVEN

Soon I was over the state line and in Ohio, which I seem to remember being known as the 'Buckeye State'.

Why I don't know. I'll add it to my list of things which I need to find out.

An 'O' at the start, an 'O' at the end and a 'Hi' in the middle.

Had I heard that saying on a commercial? Or a comedy? I wasn't sure whether I'd made it up to be honest, but it made me smile.

I was on the 76 West and the sign that I was just passing said Akron 12 miles.

Eek!

Did I really just say 'Eek'?

What was I doing here? Becoming an amateur private investigator? Is that what I was doing?

What on earth was I going to do when I got to Akron? Drive around asking if anybody knew Carrie-Ann Novitski?

I really needed to come up with something soon otherwise I might just as well keep driving.

The radio station that I had finally found amongst the endless sea of commercials was playing the opening bars of 'American Girl' by Tom Petty and the Heartbreakers. I turned it up loud and sang along.

"Well she was an American Girl… raised on promises… she couldn't help thinking that there was a little more life… somewhere else!"

I apologise if you don't know this song but strongly suggest that you buy a cd with it on. It's a real feel good song without the normal cheese garnish. If you do know it, I bet you sang along! And I bet you're wondering where your copy of it is now.

Great lyrics… "After all it was a great big world… with lots of places to run to…"

The lyrics seemed to mirror my own feelings, but then I'm sure that you could do that with any lyrics, which probably explains why people need music to get through periods of their life.

Some people need God. Some use Metallica.

It's an interesting fact, but it's true. I would lean towards the 'tallica boys as being more relevant today. And we can certainly trust in the existence of Jaymz, Lars and Kirk!

Hope I haven't alienated you now with my crazy mullings? Let's get back to the matter at hand…

"God it's so painful… when it's something that's so close… but still so far out of reach."

I had a good sing along and wasn't too upset when some commercial for a lawn mower outlet came on. And after the burst of singing came a sizeable portion of inspiration…

I was going to follow Beth's advice first and go buy a mobile phone/cell phone. Then I was going to drive around and get my bearings a little, at the same time looking for a nice motel.

When I found a motel I would get checked in, have another shower – my second of the day – and lie down on the hotel bed until I came up with a plan.

This all sounded good and I had to look at this as an opportunity to see another place. So even if I didn't round up a murderer before sundown I was still going to be better off than if I was back in the UK worrying about something stupid like whether the cats had enough food and did I need to go to the supermarket on the way home.

I looked at the clock… it was one twenty. That was when my phone rang.

I hadn't switched it off again!

It was in my jeans pocket and it was vibrating like crazy. I kept one hand on the wheel while I tugged at it to force it free, trying hard not to cancel the call as I was doing it. Don't you just hate it when you do that?

I checked the view out of the windscreen one more time, making sure that the horizon was the right way and the white lines were lined up, and looked down at my phone.

'Rachel'.

Great! Here was a call that I needed today like a rusty coat hanger in my arm!

I made another one of those split second decisions that I'm fast becoming famous for and answered it before it cut off onto the answer phone.

"Hi" I said, trying to sound as jaunty as possible.

"Mike, where are you?" she asked sounding tense and unusually cool.

I debated how to answer this. Should I be sarcastic? I wanted to show conviction that I had made the right decision in leaving, but at the same time was feeling quite smug that she was chasing me with text messages and now a phone call. I couldn't resist.

"I'm cruising through the Ohio countryside actually Rachel. Where are you?"

There was a pause.

"I'm sitting here wondering why I've just been contacted by the American police about a murder that you are involved in."

Ok. I didn't see that coming!

My life was fast becoming a whole sketch of repeated incidents. None of which had ever actually happened to me before!

Rachel took advantage of my lack of a comeback by continuing on in the same vein. Hey, when a man's down, why not kick him a bit?

"When you said that you were leaving, I didn't believe that you would really go through with it. I certainly had no idea that you were going to go to another continent and begin a new life as a murderer. I know that you were feeling bored and frustrated, but this isn't the kind of therapy that you need. And you certainly don't need to be dragging me into it!"

Great!

The odd thing about this verbal attack was the use of words and the way that I was being spoken to. This was not a person that loved me. It was as though I was being spoken to by a professional person, like a doctor, somebody detached. I had begun the conversation – if you could call it that so far – by continuing to play games with Rachel, as we had been doing for the previous few months, but it was now clear that all of this was over. We really had separated. Maybe I had been the person who had walked out, but Rachel didn't seem to be the devastated person that she had portrayed in her text messages and I wondered for the first time if it was ever so slightly convenient for her to be the wronged party here. Left behind in England! Please feel sorry for me! Then when I hook up with some lawyer or doctor who has been hiding around the corner, people will be happy for me because of all the crap that I have gone through. Maybe it's a lot to read out of a few lines and text messages, but maybe I had just woken up? This whole episode, since I headed for the airport had already begun to change me as a person and, despite the minor problem of a homicide investigation, I was feeling quite pleased with the new improved version of Mike Huntingden and I wasn't going to be talked down to by some charlatan.

"Listen Rachel, don't be ringing me up giving me a hard time about having to take calls on my behalf. If I've inconvenienced you in any way by my being chased by some asshole who is claiming to be a cop, then I'm dreadfully sorry for wasting your precious time. Bill me for it. You probably know how much it's worth per hour don't you?"

That knocked her back on her heels.

I looked out at the road in front of me. Either side of me were heavily wooded hills. I was driving through a valley, the sun was shining and there was a farm coming up on the right hand side with a huge wooden barn, which reminded me for some reason of Tom Sawyer. It was just begging for small boys to play in it, to run laughing and diving into the hay. I was a small boy for a moment; with no thoughts of continents and girlfriends, or murder.

But unfortunately, it was just a moment. Then it was gone and I was back on the phone with my ex-girlfriend, who I could picture sitting on the chair arm in the lounge with the lamp on behind her, twisting her hair in her fingers as she pondered on what to say next.

"Okay I'm sorry," she began. "But you have to understand how shocked I am. I haven't heard a word from you since you left, then I get a policeman ringing me asking for your whereabouts and telling me it's important, as it's in connection with a murder."

I thought for a second and asked, "Did he say where he was calling from? I mean which city's police force?"

More twisting of the hair.

"No, I don't think he did. He just said he was – wait a minute I wrote it down here..."

I could see her looking at the phone pad, wondering if she'd missed something important.

"...Lieutenant Saxton. He said he was ringing regarding a homicide, but nothing else."

"How about a phone number? Did he leave a contact number in case you heard from me?"

"No," she was confused now, and I guessed feeling a little stupid. "No he didn't now that you mention it. I don't understand why I didn't ask for one. I was caught off guard by it all."

"So was I when he did the same to me," I said.

It was all getting curiouser and curiouser if you ask me.

I decided this was as good a moment as any to approach what was going on between us.

"Rachel?"

"Yes."

"I'm sorry that I walked out and I'm sorry that it didn't work out but it's nobody's fault and that's the truth."

"I know."

"And you know that I'm not a murderer don't you?" I asked.

"Yes, of course I do," she said.

"Do me a favour," I said." If he rings again, which I bet he won't, ask him for his number and text me with it. I'll be in touch with you in a few days with an address and number where you can get hold of me. In the meantime I'm switching this phone off and you won't hear from me. Ok?"

"Ok Mike. Be careful."

"I will and you too."

I thought that was as good a place as any to end the call, so I hung up and switched off the phone. It seemed to go quite well, but then… unexpected events most often do. It's the planned ones that suck!

I drove in silence once more, digesting everything. This guy had rung twice now and neither time had he said where he was ringing from or given a number where he could be reached. This was not what police officers did in detective novels or TV shows. I mean… I know that these things are fiction but it would make sense that things like that are at least BASED on reality.

Surely he knew that, as soon as he got off the phone with Rachel, then she would be ringing me. So why wouldn't he leave a number for her to contact him on?

Another thought entered my head: what if he did and now she was ringing him back to say that I was in Ohio, but I dismissed this straight away. She would never do that and, even if her life had depended on it, she hadn't asked any questions as to where I was headed, or staying, so she had nothing that she could give him.

I didn't know much about modern technology, but I couldn't see how he would be able to trace my whereabouts from Rachel's call to me.

So the only reason left was that he wanted me to know that he was on my tail and that he had information about me. He was trying to unnerve me.

I'm sure that it is quite easy to find out my billing address from my phone number if you know the right people. You don't necessarily need to be in the police force to get this kind of information these days. So I was guessing that he had tried to follow me from the hotel, lost me either in traffic or at the airport and had to resort to ringing my home address. Interesting that he hadn't called me though – I wondered why that was?

Coming up was an exit for Akron.

Suburbs and the beginnings of a whole town were laid out around the highway in front of me.

I guessed that there would be several exits for the city and decided to wait for one that listed the 'City center' or 'Downtown' before I got off.

I could see a large sign that said 'Goodyear'.

I was here, in rubber town.

But what else was here?

What other dangers? I was starting to feel uneasy.

What was I going to find in Akron that was going to help me?

I might be becoming a better and more real person, but was I going to live long enough to enjoy this new life?

TWELVE

In the end I got off the 76 onto the 59 and ended up taking Market Street as it seemed to be the most promising option.

There was the usual view of contemporary American life on show here. I passed multiplexes, malls and fast food joints. Huge bright coloured signs were everywhere attempting to lure me into Jiffy Lube or inviting me to get my nails done.

This last one was ironic as, after about three years of abstinence, I had been steadily nibbling away over the last day or so quite without realising it. I had begun with my thumbs, but had soon moved onto my fingers. I kept on telling myself that this was a temporary relapse and desperately hoped that this was the case as there is nothing worse than seeing somebody's nails bitten down to the quick.

Horrible! The sign of a weak person!

I was in conflict here – big time!

There were some nice stretches to be found on Market Street tucked in and amongst the kaleidoscope of loud colour. Primarily though I guessed that this was a working town, full of working people wanting their dose of today's popular consumption items.

After a while I doubled back on myself and turned down Main Street then up Broadway and around the University before settling for a generic motel back on Market, which would give me a quick getaway if required.

I checked in and paid cash. This avoided needing I.D. so I used a false name and address, which was one of those things that I had always wanted to do. I thought a US President would be as good a name as any so plumped for John Adams.

I've always been a bit of a trivia buff when it comes to US states and US Presidents. I have no idea why, but I can just remember them. I don't even know why I decided that I wanted to know them all but it's just something that interests me. Maybe you like soccer? Or collecting beer mats? Well I like US states and Presidents. So there!

I was given a twin bedded room for some bizarre reason, but then again John Adams was wide of girth. So the story goes: he was nicknamed 'his Rotundity', which is another piece of trivia that you never knew!

Again, I had never stayed in a motel on my own. Maybe all rooms were twin bedded? Certainly all the ones that I had been in were. I suppose it made sense really, but it still seemed like the waste of a perfectly good bed. I wondered at the sanity of setting the alarm for the middle of the night and swapping beds. I then wondered how many people had wondered that. Probably not many!

I dumped my things and headed straight back out before the lure of a shower and my toothbrush became too much to resist. I wasn't in Akron to concentrate on cleanliness. I had an agenda here.

I had seen what looked like a likely store for cell phones in a mall two or three blocks down while I had been stood at the traffic lights. I headed back there now and managed to find parking space right outside the front door. This had to be a good omen?

The afternoon sun was baking hot as I stepped out of the car and I guessed that was why nobody had chosen this particular unshaded spot to park. So much for the omen! I bleeped the alarm and walked into the air-conditioned cool of the store to be greeted by a young waist coated staff member who pounced on me.

"Good afternoon, sir, and how are you today?"

Another rhetorical customer service line!

I looked at the guy. He had to be eighteen, nineteen at the most, with a short crew cut. He appeared to be a high school student. Maybe he was? Perhaps they do work experience in electrical retailers? Or maybe I was just getting old?

I remembered going to the doctors back in the UK two years before and finding that my doctor was younger than I was.

That was frightening. A milestone in my life!

Like the day when you realise you are now too old to be a professional sportsman, or a rock star, or anything else that you grow up wanting to be. Instead all of these people are younger than you and increasingly irrelevant to your current aspirations.

Song lyrics are meaningless and it's all been done before. The kind of thing that your dad used to say. I'm sure it only gets worse.

"Hot is how I am…" I looked at his nametag, "… Stuart. Hot!"

Stuart seemed shocked that a customer had spoken back to him. Maybe his profession as greeter was just a one-line gig? How would he go on if he had to develop into conversation? I decided to try him out.

"And how are you?"

Flummoxed is how Stuart was. He just stared at me, trying to smile, but knowing that he had to speak to reply he was caught between the two. His brain read 'can not compute'. He was rescued by a senior member of the team, who appeared from nowhere.

"Good afternoon, Sir, are you looking for anything in particular today?"

This name tagged individual was called 'Jerome', and was a tall, good looking African American, who was about my age and made me feel a lot happier.

"Yes, Jerome. I'm looking to buy a cell phone," I replied with a cheery smile.

I had to stop myself from saying 'my good man' at the end of the sentence.

I got a cheery smile right back, as Jerome realised he had a potential sale here, and he beckoned me over to the phone section.

"We can certainly help you out there Sir. Please follow me over here and I'll demonstrate our options today."

I love this 'autocue' way of talking. Jerome and Stuart and millions like them must go home every night with a card that tells them their lines. Deviating from these lines is to be avoided at all costs as it can lead to confusion. Confusion ultimately leads to law-suits and redundancies, both of which are not to be recommended.

I followed Jerome across the store, looking at the selection of merchandise on sale and got more and more puzzled. Frankly, I didn't recognise most of it and I was preparing to be baffled by science when we reached the phone department. Two other members of staff greeted me with a bright acknowledgement on the way and I started to wonder whether they were all trained at the retail version of Stepford.

Jerome showed me a snippet of the range that they sold and told me, very honestly, which was the low end of the range, medium and high. He pointed out the bargains of the week and made his own recommendation, which he made sure to inform me did not represent the views of the store and if I chose to go with his recommendation then it would be at my own risk. He then walked me through the airtime tariffs, or 'calling plans' and presented me with a form to fill in to get approved for credit.

Dilemma! What should I list as my address?

In the end I used my credit card as payment and gave him what was now Rachel's address. I was sure that I could amend this at a later date.

So far this hadn't taken that long and ten minutes later I was amazed to find myself sitting back in the car with the air con running on full, staring at my new cell phone which had already been activated!

Carphone Warehouse had a lot to learn!

As I sat there I noticed Staples next door and made a spur of the moment decision to purchase some index cards and a pen or two. If I was going to do this, then I may as well have some semblance of order. I remembered a novel that I had read where the female private eye kept all of her clues written down on a series of index cards, which she could keep referring back to when she reached an impasse. This seemed like a plan, so I braved the heat and popped into Staples for supplies.

Driving out of the mall I spied a deli and pulled over again, deciding that provisions were the way forward.

Finally, shopped out, I headed back to my motel room to play with my new toy and write up everything that I could recall.

When I got back and parked up I was amazed to find that it was markedly cooler than when I had left the deli only minutes earlier.

I felt the pull of the tractor beam that was the shower and gave in without a fight this time.

The shower was not luxurious by any stretch of the imagination, but it was sufficient. After drying and dressing, I popped the ring pull on a can of Tecate and split the wrapper on the first pack of index cards. This felt quite exciting!

At the top of the first card I wrote: Carrie-Ann Novitski then stopped.

What now?

I was about to write 'from Akron' when I realised that this hadn't yet been established. I dropped the pen and headed for the drawer in the table between the beds. There was usually a phone book in here as well as a bible.

Bingo!

I sat on the bed and thumbed through until I came to Novitski. There were eight listed. I supposed that I should start ringing them one by one, but exactly what to say and how to go about saying it was another thing entirely.

I got up and wandered backwards and forwards in the room, sipping my beer as I did so.

I should be as honest as possible to avoid tripping myself up and sounding insincere, I reasoned. I grabbed the remote for the TV and clicked it on.

Background TV would be good calming distraction. I perched back on the edge of the bed and clicked around the channels until I found something that aroused my interest. The only thing that I could find was an old episode of Wings, the sitcom based around the two brothers who own a small airline in some island in New England. Nantucket sprang to mind, but I couldn't be sure. Either way, I decided to forget about being Dick Tracey for a while and enjoy my Saturday afternoon in Akron in front of the TV.

I discovered after a while that either a) Wings was actually pretty good, or b) I was losing my marbles in a big way. The show was coming to an end and had gone to what seemed like its eighteenth commercial break when I decided that I was going to start making calls.

I had decided that I would say that I am a friend of Carrie-Ann's from England (note the present tense) and she had said to look her up if ever I should be in town. Hardly likely I know, but maybe not to somebody who lived here? It was worth a shot. This was going to be my road in to any conversation with a member of her family. And exactly where it went from there I wasn't sure as yet. I felt it couldn't harm to free wheel a little and try to get into the role. Let's face it, I wasn't exactly lying here, but I WAS being fairly economical with the truth. The main purpose of the calls was to establish whether Carrie-Ann was a citizen of Akron and if possible to determine whether she was alive or dead.

Wings had returned now, but only to play the credits.

Why do US shows do this? It makes absolutely no sense whatsoever. Surely nobody watches this part. They know the show is over and they now have five minutes plus to call their mom, or take a shower, or make a sandwich, before the next show. Crazy!

I punched the numbers of the first Novitski into my new cell phone and held my breath.

I needn't have worried. Nobody answered.

Nobody answered the next one either and the third Novitski, listed as 'C' answered, but didn't know anything and didn't sound particularly interested in what I was saying.

I popped the ring pull on my second can of Tecate, and rang the fourth on the list, 'Novitski, D' and this time I hit pay dirt. A guy answered with a non-committal "Hi".

I started by apologising, as I had with 'Novitski, C', and went on with my spiel about how I was a friend of a Carrie-Ann Novitski from England… blah, blah, blah, and how I was trying to get hold of her.

The other end of the phone went completely silent and I knew I had a live one.

"Hello?" I said as politely as one can say hello when trying to jog somebody along.

The guy sounded like he was collecting his thoughts and spoke in a very disjointed manner.

"Yeah… sorry, um, Hi. You're trying to get in touch with Carrie?" The familiarity of the way that he used her name had my heart beating like the clappers (whatever they are). I wasn't trained for this and I had no idea of where to go now I was here.

"Yes, sir, are you by any chance related?" I probed.

"Um, yeah, I am, well… I say I am, um… kinda. She's… she was I mean… my cousin."

"Was?" I pressed, holding my breath.

"Yeah… you didn't hear… well obviously, you wouldn't."

I decided to be silent for a second and let him continue at his own pace.

He took a deep and I mean deep, breath, then exhaled, before adding, "She died… she's… dead."

Now I was going to have to act a little here and apologies if it seems wooden, but you already knew the story, so you've no idea. You would probably have believed me… I'm a good actor, or was that liar?

"Oh my god!" I exclaimed. "I just don't know what to say."

"I know," he consoled "It was a shock to us too, believe me."

"But I only spoke to her a week ago, she was making plans to fly back for, you know her auntie's funeral?"

As soon as I said it I knew I had made a massive mistake. I'd broken the rule that I'd only made myself on the phone with Saxton the morning before. God was that only the day before? It seemed like months! But I had given information away that I didn't need to and I suspected trouble.

"Her auntie's what?" he replied immediately and I realised that I was going to have to think fast – very fast. But I wasn't fast enough to stop this guy. He was on the attack now.

"What are you talking about?" he continued. "Are you crazy? Why would she say something like that? Her aunt is dead? What aunt? Who is this anyway?"

"Hey, I'm sorry," I broke in, "I'm only telling you what she said to me. She said 'I'm going home to Akron for my auntie's funeral', I never questioned her about it." I decided that backing down was not going to get me anywhere.

I half considered ending the call here, but I had a suspicion that I was better staying on the phone as I was learning things all the time.

"Perhaps you should come over and we can have a chat over a drink or something?"

Novitski, D was changing his mood quicker than the weather in this town and I now began to sense that I was talking to a dangerous individual. His tone originally had been guarded, then had turned to grief and now it was almost as if I was talking to Tony Soprano. There was no way that I was going to his home. This had trouble written all over it.

"No… look, I'm sorry to ring you and upset you at a time like this, I truly am. I was just wanting to hook up with Carrie-Ann while I was in town and I am very sorry for your loss. She was a lovely girl. I really liked her. But I'm going to say goodbye now. I would be intruding if I took up any more of your time."

I thought I'd covered everything there.

"Hey look, don't sweat it. I appreciate your sympathies," he was talking quickly now, like he was afraid he'd lost me and I was going to hang up, "and I'm sorry if I acted weird there, it's just been an upsetting time recently as you can imagine. I hope you don't hold no hard feelings? If you change your mind about a drink and you are in town tonight, a group of us: family and friends are having a get together, kind of a wake, at a joint in town by the name of the Emerald Grill, it's on West Market Street. I hope you'll make it."

Now I was really puzzled. Perhaps he wasn't a thug after all? Maybe he was just going through all kinds of emotions? But what was that about the auntie? I needed to think some more about that.

"I'll try, ok?" I offered.

"Great, that would be good. You could be, like… the representative from England. After all, she did love it over there. You guys must have made her welcome."

"Well, you know what she was like. She could get on with anyone." I said, hoping this didn't sound too mushy.

"Yeah well, we'll be there from eight onwards, just ask for me at the door. My name is Donnie by the way."

"I'm John. John Adams. I'll maybe see you later Donnie. Nice to chat with you. And I really am very sorry once again."

And with that I pressed the 'end call' button and stared into space trying to work out what had just gone on.

THIRTEEN

After another period of silence, interrupted only by the background noise from the TV, I wrote 'deceased' next to Carrie-Ann's name at the top of the index card.

What the heck was I doing? What kind of people was I getting involved with?

I decided that I needed to write some more down to help my own understanding.

We had now established that Carrie-Ann was indeed from Akron.

We had also established that she had a cousin called Donnie who may or may not be 'unbalanced'.

That was all that I knew of her family apart from the 'dead aunt' sketch but this now appeared to have been a fabrication as Donnie clearly knew nothing about it, which he would have done as it would have had to have been his aunt who died too, right?

Actually no, thinking about it… Wrong… Donnie could have been a cousin on one side of the family, like Carrie-Ann's mum's, and been unaware of the goings on with the other side of the family, Carrie-Ann's dad's, couldn't he?

It was possible.

I'd not had enough sleep to work this out in my head so I drew out a family tree putting Carrie-Ann in the middle and her parents above her. I had no idea whether she had siblings so didn't include them. I then drew a line from her father to a fictitious brother and underneath him wrote Donnie. He was listed as 'Novitski' in the phone book so he was obviously on that side of the family.

While I was thinking I ripped the 'Novitski' page out of the phone book – just in case.

I then drew another line from Carrie-Ann's mother to a sister and sat back to look at my work.

It was still unclear. One thing was for sure: an aunt on her mother's side would have a different surname and possibly her own family. I tried to relate it to my own family to get some clarity. My father had died over ten years ago and thinking about it his brother – my uncle – and his brother's family weren't in touch with us so much any more except for the usual card at Christmas. I would hope that someone would let us know if there had been a death in the family but there really was no reason that anyone on my mothers side would get to know unless it came up at a family gathering in conversation sometime in the future. So on that rationale; it would not be out of the question for Carrie-Ann to be telling the truth and Donnie not to know about her aunt dying.

Are you keeping up?

I made a note.

What else?

What else did I know about Carrie-Ann? Nothing sprang to mind. I mentally went through events on the plane and into the airport when I rang her.

Shit, yes... the envelope with her cell phone number on it! There was something else on there wasn't there? An address of some kind! Where had I put it?

I retrieved my rucksack and opened it up, peering in for something brown to leap out at me. It wasn't immediately obvious – things never are when you want them – so I moved the other items that I could see from side to side hoping that this would do the trick but just knowing that I'd end up emptying everything onto the bed.

When I *had* emptied everything onto the bed the envelope was sat there staring up at me. I put it to one side and scooped the rest of the crap back into the rucksack, resolving to tidy it out if ever things calmed down.

I picked up the envelope and examined it.

It had seen some action that was for sure. I had not noticed when I had looked at it before just how dog-eared it was. It looked like it had been carried around folded in someone's pocket for a week. When I had first seen this, it had been thrust into my hand folded, so that only Carrie-Ann's number showed and I hadn't paid close attention to it apart from a cursory glance when I was looking for her number back in the airport in Philly. I had seen that there were other things on there, which may be private, and then I'd stashed it intending to give it back to her. Obviously this had never come about.

I'd noticed the mailing address before. The envelope had been mailed to Carrie-Ann in London. There were stamps in the top right hand corner and a postmark, which was illegible, so I couldn't get a date. That was all that was written on the front. I turned it over.

On the back was the name that I had seen before 'Mr. Lewis Pine' and an address here in Akron: 96, E.Bowery St., Akron, OH. The zip code was written underneath: 22510.

This address was written in the same handwriting as the mailing address and, from the location on the rear of the envelope it looked as if it was the sender's address.

I reached for the telephone book again and opened it near the back, flicking the pages until I came to 'PI'.

There didn't appear to be any listing for 'Pine' at all, despite my knowledge of his whereabouts on East Bowery. The phone book was for this year and Carrie-Ann had only been in London to receive mail during this year, so it had to be that Mr.Pine was either renting or ex-directory.

The only other things on the back of the envelope were Carrie-Ann's cell phone number, which I was planning to ring again, but not just yet for some reason and some scribbling. The kind of circular motion scribbling that one does when trying to establish if the pen works or not. The ink seemed to be the same colour as the number that Carrie-Ann had written so I assumed that she had done this on the plane prior to writing down her number.

This made me think... why would she carry this envelope around with her for the amount of time that she obviously had, by the state of it, only to give it away to somebody that she has just met on a plane? If she did the scribbling on it she obviously had to know what it was she was writing on. I mean, I know I was in good form on the plane but I've never exactly drawn women towards me with magnetic force, causing them to abandon all and forget all links to their past life.

So did she give the envelope to me on purpose?

And if so... why?

Maybe Lewis Pine knew why?

I was going to have to go and visit him wasn't I?

How much had I had to drink?

Only two cans.

I wasn't sure of the drinking and driving regulations in Ohio but I felt fine. Well... as fine as I had done in three days anyway.

I made the decision to go now, before I changed my mind, so I grabbed my jeans, which I had thoughtfully folded up and placed on the bed before getting in the shower and a fresh t-shirt out of the top of the case. I then threw a pair of socks on and eased back into my training shoes, which I didn't seem to have unfastened for six months. I took a quick look at myself in the mirror and decided on a baseball cap. Finding an orange Texas Longhorns cap in the rucksack, I picked up the car keys, and headed out the door, to find it was raining.

What was with the weather in this place?

I had already started the engine when I realised that I hadn't picked up the envelope with the address on it. Brilliant work!

I cut the engine and headed back to the motel room through the rain, which was really getting heavy now, and fumbled, in my pocket for the card to open the door.

Once inside I grabbed the envelope off of the bed and my cell phone, which I had also forgotten in my rush to get on the trail.

I hadn't yet called Beth, as I had promised, so while the rain was bucketing down outside I decided to get her number out of my old phone, and put it into my new address book then I could ring from the Dodge if I had five minutes while on stake out.

It occurred to me that I had absolutely no idea where Bowery Street was, never mind East Bowery, so I made the decision to check with reception to see if they could direct me.

When I finally got out of the room again I headed to reception underneath the covered walk, which also served as the upstairs walkway.

There was a different person on duty now to the lady who had checked me in. Staff at motels always look so bored with life don't you think? Occasionally you come across somebody who is happy and friendly, but that's probably because they have just started, or are just about to end their shift. The rest of the time they seem to have just about enough energy to lift up their heads to look at you for any length of time.

This guy fitted the bill entirely. I got no greeting as I approached the desk and he simply looked up with his eyes from the magazine in front of him. He was probably in his late twenties, white, with a church goer's haircut which his mother probably did for him and he looked as if he lived on pizza; big chubby cheeks which went straight down to his chest, avoiding the need for a neck, and huge podgy hands.

'Hello' was implied so I just picked up a card off of the desk in front of him with the hotel's name and address on it and went right to the point.

"Hi, can you tell me how to get to East Bowery please?"

He stared at me for at least twenty seconds with his mouth slightly open and I was starting to wonder if he had passed out when he finally spoke.

"Are you on foot?"

I looked out of the window where rain was falling in biblical proportions and briefly considered a sarcastic response but decided against it.

"No, I have a car," I said.

"You want to head right on market, under the inner belt and take Broadway south. Bowery is your second or third turning. I don't remember which."

With that his eyes dropped back to his magazine and he turned a page with his big hand as if to illustrate that the exchange was over.

I resisted the temptation to thank him as he evidently wasn't expecting further conversation, turned on my heel and walked out of the office. Oddly it felt quite liberating, being rude.

I climbed in the Dodge, started her up and released the parking brake. Then I headed out of the car park, back towards the freeway and the shopping mall and Broadway, which I had driven down earlier. When I got to Broadway I stood at a red light in the rain, which was petering out noticeably now, before turning right and started to watch out for Bowery. With the address being East Bowery I knew it would be a left turning when I reached the intersection and pretty soon I had taken the turning and was looking for numbers. I could see the Akron railway station in front of me and that was plainly where Bowery reached an end, so the building that I was looking for was any one of the ones immediately alongside me. I saw number 84 in gold on the door of one property, which looked like a solicitor's office or an accountant's.

There were cars queuing up behind me as I strained to look for numbers and more than one honked a horn in annoyance. I speeded up, resolving to park in the station car park and walk back. Just as I passed the last building I noticed the number 94 on the window above the door which meant that Mr. Pine was back one, next door.

Dropping the window I reached for a ticket from the automated machine as I entered the car park and as I accelerated away to look for a parking space my mind caught up with my eyes. The numbers on the buildings had been going up, not counting down, which meant that if 94 was the last building then 96 was... where?

I came to a stop and turned off the ignition, staring at the railway station in front of me.

It didn't look new. Ok perhaps it had undergone some renovation recently, but the actual structure had clearly been there for some time. It was an imposing stone façade which looked to have been steam cleaned in the last couple of years but if I had to guess I would say that it had probably been there as long as Akron and was probably the main reason that Akron became a city. So this meant that I was looking at number 96 East Bowery... a railway station. This made no sense.

But it wasn't exactly the first time that things had been a tad unusual so I decided to get out and have a wander round while I was there.

I walked in the main entrance and tried to take everything in. There were the usual things that you would expect to see in a station: payphones, restrooms, a sign pointing to a waiting room and platforms, automatic ticket machines, a digital information board with train times and helpful maps on the wall. It wasn't over busy and there didn't seem to be any staff in sight to speak to.

While I was there I decided to pay a visit to the restroom and gather my thoughts while draining off some of the Tecate.

On my way to the bathroom I walked past a wall which was clear except for posters advertising local events, a notice board with a lot of official looking typed documents and some flyers which I guessed were stuck there by bands and escort girls. I resisted the temptation to read through all of this literature as my bladder was calling.

The restrooms were very clean and quite impressive, if you like that kind of thing. I stood on my own staring at the wall in front of me, wondering what options were now open to me.

Why would anyone leave his or her contact address as an unmanned railway station? There didn't even seem to be anybody here to open mail.

Somebody obviously did come here to clean and keep an eye on things, but even if Lewis Pine worked here he surely wouldn't leave this address for people to get in touch with him.

I walked around the interior for five minutes hoping that something would happen or I would catch sight of a secret door leading to an upstairs apartment, but there was nothing doing. This clue was a dead end for the moment.

I got back to the car, surprised to see that the sun was now out again and the temperature appeared to have risen by more than a few degrees. I remember reading about Melbourne in Australia having weather that changed every half hour. Maybe Akron was twinned with Melbourne? If not, it should be.

I had reached what appeared to be a dead end and I sat in the Dodge staring out at number 96 East Bowery Street hoping for a light bulb to appear over my head. But nothing happened.

Short of divine inspiration the only course that appeared open to me was to head back to the motel and finish the Tecate.

FOURTEEN

As I opened the last of the six cans of Tecate that I had bought earlier I remembered that I still hadn't rung Beth. A friendly voice would probably help at the moment so I took out my phone and placed the call.

I had been sat in my room for the past couple of hours steadily working through the beer whilst trying to think of things to write on my new white index cards which might help. Unfortunately I hadn't come up with a great deal.

I had made up a card titled: Lewis Pine, but all that I could put underneath was his incorrect mailing address on East Bowery Street. I knew absolutely nothing else about the guy. He wasn't even in the phone book. I briefly mulled about the fact that if he shortened his Christian name then he would be Lou Pine, or 'lupine' – as in 'wolf-like'. But then I dismissed this as beer talking.

I next made up a card headed: Lieutenant Saxton and wrote down that he had called me in the early hours of Friday morning regarding a homicide, saying that he would get somebody to get in touch with me at the hotel in Pittsburgh to arrange an informal chat, or something.

At this stage I had rung the hotel from my cell phone to enquire whether anybody had left me any messages and, when I had finally got to speak to somebody who understood what I was trying to get across, I was told simply, "No, you have no messages, Sir". I wasn't entirely convinced with the accuracy of this but there was nothing that I could do. I could only assume that neither Lieutenant Saxton, nor one of his merry band of men had attempted to get in touch.

I had also switched my old mobile phone on for a short while to see if anybody had tried to reach me on it but again this was a negative.

I wrote underneath that he had telephoned Rachel, in England today to inform her of my involvement in a homicide and ascertain whether she knew my whereabouts. To which he had got no further information and despite this, had not left a contact number.

Then I had made up a card for: The guy in the red and black shirt. That way I was covering all of the bases, as it was quite possible that this guy was not Lieutenant Saxton. I wrote about my first sighting of him at Philadelphia Int'l Airport on Thursday and his apparent hold over Carrie-Ann, then about his appearance at the hotel in Pittsburgh this morning.

The fifth, and final card I made up for my new friend Donnie Novitski and wrote that I had contacted him this afternoon and that he had invited me to some kind of a wake at a local bar. I also wrote that I suspected him of having an 'excitable' temperament. A nice euphemism I thought just to round things off.

After my work was done I had put the cards out on the bed in front of me and looked backwards and forwards at them, in the hope that something would click into place. There had to be something that I was not seeing!

But after a while I gave up, thinking that maybe I wasn't going to be very good at this detective lark. I'm the kind of person who needs immediate results or I get fed up pretty quickly.

Beth's phone was ringing now and I was more than a little excited in anticipation of speaking to her.

However it appeared that I was going to be thwarted in everything I turned my hand to at the moment, as she didn't pick up and her message came on. I checked my watch: it was after eight. She was probably working at Harry's bar.

"Hi, this is Beth. Sorry I can't talk at the moment. Please leave me a short message and I'll call you right back. Thanks."

The message cheered me up anyway. I felt a rosy glow in my cheeks. But again, that could have been the beer.

"Hey Beth," I began, in as jaunty a voice as I could muster, "Mike here, just calling in as promised on my new cell phone. Sorry I missed you. You can ring me back on…" and at this point I realised that I had no idea what my number was, "… I have no idea what my number is… well maybe I'll get hold of you later. Thanks. Seeya!"

Sausage!

I should really have made that call earlier, as promised. Oh well, what the hell!

I stood up and drained the last of the beer. I then walked over to the mirror and leaned against the vanity cabinet, staring at my reflection. It took all of five seconds before I began to question myself.

Did I really have any idea of where my life was going at this point?

Was I making a big mistake?

Had I been too hasty in leaving England? Rachel had certainly sounded friendly enough on the phone today. Maybe there was a chance for us? Perhaps this distance between us would give us both a bit of room and space for thought about what we were throwing away?

Should I call her? No, it'll be the early hours of Sunday morning at home now.

Home… where was home? What had I done? Was everybody right, was I just going through some kind of mid-life crisis? Was all of this about me and not Rachel, and how we had drifted apart? Perhaps I was being selfish! And here I am playing detective in some town in Ohio.

I was starting to feel sorry for myself and I knew it.

I also knew in my heart that Rachel wasn't an option anymore. That boat had sailed. I had to get on with things.

Perhaps getting on with things by getting involved with a university student was taking the Mickey a little bit, but I was confident that I could start making the right choices.

Couldn't I?

I didn't seem to be answering my own questions very well, never mind looking into other peoples' lives and trying to sort out a murder investigation in a foreign country.

I was in a motel room in Akron, Ohio with some guy, who could be a killer, chasing me across the country.

Oh, and a woman that I had spent a few hours with on a plane was dead.

Where was I gonna go from here?

Back to Pittsburgh? To see Beth and Stevie, and start a new life as a hotel clerk? Checking over my shoulder for a red and black shirted pony tailed individual every five minutes?

Home to Rachel on my bended knees, begging for her to take me back?

Or maybe I should take a walk to the liquor store for more beer? Or perhaps some bourbon?

But I looked hard at myself in that mirror, and I knew where I was going to go… I really only had one possible destination tonight.

Maybe I had messed up and perhaps I was making a mistake, but whatever I was doing, I was going to do all I could to do it right. And if I went and just had a few beers and socialised, and came back here later with nothing more, then at least I'd exhausted all my options. But that was better than not going and simply wondering. I'd made it to Akron so I might as well pay a visit to the wake of the girl who got me started in this whole mess.

I was still staring at myself. My eyes were a little red. I looked tired.

I would need to get showered and cleaned up before I headed out to the Emerald Grill.

So I made the decision and jumped to it. I took my third shower of the day and threw on a clean shirt with a collar. I had no shoes, or smart trousers, so this would have to be my token gesture. I decided that I would call my own cab, rather than ask for assistance from the blimp in reception, so I found one in the phone book and asked him to come as soon as possible. Before I changed my mind about where I was heading.

Time was flying now, but that could have been the beer also. It was just turning nine as I paid the cab driver and climbed out onto the pavement in front of the Emerald Grill. As the cab pulled away I had a momentary wobble, questioning my sanity once more. But I'd come too far now. Best foot forward!

The place was very cool, in a laid back 50's kind of way.

Very straightforward, no stupid colour schemes or geometric shapes. Stone walls and big windows with no clutter in them save a couple of obligatory neon beer signs. A 'real' place, which looked like it had been a fixture in this town since Benjamin Franklin Goodrich decided to start producing tyres, or 'tires' as they call them here.

I walked up to the greeter and told her that I was here to meet Donnie Novitski and his party. She asked me to please wait a moment and disappeared over to a party of about fifteen or twenty individuals who were stood around chatting by the bar.

The bar was a big slab of polished wood that ran down the whole length of the left hand wall, probably about thirty feet or more. There was a scattering of heavy looking wooden tables in the centre of the room made up with table cloths and cutlery, and the walls were painted a soothing pale cream colour with the occasional framed black and white photograph of what must have been Akron in days gone by. It really did look a great place and I wished that I was here for a different reason. There was a general hum of voices chatting above music, which played quietly in the background. I couldn't be sure, but it sounded like Bruce Springsteen. If it was, it certainly fit the place. And if Bruce himself had have been here he probably would have done too. I was definitely glad that I hadn't brought a suit because I would have looked like I had arrived to shut the joint down.

The greeter, who was a tall lady of about forty, was walking back towards me now, with a smaller guy following close behind. I guessed that this must be Donnie Novitski. The height of the greeter made him look smaller than he probably actually was, but as he got closer I could see that he was built like a tank. He looked like he would have no problem handling himself if it was called for. Maybe I should start being cautious again? I really did not want to get into a situation in a place like this. I don't think that many people would be jumping in to help me out. I guessed that he must have been a good ten or more years older than his deceased cousin but he still had a full head of thick black hair cut in a very neat style short over the ears with a little fringe, and he had dark brown eyes that seemed to burn right through you, looking at your inner soul. This guy was not to be messed with.

"This is Mr.Novitski here," smiled the giant greeter, who was in fact taller than I was when I thought about it. I smiled up at her and nodded thanks, then turned to face Mr.Novitski.

His hand pumped out towards me and for a moment I was startled, then immediately realised he only wanted to shake my hand.

"It's Donnie to you. None of this Mr.Novitski crap!"

I took his hand and shook it firmly. God, he had hands twice the size of mine. Boxing? Bouncing? The scrap metal business?

I forced a smile, but seemed unable to speak for some reason. I could sense the same kind of aggression in him that I had picked up on over the phone, but close up he was almost wearing it like aftershave.

He didn't seem to notice my apprehension, or maybe he was used to it. Perhaps everybody was like a bunny in a car's headlights around him? Instead he threw a big arm around my shoulders, despite being a good five inches smaller than me and turned me around to face the bar so that I was alongside him, then he began to march me over towards the expectant faces.

"Come on in Johnny, let's get you a brewski and you can meet some of the other folks. They're all dying to get to know you."

Why was the music from the Godfather playing in my head?

By the time we'd walked the twelve or fifteen steps to the waiting Corleone family I had sobered up and was wondering how I was going to get away. I needed to stay long enough to be polite, but not too long, otherwise the concrete they were mixing in the kitchen for my new shoes would be ready.

I still hadn't spoken since I had met my new friend, but he didn't seem to notice as he introduced me to Sonny, Connie, Fredo and the rest of the family. He still had a heavy protective arm around my shoulder and I could only nod and try to smile at the people that he was pointing me at. He barked at somebody to get me a beer and one was duly produced without a moment's hesitation. I could see that this guy was in charge. I wondered what his line of business was. I didn't think I'd be asking him anytime soon.

"So how long are you gonna be in town then Johnny?"

It took me a couple of seconds to realise that I was Johnny and he was talking to me. I was going to have to be on my toes here and keep up with the lies. I was also going to have to be careful with what I said and gave away. Jeez there were a lot of rules in this private eye gig! The crowd of dark clothed mourners looked on, awaiting my reply as if their livelihoods depended on it.

At that moment my mouth was dryer than I had ever known and I felt like the tin man in the Wizard of Oz. I desperately brought my beer up to get a swig before I answered, trying to control my arm which was shaking under the pressure of the fish tank that I now seemed to be living in.

The beer was just the tonic that I needed and flicked a switch in my brain that got the circuits all going again. Now just be careful in your replies Huntingden! Or should I say 'Adams'?

"I'm literally here for a couple of days," I said and felt everybody exhale at once, or maybe that was me.

"And you came all the way here just to see Carrie-Ann. She would have been so happy," said Donnie, throwing his arm back around me and looking almost tearful. This is a big, plainly well respected, almost feared individual and tears were welling up in the corner of his eyes!

As if on cue, I heard a sniff and looked at the rest of the family, to find that a couple of the women had got handkerchiefs out and were weeping into them.

How confusing!

The different emotions in the room were stifling and I gulped more beer down whilst there was a natural break. Donnie would have been a tremendous ally, but one that you'd always be waiting for to call on you to do him a favour. Surely better your ally than your enemy though? I wondered whether he was capable of the murder of his cousin? He clearly wore his emotions on his sleeve. I had witnessed his sudden changes of temperament on two occasions already. I was no expert on criminal psychology, but this guy had to fit the bill of some kind of perp. I was one hundred per cent certain that he was a man who could kill if the occasion warranted it. The only question was motive. Why would the man kill his cousin?

The outbreak of emotion had caused the group to split off into small sympathy sub committees and I was beginning to wonder which group I should be joining when I felt the same old arm around my shoulders. Again I was being lead away, almost as if I had no feet of my own and I was hovering two inches above the rough cut wooden floor.

"Let me get you something a little stronger Johnny. You don't mind me calling you Johnny do you?" said Donnie, and without giving me chance to answer, enquired, "What do you friends call you? What did Carrie call you?"

He looked at me as we came to a stop further down the bar back towards the front window and it was clear he expected an answer to this question. I hoped that this answer wouldn't bring on a fresh bout of the water works.

"She called me Johnny as well."

This sounded contrived, but then it would... because it was. I decided a little embellishment was called for and went for it. "Which is why you caught me off guard when I got here, when you called me Johnny. Nobody else has ever really called me by that name. Back home I'm simply known as John. So I was kind of choked back there. I hope I didn't come across as rude in front of your family?"

The hand was back on my shoulder before I finished. Then he pulled his lips together and nodded his head like a sage. "That's a beautiful thing you just said Johnny. I will take that with me to my grave."

He was still nodding, as if having a private conversation with himself about me, sizing me up. Then in a total change of emotion which shouldn't have made me jump, but did, he turned towards the bar keeper, who was waiting attentively a discreet six feet away, and bellowed, "Get us a bottle of brandy over here, will ya! And none of your cheap stuff!"

He turned at me with a paternal look in his eyes and continued talking to anyone who was listening, "Only the best for me and my good friend Johnny."

Oh boy!

FIFTEEN

Despite the constant threat of a violent outburst hanging over us, Donnie soon had me relaxed enough that we were able to have a sensible conversation in which he told me all about his car sales business and his relationship with his cousin, Carrie, who he had clearly doted on all of her life, with him being in his teens when she had been born and how he'd felt like he should look out for her, as Akron wasn't always like it is today and used to be a place of senseless violence and open warfare.

'Take a breath,' I kept thinking.

It was a slightly one-sided conversation.

I wondered just who was playing who here. Donnie clearly wasn't stupid. He had street smarts and hadn't got where he clearly was by being taken in by a novice like me. But he seemed to be buying into my character and was quite happy to volunteer all of this information.

Perhaps it was grief? Or maybe he just hadn't come across an English guy who had decided to become a sleuth overnight?

He kept topping up the brandy and I kept sipping politely, keeping him company throughout his monologue. He didn't seem to realise that my brandy wasn't going down very much. He just kept throwing his back and filling up both glasses.

I was listening to him, but my mind kept wandering. At one stage I came up with the realisation that I didn't actually know how Carrie-Ann had died. And once I'd come up with that thought I spent the next five minutes wondering how I could bring the question into conversation without being disrespectful. I needn't have worried as eventually he came around to the subject on his own. I guess he'd run out of topics that involved either one of them and it was on his mind.

I don't remember how he began the sentence, I just caught the trail end of it, "… and then some bastard murders my own little cousin, who never hurt nobody in her entire life."

I thought quickly and tried to sound as confused as possible, "Murdered?"

He looked me right in the eye and I almost had to turn away such was the strength of his gaze. I could feel him analysing me for a moment, then he said, "If I ever find out who did it, I swear to God… with my own hands…" and left the rest unsaid.

It didn't need to be. And by not saying it, a whole lot more was said, if you see what I mean?

I decided to press on, "So they don't know who did it? I don't understand. How did it happen?" I tried to look as concerned as possible, as if I too wanted retribution, which I suppose I did, only clearly not in the same way as my new drinking partner.

"The police found her body at the train station here in town on Thursday last, late at night. She'd been strangled. Nobody has any ideas as to why, or who did it." He looked into space above my head, as I thought: 'THE TRAIN STATION!!!!!'

I would not have been surprised if the words had been written in flashing lights over my head. I hoped he couldn't read it in my face, because from my expression it must have been obvious that these three words had shaken me. All I could think was that I was just there! What was the connection?

I couldn't think of anything intelligent to say that wasn't going to give the game away so I lifted the brandy to my lips and took a swig.

Then he changed the subject again and I found myself tuning in even more. "Oh, by the way I asked around and you were right about the Aunt."

I just kept quiet and looked at him. I must have looked kind of gormless, because he continued, "You know, you were saying that Carrie came home for her Aunt's funeral?"

"Oh, yes. Well that's what she told me," I replied.

"Yeah, well it turns out that you're right mostly. Her mother's sister, Sarah died. We didn't keep in touch with that side of the family much after Uncle Andy died. Just Carrie really. I suppose that's another reason I looked out for her so much. She was only about ten, I think, when her pop passed on. We dropped in from time to time to see Aunt Nancy and pay our respects, but after a while we stopped going and once Carrie left home we never heard no more from them. Aunt Nancy passed just last year, which is probably what caused Carrie to go globetrotting. The last time we all saw Sarah was at Aunt Nancy's funeral. I never said more than three or four words to her. She was very standoffish. Always looked like she was carrying the world's problems on her shoulders."

He paused and seemed to be collecting his thoughts. I decided against interrupting, hoping he'd pick up from where he left off and eventually he did, but it was odd that I hadn't seen any other breaks of silence while he was telling me his life story. Nothing was going to shock me too much anymore though. Or so I thought...

"Sarah's husband was in with a bad crowd. And they weren't too clever about it either. They were always bragging about having done this and that, and the other. I don't think my folks liked being around them too much, especially when me, and my brother Leo were younger. Leo couldn't make it tonight," he explained. "He lives out on the east coast. He'll be here on Monday for the funeral."

He paused again then went on. "Anyway in the end Tony, that's Sarah's husband, ended up going away for armed robbery. So I guess after that we just never talked about them. I never knew nothing about her death until you mentioned it this afternoon. I rang a couple of people and it turns out she walked in on burglars in her home, and one of these guys gets panicky and pulls out a gun. Poor woman, she always seemed very serious and reserved. I don't think she enjoyed life too much."

My brain was working at triple speed here and the brandy was not helping at all.

I was frantically trying to process everything and to make sure that I remembered it all for later. I would have paid a kings ransom at that moment for an index card or two!

Two murders!

In the same family! How did this not seem strange to him? Was murder so prolific in this part of the world?

I needed to ask some questions. "You said that her husband… was it Tony?"

"Yeah, that's right Tony," he interrupted.

"You said he's in prison?"

"Right, but he's out now. Turns out that he got dispensation when Sarah died, as he'd been a model prisoner, all of that shit, and he was a reformed character you know. And it seems so, cos I spoke to the guy this afternoon after I talked to you and I gotta tell you, he couldn't have been more pleasant."

"You spoke to him?"

"Yeah, well it seemed like the respectful thing to do. Guy loses his wife while he's inside to something terrible like that. I thought the least I could do is call and tell him I'd heard, and pass on my respects. He was really low and not the loud wise guy that he used to be. He may turn up tonight, I told him to come along if he fancied it. Much like I said to you."

"Wow," was all I managed.

He took a big gulp of his brandy and looked at me again, in that way of his. I knew I was in for another revelation. I was starting to get a handle on this bloke.

"But here's the strange thing... I said that you were mostly right. Well it turns out that Nancy died, like, three months ago. So why do you suppose Carrie would tell you that she's going home for her aunt's funeral, when she missed it by like three months?"

Questions, questions and more questions.

Answers, unfortunately, were harder to come by. I just looked back at him and shook my head.

Just then somebody tapped Donnie on the shoulder and after a brief discussion in lowered tones, he turned back to me, "Johnny, I'm being summoned back to the bosom. Stick around a while and get to know some of the folks. The bar tab is on me, so enjoy yourself. We'll catch up later."

And with that he wandered away, leaving poor Johnny with a bottle of brandy and another murder to mull over.

I didn't have long with my thoughts as a buffet had been laid out on a couple of the tables, that had now been pushed together and I was beckoned over by an elderly lady who turned out to be Donnie's mother in law's sister. Are you following all of this? Quite why she would have been there was anybody's guess. Surely she didn't know Carrie-Ann that well? And if my memory served me well, she had been one of the weepers when I had arrived.

I had read about Americans getting very interested in death and wakes and funeral parlours as they got older and had assumed that this was rubbish, but maybe there was a hint of truth.

She was a quite lovely lady anyway and we chatted as we loaded our plates with cold meats and some strange looking warm pastry type things which didn't seem to taste of very much.

The food was very welcome, as I'd not really eaten anything of substance since breakfast and as I ate I was questioned by some younger members of the family about England and put them right on some things that they said they had been taught at school about our history. Whether it is true that the curriculum in US schools teaches children that the Kings and Queens of England live in the Tower of London, and that Buckingham Palace was only built as a decoy for the German fighter planes, is now purely decorative and used only for tourism is all debatable. Perhaps I was being set up? But it was fun. I got my own back. I told them that under the terms of the Declaration of Independence, King George made a deal to allow the US their own republic after the revolutionary war, but only for a five hundred year period, after which it would revert to British rule unless a fixed sum could be agreed to buy out the contract. I don't know if it's the British accent, but they seemed to totally believe me and I was sure that they would have their hands high in the air in the next history lesson.

One guy who had plainly had far too much to drink started baiting me about the war and telling me that without their help we English would all be speaking German. I considered telling him that without the French navy they would still be British subjects but it would have been pointless, so I just laughed along with him until he forgot what he was talking about.

When I checked my watch as I stood in the bathroom I was shocked to find that it was eleven thirty and my quick escape had, in fact, turned into an enjoyable evening.

The man stood at the next urinal must have noticed me check my watch as he commented: "Is the jet lag catching up with you?"

I glanced at him quickly. It's hard to study somebody when they are urinating. It seems a bit rude, don't you think? I managed to take in that he was about my height, slim, with thinning hair. He looked a bit pale, like he could do with a good trip to the Caribbean.

"Maybe. It's been a long weekend already and there's still Sunday to go," I answered.

He made a noise like a polite laugh and continued as he pressed the flush and turned to the sink behind us, "Are you visiting anywhere else on your trip over here, or just sunny Akron?"

"I'm not sure where I'll head next, but I'm not planning on going back to the UK just yet," I said, pressing the flush and turning towards him.

He seemed a friendly chap, with a worn, but happy look to him. He had the palest blue eyes, like the colour was slowly running out of them. He looked at me in a shy manner, never fully turning towards me, while drying his hands on paper towels from the dispenser.

"You must have known Carrie-Ann well then, to come all the way out here?"

I washed and rinsed my hands, and reached for paper towels while trying to come up with the right response.

"Yes, we had more than a few laughs together. She was a good girl." I hoped that this would suffice.

"And did I hear that your name is John?" he asked.

"Yes, that's right. John Adams," I answered.

He opened the bathroom door and turned back to look at me, before saying, "John Adams, eh? Like our President?"

And with that he was gone. I wondered what he meant by the tone in his last comment. Was he checking up on me? Was he sent to check up on me? He didn't appear to trust me otherwise he wouldn't have made a remark like that before walking away.

And why ask for my name, then not tell me his?

It was late and I was starting to get jittery again. Enough had gone on today. I needed to get some rest and recharge my batteries.

I walked out of the bathroom and looked around for Donnie. I spotted him, stood over at the bar and was alarmed to see him talking to the guy who I had just had the conversation with in the bathroom. I hung back and watched for a second, as they finished their chat, shook hands and the other guy walked out of the bar onto the street. What was going on? Had I been rumbled? I needed to leave. I'd find a cab outside somewhere.

I headed straight over to where Donnie was stood and put my arm on his shoulder. "Donnie, you've been very kind and it's been an honour to have been invited to be part of this, but I'm bushed. I have to get to bed before I fall asleep stood up."

He laughed and took my hand.

"Johnny, I'm glad you came, and I'm sorry we started off on the wrong foot on the telephone earlier today. I hope that you understand?"

"Of course. I'm just sorry to shock you with all that news," I said.

"It's water under the bridge, and hey, I hear you met him." He picked up a beer and drained it, before slamming it back on the bar.

What did he mean?

"I'm sorry," I said, "I don't understand. Met who?"

"Sarah's husband. Carrie's uncle. He said he chatted to you in the bathroom just now."

SHIT! That was him? The guy who just got out of prison. No wonder he was so pale.

"I wondered who that was," I said. "He never introduced himself."

"Yeah prison'll do that to a guy. You get real choosy about who you trust. But that was him alright. Tony Wolf."

Wolf!!

As in 'lupine'!!

SIXTEEN

I made a polite promise to call Donnie and arrange to get together before I left town, knowing full well that I would do no such thing. He pressed me to stay for the funeral, which was planned for Monday, but I was non- committal in my answer and made it clear that funerals upset me. I over exaggerated about my father's funeral and how at every ceremony since I had been reminded of it, to the point that I had stopped attending them. He seemed to buy this and to an extent appeared to like the sentiment involved, so he settled for me getting in touch, gave me a bear hug and sent me on my way.

All I planned to do now was get some sleep, then get the fuck out of Dodge (in the Dodge) before I met any other strange characters. I was going to ditch the John Adams persona and get back to being Mike Huntingden as soon as I was on the road back to Pittsburgh.

I was out on the street now, scanning up and down furiously for a cab. There didn't seem to be much traffic at all, never mind cabs and I wondered whether I'd be better finding another bar and calling one from there. There was no way that I was going back in the Emerald Grill.

I headed left, which must have been west, as I reasoned that I had come from that direction in the cab and there seemed to be more lights in that direction. There was a building up ahead that seemed like a bar, but once I reached it I realised that it was a fancy dress shop, with lights flickering in the windows and costumes on display.

I stopped for a minute and was about to walk away when suddenly I was grabbed from behind and a hand was clamped firmly over my mouth.

It was a big hand, and whoever owned it was very strong and a lot taller than I was.

The shock combined with his strength led to me being dragged down the side of the costume shop and my efforts at resistance proved simply useless.

Eventually we came to a stop and I was thrown up against the wall.

The sheer force of the action knocked the wind out of me and caused me to bend double.

Then, while I fought to try and get my breath, a large fist smacked into my mouth making things a whole lot worse!

I got the metallic taste of blood in my mouth immediately and knew that I had a split lip at the very least.

Instinct threw my arms up around my head to protect myself, as another fist slammed into the side of my chest.

As I mentioned earlier, my own personal experience of events like this was limited to one and I had no natural sense of what was the right thing to do here. All I wanted to do was avoid any more hurt, slightly behind that feeling was the notion that I would like to escape. But I was still having problems breathing and couldn't lift my head, so I had no idea who my attacker was, or where he was, never mind where the escape routes were located. Everything was happening so quickly and there were so many thoughts and feelings going on that when he spoke it caught me by surprise.

"I know why you are here and I know what you came for. If you tell me where it is there's no need for any more trouble."

He spoke rapidly, in bursts, with a heavily accented voice, almost German sounding. Nothing like any accent that I'd heard that night.

He must have got the wrong person, I was thinking at that point, but how to tell him that?

I tried to speak, but had trouble getting my words out. I attempted to stand up and held my hand out in front of me as I lifted my head.

I needn't have bothered, as another fist dug into the same area at the side of my chest, which had taken a previous hit and I doubled up coughing again.

"WHERE is it?" he demanded, and he hit me again.

This time the punch landed on my temple and the next thing I knew I was lying out on the tarmac. I was dizzy, hurt, and shocked and I had absolutely no idea what it was that this man wanted.

I didn't have long to wait as two hands grabbed the front of my shirt and lifted me back up.

I tried to protest but still couldn't get the words out. My mouth was full of blood and grit and for some strange reason, at that moment I clearly remember worrying about how I would look the next day. Important stuff!

My eyes had been screwed shut since the first punch had hit me and I gingerly tried to open them now.

I was being held up against the wall, my feet barely touching the floor and as I fought mentally to prise my eyelids apart I found that I was looking directly into a pair of eyes that were six inches away. Instinctively I shut my eyes again then opened then slightly, as if, somehow that made what I was looking at, less frightening, like peering from behind a cushion at Freddy Krueger.

His face was in darkness, obscured by the shade from the shop, but I could see the top of his head, where he appeared to have short blond hair. He was very tall, with a large head to go with his hands and he was breathing oily breath right into my face. I tried to look away, but wasn't able because of the grip that he had on me. Shit this guy was strong!

"That money is mine," he said in the same accent, with a growl for good measure.

I didn't dare reply.

"My brother died for that money. I'm not stupid. You've not come all this way for nothing. You know WHERE it is."

"I ... I don't know what you're talking about. Honestly," I managed to say before he let go of me with one hand then immediately brought it back, slamming it into the middle of my chest.

Aside from the obvious pain, this punch caused me to throw up all of the brandy and the small pastry things that I hadn't been sure about earlier. I hate throwing up. It is not a pleasant experience at all, but I soon forgot about it as I was hit very hard on my jaw and I went down.

Hard!

I must have passed out momentarily, as things got a little fuzzy from this point on. I remember shivering and I can see his face staring down at me as he said something else.

But I don't know what it was that he said.

The next thing that I recall was hearing two voices and opening my eyes to find two guys knelt in front of me, talking to each other. I don't know how long I had been out, or where my attacker had gone, but I was now curled up in the foetal position and can't have looked very clever.

The two guys helped me to my feet and spent a period of time discussing getting an ambulance or taking me to the hospital. One of them had a cigarette, and I remember thinking that this was the only thing that I needed at that moment, despite not having smoked for well over two years.

I was having even more of a problem speaking as I must have been in shock, but the one with the cigarette understood what I meant and got me a fresh one out of his pocket. After trying to light it for what seemed like an eternity I gave up and he took it back off of me, lit it, and put it into my hand.

"Thank you," I said, managing speech for the first time.

I took a drag and leaned back against the wall, as the rush hit me. They both went to grab me, but I steadied myself and held up a hand.

"I'm ok. Honest," I said.

"Shit man," the one who had given me the cigarette said, "you scared us to death, man. We thought you were dead there for a minute. We saw this huge dude stood over you and you weren't moving. Who was he?"

I just shook my head in response and tried to shrug my shoulders. The pain that this caused in my chest made me drop the cigarette onto the floor and one of them made a noise as if to say don't worry, as he picked it up and gave it back to me.

"You look terrible man," said the other guy, the smaller of the two Samaritans, "you need to see a doctor and get yourself checked out. You could have a concussion or something."

I have absolutely no idea what these two characters look like to this day. My memory of this whole episode is sketchy to say the least. What I do know is that I managed to talk them out of getting me an ambulance and one of them used my cell phone to ring a cab company that he knew.

I then remember them telling the cab driver that he should take me to the hospital and I don't think that I even thanked them before we pulled away.

I spent an age in the cab trying to find the motel address that was on the card in my pocket, before thrusting it at the driver. He didn't seem interested at all whether I died, went to hospital or whatever. This must have been a regular occurrence for him. It certainly appeared that way.

He dropped me back at the motel and I fumbled about in my pocket for some money to give him. I remember spending an inordinate amount of time working out the tip, which is strange for me, as normally I totally over tip rather than get into the maths. Then I looked around cautiously before heading to my room, but there didn't seem to be anybody about. It was dark now and the wind had gotten up. I was still at sixes and sevens, and very scared.

I let myself into my room, then shut the door and locked it before turning the lights on.

The room looked exactly as it had when I had left, but that was not tremendously comforting at this stage. I went to sit on the bed but even the act of sitting was painful. I stood up again and leaned back against the television set, which caused it to turn sideways because of the pressure that I was putting on it, and I wheeled away towards the mirror and the vanity unit, which I had rested on earlier.

When I looked at myself in the mirror I was the most frightened that I have ever been in my life. Dried blood had matted my hair, sticking it to my forehead and one of my eyes was partially closed.

I looked a lot worse than I felt.

Remarkably, my nose looked to have come out unscathed, but my lower lip was fat and had split.

Again there was dried blood all around my mouth and bits of gravel that I had picked up while lying out on the floor. I looked like Rocky after one of his epic battles with Apollo Creed and the thought made me laugh, while at the same time I could feel tears welling up.

This was not for me. I didn't like this one bit. I wasn't cut out to be a hero.

My shirt was ripped in several places and there didn't seem to be much point in trying to rescue it, so I unbuttoned it and tried to let it drop off by using the force of gravity, as moving my arms was very painful. I looked at my chest, which was already bruised and wondered if I had broken a rib. Maybe the two guys were right. Maybe I should get to a hospital? But I couldn't go to one here in Akron. I'd have to go to another town, maybe Canton? That wasn't far away.

The shock of seeing all of my injuries had apparently woken me up a little from my earlier shock. I don't know whether this is a medically approved theory, but it has plausibility to it. I recognised that I may well have concussion, but I also knew that there was no way that, tired as I was, I was going to get any sleep in this town tonight, or maybe ever again. I was fairly confident that my injuries were not life threatening and made a promise to myself to visit a hospital the next day, but for now I needed to get out of town as quickly as possible.

I don't condone drunk driving and abhor anybody who attempts to justify it, but at that moment I was frightened for my life and didn't feel confident in ringing the police, as they could well have been after me also for all I knew. I also firmly believed that I had gotten rid of most of the brandy that I had drunk when I had thrown up while under attack. I knew that I had drunk six or seven beers, but all but one of those had been between the hours of three, and eight.

I looked at my watch… it was now just coming up to half past midnight. I could stay here, and work out pros and cons, or I could pack up my shit and get out.

I went for the latter.

I carefully washed away as much blood as possible and tried to sort out my hair, before deciding that a baseball cap was the way to go.

My jeans had withstood the attack very well and didn't appear to need any attention, or changing for a clean pair. I endured the pain of putting a clean t-shirt over my head. I won't lie to you, it hurt like hell and I screamed out loud, having to stand still and take deep breaths afterwards, but it was necessary. I didn't look like I'd win any beauty pageants at this stage, but I still looked more normal wearing clothing than not.

I threw everything else, including the ripped shirt into my bag and put the index cards and pen into my rucksack. I made a last sweep of the room and then put on my baseball cap and picked up the keys for the Durango.

I turned off the lights before unlocking the door then eased it open slowly, peering out into the parking lot. All was quiet, so I opened the door fully, stopping again to listen for any strange noises before I clicked the remote for the Dodge and picked up the bag and the rucksack. I lifted them one by one into the back seat of the car. This was also a painful experience, but I got it over with as quickly as possible and climbed in the driver's seat, wincing as my bruised battered chest protested at me. I was going to have to get some gas at some stage anyway so I would get some painkillers at the same time.

I was not going to be sorry to see the back of Akron and hoped that I would never have occasion to come back here again. I let off the parking break and took a deep breath before easing forward, out of the car park and back onto the street.

There was very little traffic and pretty soon I was making the turn back onto the 76. I was not comfortable by any stretch of the imagination. The seatbelt was digging into my bruised ribs and I was starting to get a headache. In addition I was not particularly in great mental shape. I was running on empty and was so tired both physically and mentally that I was surely in danger of falling asleep at the wheel. But even though I had been in Akron for less than one day, it seemed like I had spent a week of my life here and every bone in my body was urging me to get out.

SEVENTEEN

I had not made a conscious decision to return to Pittsburgh but I soon became aware that this was, indeed, where I was heading.

A lot of things were happening that I didn't seem to have much control over and I pondered fate for a while as I drove in silence.

My mind had shut down on everything to do with Carrie-Ann and I didn't think about it once during the whole ride back. I guess it was like when people get selective amnesia. I wasn't ready to even attempt to work out what was going on and what had gone on. My mind was protecting me from it all.

I breathed a huge sigh of relief when I passed the state line and was back inside Pennsylvania, and soon after that I stopped at a twenty-four hour gas station, where I filled up the tank and bought some Gatorade, some coffee and some crisps/chips to munch on. I also bought some painkillers, two of which I swilled down with my coffee before leaving. If the guy who was working the till at this late hour had been surprised to see somebody with a fat lip, a mangy eye and a bruised face he did an excellent job of hiding the fact. Perhaps this is the normal traveller that they see at this time of night?

I had kept an eye out while I was pumping gas – as they say – just in case I was being followed, but not one car stopped the whole time that I was there.

Before I drove away, I dug through the rucksack and pulled out the Izzy Stradlin CD. I then listened to Izzy for the remainder of the journey, playing it through maybe three times, until I finally reached the outskirts of the city and saw the skyline in front of me.

I don't want to labour this point, but I did feel like I'd been on a mammoth journey and was more than a little elated to be returning to Pittsburgh. It was a similar feeling to returning home, which was slightly odd, as I'd only spent three nights here in my life and now here I was at three am with no place to stay.

I got off the freeway and followed the signs for Heinz field, knowing that it would lead me to the neighbourhood where Stevie and Beth lived, and hoped that I would recognise the streets and be able to catch somebody awake who would let me in, though I realised that most sane people would turn me away, looking like I did.

Fortunately I found the Inn more or less straight away and as I approached I saw that there was a parking spot literally twenty yards from the front entrance but on the left hand side of the street. I pulled across the road and parked without turning the car around, which meant that technically I was facing the wrong way, but this was a minor indiscretion to my mind at the moment. I turned off the engine and wondered what my next move was.

As I was mulling over my options, I saw somebody walk out of the gates of the inn and head towards me. It was Ray, the grungy looking bartender, who worked at Harry's with

Beth. He was obviously heading home for the night, which gave me hope that there were still people up and about at the Inn.

I was so relieved that I threw the car door open with a little too much force and forgetting my ailments went immediately to rectify the fling by grabbing hold of the door. Despite the painkillers this activity was too much to bear and the pain kicked in before I reached the door handle, which led to me falling out of the Durango and onto the pavement.

Fortunately I landed on my shoulder, but this still wasn't what I needed after everything else that I had been though. It was dark, I was cold and in pain, and to top it off, the pavement was wet. I lay there and just gave in. At that point I really had just about had it with everything and there was a moment there, staring up at the sky not being able to hear anything at all except my own breathing, which was almost an out of body experience. I would not have been surprised if I had floated up into the air away from my body. Looking back, as I have done several times since, I often wonder whether this was a spiritual moment. I'm not going to get all new age on you here, but it was as close to how people explain their own personal 'moments' as I have ever come across and it came from nowhere, whatever it was. I have no idea how long it lasted, but from somewhere I seemed to get the strength to continue.

I looked up and saw that Ray had jumped backwards and looked like he was getting ready to defend himself, but then he started to shape up as if he was going to hurry away from what, to him, must have appeared like some crazy drunk driver arriving home in the early hours.

I tried to work myself in to a position where I could stand, "Ray," I managed breathlessly, "I'm sorry... Please. It's me, Mike."

He stopped in his tracks and was now staring at me, clearly still trying to work out exactly what was happening.

"I'm hurt and… I'm gonna need some help here," I continued.

After another second of contemplation, Ray seemed to all of a sudden realise who I was, and then hurried up towards me. "Mike?" he said as he crouched next to me, anxiously trying to ascertain where he should take hold of to try and lift me up.

I was lost for words again as I tried to summon the strength to work with him at getting me back on my feet. All I could manage was, "My ribs… my ribs… please…"

After a bit of a struggle and a lot more agony I was leant up against the car sucking in air frantically. Ray caught a look at me as the light from a streetlamp shone on my face for the first time.

"Jeez!" he exclaimed, stepping backwards again. "Tell me you didn't do that just falling out of the car!"

I managed a grunt in response.

"You look like you've seen a little action tonight, my friend. We heard you were in Ohio though. What are you doing back here?"

"I got run out of town," I said, "and didn't have anywhere else to go. Do you think you could help me inside? Is Stevie around?"

"Sure," he said, "… let me get an arm under your shoulders here and I'll come back for your bag in a minute."

Walking wasn't half as hard as I expected, but the extra help was bliss and I was not about to turn it down. When we reached the door to the Inn, it opened for us and Stevie was stood there ready for action.

"I saw you two heading up the pathway. What the hell went on here? Are you ok?"

I forced a half smile, as Ray helped me over the threshold and I concentrated on negotiating steps and doorways before answering.

In the meantime Ray filled Stevie in on what had gone on outside. Stevie asked Ray if there was anybody else out there and Ray told him that I'd arrived alone in a car.

"Where did this happen?" he asked. I think the question was to either of us, but I elected to answer.

"I got jumped by somebody in Akron tonight and I had to get out of town. I didn't feel safe and I didn't have anywhere else to go."

Before I'd even got the last word out I was overcome by it all and found that there were tears rushing down my face. I almost fell again, as my body shook with the emotion that was trying to escape. Ray had let go of me by now, but grabbed back hold as soon as he saw what was going on and Stevie was less than a split second behind him.

They helped me into a large substantial chair in the reception area and I just let it all out.

I couldn't help it. I had no time for embarrassment at this point and I had no control over what I was doing. It was my body just telling me that it was overworked, overtired and abused.

Up until that point my mind had held it all together, but now, as I was feeling like I was in a safe place, it just let go.

Ray must have gone out to my car and fetched my gear in, and at some point I heard him ask Stevie if he would be ok with me, then he knelt in front of me and said he'd see me tomorrow and that he was glad I was ok. Something along those lines.

It took a while to compose myself and when I finally did I found that Stevie had poured us both a large measure of brandy and was leant on the counter looking at me. He would have been quite within his right to have asked me to leave. Shit, he could have called the police, either as a way of getting me off of his property, or in order to help me. But he didn't and I'll never forget that. I knew that this guy was for real when I first met him, but his complete acceptance of what was in front of him without showing any sign of judging me, or pushing for an explanation showed me that he held me in the same regard. I don't know whether he took my outpouring of emotion as a compliment, or whether in da Burgh men are supposed to be men and hide their feelings, but he wasn't looking at me like he couldn't wait for me to get out of his sight.

I took a swig of the brandy. This, for obvious reasons, brought a lot of turmoil back to me, hurtling at me all at once, along with the usual rush that you get from a first swallow of brandy. I felt my eyes open wide and I grabbed at one of the chair arms for support.

Stevie was alongside me as quick as a flash and had the brandy glass in his hand before I let go.

"Whooa there, big guy!" he said.

I sat back, in the chair, steadied myself and looked at him. "Sorry" I said.

"You don't need to be sorry," he replied.

"You know, the crazy thing is, you mean that and I actually believe you mean that," I said.

He just smiled and put the brandy glass on the reception desk, before saying, "Let's get you up to your room. Get a night's rest, you clearly need it. Then tomorrow we'll discuss my elevation to sainthood. Yes?"

That sounded great.

"That sounds great," I said.

I have no idea what the time was when I walked back in the room that I had last had a night's sleep in. Stevie said goodnight and left me to it, after telling me that he had a friend who was a doctor and that he'd get him to check me out the next day.

I didn't bother putting the light on in the room. I just headed over to the bed and kicked off my shoes. I then pulled my belt loose, undid my jeans and let them drop. I was passed caring about washing, or cleaning my teeth, which shows you the state that I was in and I knew that trying to get my socks or t-shirt off would be stupid, so I climbed in bed and found a position on my back that was half comfortable. I did count my blessings before I fell asleep, but this wasn't in a 'thank you God' kind of way and I didn't do any praying or anything so I can only assume that my moment of enlightenment was just that, a moment. I'm not ruling anything out for the future though, because something outside of me was doing the guiding for a time out on the sidewalk of Pittsburgh and maybe this will revisit me when I have the time and inclination to think some more about it.

Sleep enveloped me while I was awake and I felt myself drift away. I am sure that you know this feeling, it's not something that you experience all of the time, but when it does it's almost like the moment before orgasm. You can feel it washing over you. If it ever becomes available as an illegal drug, I will be queuing on street corners to buy it before my stash runs out.

I don't know how long I slept, but I awoke at one stage in the night and needed to piss. I tried to fight the feeling for a while but knew it was pointless, so I got out of bed, which brought a whole lot of pain. On my way to the bathroom I snagged my rucksack and while I sat on the pot I managed to find the painkillers and the Gatorade, which I had not even opened on my journey back from hell. I took two more tablets and concentrated on trying to remain in a half sleep, worrying that I was now going to be wide awake for the remainder of the night.

I needn't have worried about that because the next thing that happened was a light rapping on my door and when I opened my eyes I could see that light was pouring in through the windows.

I really needed to learn how to use the curtains at some stage!!

I quickly snapped my lids shut in reflex and the pain around one eye reminded me of my big night out.

I groaned and lifted my head, opening my good eye, and looked towards the door which had been pushed open a little way. Stevie was looking back at me.

"Hey man, it's after two in the afternoon and my buddy the doctor just dropped round as I promised. He's happy to take a look at you if you're up for it?" he asked.

I exhaled, dropping my head back onto the pillow, as if the effort of holding it up had taken every last drop of strength.

Two in the afternoon?

"I think it's wise, dude," Stevie continued, "after the state you were in last night. And don't worry; he's doing it out of kindness. You won't get billed."

I lifted my head back up to look at him, "Ok," I started. "That's very kind of him… and you… really. If he doesn't mind…"

"He doesn't," Stevie interrupted as I lay back down. "I'll send him right up."

With that, he disappeared and I lay there wondering if I should get up for the doctor. What was the etiquette, I wondered? I mean, he knows I'm in a bad way, but will he be offended if I don't at least try to get out of bed and shake his hand?

I decided I should make an effort. And an effort it was! After I got myself to a sitting position I gave up and leant forward with my palms face down on my knees.

This is how I greeted the doctor.

"Hi Mike, I'm Robert," said Robert as he breezed into the room.

I looked sideways at him and tried to smile with one eye open. He took a look and smiled right back at me.

"Don't worry; I'll just take a quick look at you. If there's no need for a visit to the ER we'll be through in no time. Now… where does it hurt?"

I had to laugh. I quickly discovered that Doctor Robert had what can only be described as an excellent bedside manner. He looked about my age and had short sandy hair which stuck up on top and made him look a bit mad, but in a good way. He had smallish green eyes and quite a full nose. Not a good-looking bloke, quite big built and clumsy looking to boot,

159

but I couldn't help taking an instant liking to him. I don't think I stopped smiling the whole time he was there, even when he helped me to pull my t-shirt over my head.

He checked out my ribs and pronounced them badly bruised, but not broken. My wounds were superficial apparently and should heal up in no time. I was in need of some rest and relaxation. Painkillers were the best solution, but I was to keep an eye on how many I was popping and try to be sensible. Other than that he had nothing else of wisdom to pass on, he said and with that he bade me farewell, actually waving in the process, even though at the time he was less than two feet from where I was stood, and he departed, leaving me with an arm half in the air returning his wave. I slowly lowered my arm, wincing at the pain and imagined him already breezing into see the next patient. Speed doctoring… it should catch on!

I ran a bath, knowing that it was not going to be easy to bath myself, but also in the knowledge that I would get a lot out of the experience.

Climbing in was harder than climbing out. I felt like a new man, until I looked at myself in the mirror again. The bruising around my eye was looking good. I wasn't sure how I was going to be able to eat without reopening the cut in my lip and wondered whether Robert the express doc had missed this in his speed analysis. Oh well, at least nothing was broken.

I fished my soap bag out and cleaned my teeth, then had a shave and popped another painkiller prior to getting dressed.

I found some clean-er jeans and managed to ferret out my only other shirt which buttoned up the front, thus avoiding lifting my arms again unnecessarily. I pondered the socks and decided that much as I hate not wearing socks, today was a day for simply working my way into my shoes from up high. Bending down that far was going to be something that I would put off till another day.

When I was as happy as possible with the way that I looked I checked my watch. It was three oh five on Sunday. Sunday – so far – had most certainly been a day of rest.

But now I knew that I was going to have to go and face the music. I owed Stevie a proper thank you and, more importantly, an explanation for what I was bringing into his Inn, then he could decide if he wanted a friend with these kinds of complications or not.

EIGHTEEN

Despite my bruised and battered body, it felt good to be up and about. My nights sleep had been well overdue and whilst I could have probably done with a few more I was better for it.

I went downstairs and, seeing there was nobody around in the entrance hall cum reception area on the left, I headed to my right into the large kitchen that I had been in before.

I walked in to find Stevie and Beth both sitting around the kitchen table expectantly in silence and immediately felt like I had walked into a job interview. All that was missing was the firm handshake. I had been looking forward to seeing Beth again, but had not expected to see her quite so soon and certainly not looking as she did, which was cold and businesslike. Again, like a prospective employer. In fact she made Stevie look positively warm by comparison and my mind immediately jumped back to the conversation that I'd had with Stevie when I was entering the Inn for the first time and his exception to my mentioning

Beth's concerns about his workload. Maybe this was the side of her that gave him wrath?

They were both soberly dressed with cups of steaming liquid in front of them, tea, or coffee, I couldn't tell and the silence from around us, echoing around the Inn, with its high ceilings and large rooms added to the 'Sunday best' feeling. It was almost Dickensian in a way and I wondered if it was too late to pop back upstairs to don a waistcoat and cravate. I had to remind myself that, despite the kindness that these people had shown me, I was not their son, home from boarding school, but in fact, a 35 year old man from another country.

I attempted to break the ice with a breezy, "Good Morning!" and it worked, partly. Stevie made a joke about my beauty sleep and how well I was looking then offered me a cup of coffee, which I accepted gratefully. Beth ventured a half hearted, "Hi", which was a far removal from the conversation we'd had the day before when I'd dragged her out of her lecture for a flirtatious chat.

Eventually we were all sitting around the table in uncomfortable silence and I could see Beth looking at her brother, as if willing him to begin the meeting. I knew, at that point, that they had rehearsed in detail what they were about to say. I could also hazard a guess that, from the vibes I was getting, Beth had decided that I should be told to go and Stevie was the one who was unsure. I wondered how long they had spent discussing this.

I made the decision that I had nothing to lose but to tell them everything, so, after another moment of silence and some much needed coffee, I put my cup down and began my oratory.

"Well… first of all I'd like to thank you both for your hospitality, which I will be paying you for. Secondly I would like to apologise, to you Stevie, for my display in the early hours of this morning and to you, Beth, for disappointing you in some way."

At this point Beth tried to jump in but Stevie held up a hand to stop her and looked at me with a look that I could almost be sure read, 'you're doing just fine, carry on'.

Did I tell you how much I liked this bloke?

I continued while the floor was mine, "I can say to you with complete honesty that I have done absolutely nothing wrong, nothing illegal and nothing immoral, depending on what your standpoint is. But for some reason, which I have been trying very hard to work out, I am being pursued by somebody, or some people, who want something from me. I have no idea what this 'thing' is, but whatever it is, it's clearly dangerous, as I found out last night."

I stopped and had another mouthful of coffee. Beth was looking at Stevie for a lead, whilst chewing a nail and Stevie was still in the same position, arms crossed in front of him on the table, leaning forward slightly towards me.

I had been speaking very slowly and clearly, which is unlike me. When I'm trying to say, or explain something, I normally speak quickly, animatedly, in my hurry to get everything out, lest I forget something. I've always admired the quality in others of being able to get everything out in a clear concise manner, without forgetting a vital point, which only returns to mind later. I felt remarkably calm and again I put this down to Stevie's manner, but also maybe the Inn itself and perhaps the city of Pittsburgh? Maybe I could go on to include the state and the country? I don't know.

I once heard a very interesting story about a man who, for a fee can read in the stars where you are supposed to live. This is for real. It's a legitimate business. This guy takes information from you about your birth date, etc, and through astrology tells you where you would feel happiest living, where you would get the most inner peace. A lot of people have followed his advice and literally moved home, sometimes to another country or continent and allegedly he's spot on. I've always felt like when I'm near water I feel more at peace than in the middle of the countryside. I'm sure that you can think of something similar in your own life. But my point is, since first stepping foot in Pittsburgh and now returning to Pittsburgh I felt a calmness which I can't remember feeling before. Now you may say, just how calm were you when you were fleeing town yesterday? And you'd have a point, but in my defence I was being pursued. Anyway you get the point… I've left England because I felt like I was missing something and more and more, despite the pandemonium that is going on around me, I was feeling like I'd found it. Maybe I hadn't? Maybe it was an illusion. But I felt better, happier and more alive, and this positive feeling was doing good things for me in lots of ways that I've pointed out in the last few days. If Beth was going to try to run me out of town then she had a fight on her hands and if I could change her opinion of me at the same time then I would go to bed tonight at the Inn confident of another good nights sleep.

So I assumed the 'Stevie position' arms crossed in front of me, declined a refill on my coffee and started my tale. I began with the flight from the UK, too many vodkas and my meeting Carrie-Ann. I went on with the incident in the airport and the expression on her face when the guy in the red and black shirt appeared, how she had ignored me in the bar when I had gone in, despite us arranging to meet and the genuine fear that she had in her eyes. I told them about the early morning phone call which I had initially dismissed as a prank and the knocking on my hotel room before I had gone out. Both Stevie and Beth were sat forward listening to me now as I tried to explain how much meeting them both and the subsequent gathering back here had meant to me. I was open about the fact that I had woken up on Saturday morning excited about moving into the Inn and where the relationships between us all were going to go.

Then I began the dark part, about the recognition of the guy in the black and red shirt and ponytail and the chance getaway in a cab, my quick thinking on the way to the airport about renting a car and the decision to go to Akron. I apologised for holding out on the information to Beth during our conversation, but pointed out that I had tried to ring her later. I told them about the call from Rachel and briefly explained who she was, feeling able to slip this information in while I was unburdening my soul and I told them about Saxton ringing her. Then I moved onto remembering the envelope that Carrie-Ann had written her number on, the name and address that I had found on it and my fruitless trip to the railway station, about how I had decided to try to be professional and write everything on index cards and had then come to the decision to follow up all of my possible leads before coming back to Pittsburgh and how this had led to me going to Carrie-Ann's wake, totally unplanned. I told them about meeting Donnie Novitski and Carrie-Ann's uncle Tony, who had just got out of prison for armed robbery. How he had made me feel very nervous and how I had a strange theory about his name, 'Wolf' being like the name on the envelope, 'Lewis Pine – Lupine'.

I took another moment before finally giving them what I could remember about being dragged down an alley and beaten up by a huge guy who kept demanding I give something to him, that whatever it was, his brother had died for it. The two men helping me to a cab and then hightailing it out of Akron frightened for my life.

I had speeded up in my narration at this point and was starting to get a bit worked up. Beth noticed and grabbed me a bottle of water from the fridge, which I took from her very gratefully and drained half of before continuing. In the whole time that I was composing myself neither of them moved a muscle, other than Beth fetching me the water then sitting straight back down again. I don't think they quite knew what to make of things.

I ended my story by trying to explain how my relief at being safe and seeing Stevie had caused my breakdown and made it clear that I did not want to bring any pain, or danger into their lives, so was quite ready to move on if they wanted, but that I really did value their friendship and would like to stay, until I REALLY overstayed my welcome.

When I finally finished the silence returned and it was clear that they were trying to take it all in. I had sympathy with this position, as I had suffered similarly, so I busied myself with taking the empty cups over to the sink and finished the water, before tossing the empty bottle into the bin.

It was Beth this time who broke the silence, standing as she turned to speak, "Mike I can't believe what you've been through! I don't rightly know what to say now after that, except that I'm sorry that we put you through this entire charade on top of everything else."

She had kept walking towards me as she had been speaking and ended up so close that I could feel myself being pulled towards her with some kind of magnetic force. She obviously felt the same as we were hugging each other tightly before I knew it. My ribs were hurting me, but in a very good way. I think I might have moaned out loud, but it may not have been entirely pain that caused it. Beth suddenly realised what was going on and stepped back, and not completely letting go of me, she exclaimed, "Oh my god, I'm so sorry!"

"That's ok, they're only bruised. Doctor Robert is sure I'll make a full recovery."

Stevie was stood now, with the ever-present smile on his face. "While I'm thinking, Doctor Robert, as you call him, says that you might want to think about counselling or some kind of self help group. Violent attacks can lead to all manner of repercussions and if you need any names or numbers I can get them from him," he said.

"That's great, thanks. That's something else I owe you for," I replied. I reached to pat him on the shoulder, but didn't quite get there before the pain hit.

I winced and they both stepped forward, so that we all ended up in a little group hug like situation. This brought laughter from us all and brought a natural conclusion to the meeting.

"I need a beer after all of that," said Stevie, heading for the fridge, "How 'bout you two guys?"

A beer… god that sounded good. "That is a great idea," I said, "but I reckon I should pop a painkiller first before I start with the alcohol. Or is that dangerous?" I looked at them both for guidance.

"I don't think you should take anything if you're going to have alcohol," said Beth, "and to be honest, if you have enough alcohol, will you really need painkillers?" She smiled.

That smile! Wow! What pain?

"Amen to that," said Stevie, opening the fridge, before exclaiming, "Goddammit!"

"What's up?" asked Beth who, by the way, still had a hand lingering on my arm. It felt good.

"There's like two beers in this fridge. I didn't realise just how much we had got through!"

I checked my pockets for my wallet, before realising that I'd left it upstairs in my rucksack… I hoped… I would have to check. "I'm heading upstairs to get my wallet and then I'll ride out with someone to get more beer. I'd go alone, but I'm not sure how much they'd sell me looking like this."

They both laughed and Stevie spoke up, "I'll go, there's no need us all going. I can pick up a crate."

"Well I'm paying," I insisted, "so wait right there. I'll be right back," I said, as I headed out towards the stairs.

"I'm not arguing," shouted Stevie after me.

"Me either," called Beth.

I hobbled upstairs and found my wallet straight away at the top of my rucksack, which was handy. I also grabbed the painkillers and decided I'd keep them in my pocket just in case the beer didn't work.

"Do you fancy pizza Mike?" asked Beth, when I got back downstairs. "I'm gonna ring and order. They deliver."

I thought back and tried to remember when I'd last eaten anything as heavenly as pizza. Just what the doctor ordered. I wasn't sure how I'd go about chewing without opening up sixteen wounds, but I'd give it a good go.

"That sounds great!" I said. "Pepperoni?"

"Sure, I'll order that, and you want ham and mushroom right Stevie?"

"Exactamundo chica!" replied Stevie.

I handed him fifty bucks and he looked at me in amazement. "Dude… how much pain are you in?"

"I figured that now I've made my peace with you two that I may be around a while, so I may as well stock the fridge."

They both looked at each other then Stevie looked back at me. "Okay. Your call. I'm not going to protest at somebody filling my fridge with beer. No never! Any particular brand?"

"Something imported" I replied. "None of your US domestic 3.5 per cent fizzy pop. Dos Equis, or Tecate."

"You got it," he said. And with that he was on his way.

I turned around to find that I was alone in the reception area and so headed into the kitchen, assuming that this was where Beth had gone to phone for pizza. The kitchen was bare however and I was about to go back to the reception when I met Beth coming into the kitchen towards me.

"Hi. Sorry to disappear. I just popped to the little girl's room."

"A-ha. I was wondering where you went. I thought you were scared about being left alone with me and had barricaded yourself in a bedroom."

She looked at me for a minute and I thought she was going to burst into tears so I added, "Hey I'm only kidding," and cupped a hand around her upper arm.

This quickly led to us coming together again and Beth, carefully this time, wrapping two arms around my chest. I held her in my arms for what seemed like forever, saying nothing. Beth is about five to six inches smaller than me and with a slight tilt she can fit her head snugly into my neck and shoulder. It was a very welcome feeling at the time and I think I involuntarily closed my eyes for a second, just happy with the feeling. When we parted she looked up into my eyes and brought one of her palms up to my cheek, lightly stroking it.

I gazed into her sky blue eyes and realised that we were stood next to the island in the middle of the kitchen where we had spent ages chatting in the early hours of Saturday morning, before leaning in towards her. The movement was reciprocated and we kissed. Not a long hard passionate kiss, but a tender, exploratory kiss, neither of us sure about our exact expectations or needs, but both of us knowing that we were feeling the same way.

We parted, smiling at each other. Even though I was only staring into Beth's eyes, I had already learned to read that they were smiling.

"I'm sorry that I didn't trust you," she said.

I gingerly brought up a hand and pulling her head forward, kissed her on her forehead.

"Don't be," I replied. "I didn't exactly give you any reason to trust me, did I?"

"That's what trust is about though isn't it? I feel like I've betrayed you and I'm sorry, but it's only because I really like you and… well, to be honest, it's not often that I find myself in this position."

Beth looked like she was trying to decide on what she wanted to say next. I was starting to get a read on her a bit, especially when she was feeling uncomfortable, so I decided to break in again, to reassure her, "Beth, don't worry. You've done nothing that I'm gonna hold against you, I promise. I really like you too, I already told you that. I'm not expecting anything from you, so you don't have to warn me, or prepare me for anything. Let's just take things steady and things will just happen when they feel right… like they are doing already."

The smile crept back. I'd obviously said the right thing again. The new Mike Huntingdon seemed to be back in the building and it WAS the building, and the people in it, that seemed to be the making of me at the moment. I hoped that this was going to be how it was going to be from now on.

Unfortunately the events of the last few days had prepared me for the fact that it probably wasn't going to be total plain sailing from here on in, but I just hoped that I was going to get the chance to relax and recharge with Beth, and get to know her and Stevie before anything else dramatic happened.

NINETEEN

Beth and I drank the remaining two bottles of Yuengling that remained in the fridge, while waiting for Stevie. We then realised when he got back with two cases of Dos Equis amber and one case of Corona, plus five limes, that we hadn't held up to our side of the bargain, as we'd clear forgotten to ring up and order the pizza!

Stevie pretended to be really pissed off about this, but I was learning to understand this guy too and we all had a bit of fun over it.

This rectified and the pizza ordered, we found ourselves back around the kitchen table, limes chopped up on a wooden chopping board in the centre and three bottles of Dos Equis open in front of us.

The next two or three hours just flew by. We drank beer, ate pizza and just chatted about stuff. Stevie regaled us with stories from the Far East, including a couple of very amusing ones about a place that he'd lived in for three months whilst in Vietnam.

I gave them a potted history of my life. I'd given a similar story to Stevie the other night in Harry's but he seemed more than happy to hear it again and pressed me with questions about my job and my family. Beth didn't seem to be fazed by my mentioning Rachel. I tried to be as frank and honest as possible, and I was confident that I was doing the right thing.

Beth then started to explain about her choice of studies, she was doing a degree in psychology and psychoanalysis, and was obviously extremely into both subjects. I wondered why I'd not picked up on this before and made a resolution that I'd ask her more about it on another occasion. It seemed an area that took in a vast amount of material and she was not going to be drawn as to what she wanted to head into career wise when it was all over.

They told me about their grandparents and shared several reminiscences of them, childhood memories and such, and then both made a firm commitment that they would make time soon to go down to Florida to visit with them – or visit them, as we say in England.

We'd all kept steadily on drinking and it was having a magical effect on my aches and pains as predicted. However it did have the usual effect on my bladder and after I made yet another trip to the bathroom, my third to everybody else's one I think, I came back to find that the mood had changed and an awkward silence was hanging over the kitchen again.

Something had gone on while I was away. I got the feeling that these two had more family meetings than the Ewings. And so far it was me who always got the brunt of their ruminations.

"What? What's up?" I asked straight away, looking them both in face alternately.

It was Stevie who kept quiet this time and Beth who took the lead, "We were talking about, you know, your adventures and what went on?"

Relief! "Oh, ok, just that… I thought you'd changed your mind and decided that I should pack my bags," I said, joking, but they only half laughed.

Beth spoke up again, "What happens now?" she asked. "What happens if this nightmare follows you here?"

I stopped short.

Didn't I just say that this was all too good to last? I don't know, I can't honestly remember, but if I didn't, I should have!

"How would it?" I asked them both, with a slight hint of defence in my tone. "How would anybody know that I was here?"

Next up was Stevie, "Don't worry Mike, we're not hounding you out here, or trying to frighten you. We just got to talking and were thinking that maybe we could help."

I was getting confused now, what exactly were they offering here? "Help how? What are you proposing? That I turn myself in?"

Beth jumped in again, "No! God! Nothing like that! At least not at the moment... until we know for sure that you would be safe. That's the last thing that we want. What we're suggesting is that we help you figure it all out. What do you say?"

I couldn't say anything for a moment. I just wasn't prepared for this at all. My emotions were up and down. One moment I'm down an alley getting seven bells kicked out of me, the next I'm kissing a beautiful girl and now they were thinking about...

"No!" I said, quite definitely and pretty loudly too. I startled myself with the force that I spat it out.

Beth approached me tentatively, but didn't quite get as close as before. "We could help. We may have some ideas. Things that you didn't think of..."

I sat back in the chair, picked up my beer and tried to think calmly, before saying, "I... I can't get back into this. I can't get you both involved in something like this. It's dangerous. Besides which... I just don't think I've got it in me to do this."

I was speaking quietly to begin with, but by the end of the sentence it was barely a whisper.

Now Stevie spoke. He sat down in the chair opposite me, where Beth had sat for the past couple of hours while we'd laughed and joked.

"We're not going to do anything stupid here Mike. We're not even planning to leave the Inn. At the moment, all we're suggesting is that we throw a few ideas about. Didn't you say you had some index cards with everything written down on them?"

I didn't speak. I just listened, while looking at him. He continued, "Well why don't we just look at them and see what comes up? It'll be like a party game… like we're playing Cluedo or something."

They were both looking at me. I didn't know what to say or do here. In my own head I knew that this was not a particularly bad idea, but it was what it could lead to that worried me. Events can quickly snowball, as I had found out already to my detriment. Now I was back in a protective environment, a place where I felt safe and content. Did I really want to ruin it by bringing all of this hurt, and anguish?

Maybe to them, Stevie and Beth, it was already here? Perhaps they would always think that I'd brought it along with me? To me though this was the only place that I had felt safe in the last few days.

Beth spoke again, putting her hand on my arm, in a caring way that could not have been lost on her brother, "If you really don't want to do this Mike, we won't. But all we're suggesting is talking about it here, in this room, between the three of us. Even if we do come up with anything that could lead somewhere else, I promise that we will not act on it unless all three of us agree on it. How does that sound?"

I looked at Stevie, he was nodding along with her. Beth still had her hand wrapped around my arm and I wondered how much of her psychoanalysis was in operation here.

What was this? Was I questioning Beth now? Jeez Mike… you gotta start trusting somebody here.

"Ok… but it stays here," I said finally.

"Agreed," said Stevie.

"Nobody else involved," said Beth.

Where was everybody else, come to think of it?

"Where is everybody?" I asked.

"Oh… it's midterm break," answered Stevie, "and most people tend to head home to see family."

"But didn't you have a lecture yesterday morning?" I asked Beth.

"Yeah, it was like a special event before break and was supposed to be really something, but as I told you on the phone, it was a bit of a letdown really. I should have stayed in bed."

There was a lull, while we each wondered what was going to happen next.

"Anybody want more beer?" asked Beth, removing her hand and standing.

"Great," said Stevie.

"Me too," I said, standing, "and I'll go get the index cards." I could almost feel the relief in the room, and maybe a little excitement too.

The index cards were loose inside my rucksack, where I'd flung them in my rush to escape Akron. I gathered them all up and started back downstairs. This couldn't really be a bad idea could it? I mean, we may only talk about this on a night occasionally for the next six months and get no further. On the other hand they were sharp cookies and it was quite possible that they would see things that I hadn't. With the three of us banging ideas about, something could jump out that I'd not considered before. But what would happen if we did come up with a new direction? This was what worried me. Would we end up like the Hardy Boys and Nancy Drew? Amateur sleuths chasing crooks across the rust belt? It may have been fun back then, reading those books, but bad dudes tended to be better armed these days. And I'd already had one pasting too many. I really didn't want to meet that guy again in a hurry. Aside from that, I really couldn't imagine leading either Stevie or Beth into a situation where they ended up confronting him! I had to try and keep a hold on where this was going and try not to let the excitement get them carried away. Easy for me to say though, I'd not exactly been restrained myself.

On the plus side we might discover hidden treasure, or lost inca gold! That would be nice. I mean, the guy who whupped me was after something. Maybe it was the heist from the armed robbery that Tony Wolf went to prison for?

Wait a minute!

Maybe it was.

I was already back in the kitchen doorway at this stage and now stood stock still as I attempted to keep this thought process going. You know what I mean here? When you all of a sudden get a flash of inspiration, or remember something and need to get it all worked out there and then? Unravel it quickly in your mind, otherwise it will go, lost without a trace and you'll end up retracing your steps, and trying to recover the original thread.

Well there I was and Tony Wolf had committed armed robbery, he'd left the Emerald Grill just before me and then I'd been jumped by a guy who wanted to know where the money was. Now I knew that the guy wasn't Tony Wolf, but I also knew that Tony Wolf had thrown some remarks at me that had lead me to think that he didn't trust me, hadn't he said something similar to the guy in the alleyway, about me coming a long way? Carrie-Ann had obviously been murdered for some reason and the railway station and Tony Wolf seemed to be a strong lead.

I came back from my thinking and refocused my vision to find Beth and Stevie staring up at me from their positions around the table, anxiously, almost like two chicks in a nest waiting for their parent to bring food. No, scrap that last analogy, it's awful, but that is the thought that came to mind at that moment. I was stood in the doorway with the five cards in my hand and I wondered just how long I'd been stood there, lost in my investigative thoughts…

"What?" asked Beth. "You've thought of something haven't you?" She was smiling. Such a lovely smile.

I spent the next however long it was explaining my thoughts and the rationale behind them. I passed my index cards around and tried to go into as much detail as I could remember behind each of the points on them. Then I let them ask me questions and I answered what I could, leaving us with a bunch of new questions, which we wrote down on a piece of paper that Beth had found behind reception.

The main question that we had was 'who was the guy that had attacked me?'

We all pretty much agreed that he had more than likely attacked me for the money that was stolen in the armed robbery, which Tony Wolf was responsible for and that there was a distinct possibility that Tony Wolf was behind the attack, as he had just left the bar before me. Which lead to the next question, 'exactly what did he steal?' and 'how did he get away with it?' as we were presuming that there must have been an 'it' that everybody was chasing.

Right behind those questions was 'what is there at Akron railway station?' and 'who killed Carrie-Ann Novitski?'

We had a theory that whoever killed Carrie-Ann was the same person that killed her aunt Sarah, Tony's wife. They were obviously looking for something, maybe the haul from the armed robbery, or something that would lead them to it. If so, then logically it could have been the guy who had attacked me. But then surely it couldn't have been anything to do with Tony Wolf, as he wouldn't have killed his own wife… would he?

Somewhere behind all of this we still had to figure out what the guy in the red and black jacket had to do with all of this and if he was Lieutenant Saxton. If he was, then why had Carrie-Ann been so obviously disturbed by him, and how had she been murdered if she was with him at the time? Unless he had been the murderer and was now trying to pin it on me?

Stevie had asked me about the possibility that my attacker and the guy in the red and black jacket and ponytail was the same person, but I was fairly sure that they weren't. I know it was dark and I was confused at the time, but I'm confident that, although the guy from Philadelphia airport and the hotel was tall and strong, he wasn't as tall as my attacker, plus I had seen the guy who was beating on me close up and I remembered that he had blond hair. I just didn't think that it was him.

We were all sat mulling, sipping our beer, when Stevie announced that he was going to Akron, just like that.

"But you can't go to Akron," I said defiantly. "You promised that this was not going out of this room".

"Listen," he began, "I have a buddy in Akron, Callum, he's an Irish guy that I met out in Hong Kong and he's in Akron studying polymers or something. He's only there for a six-month period then he's back to the Far East. He's been on at me to meet up, but I've been putting him off because of the Inn and my work. Now seems like a perfect opportunity for me to go see him. And while I'm there I'll go check out the railway station and see what I can find. It's perfect. Nobody knows me, so nobody will suspect a thing."

"I don't know," I said. "What happens if somebody is watching the station for people who are snooping around? This could be dangerous. Look at me for chrissakes!"

"Plus," said Beth, "how do you even know that Callum will be there? There won't be any classes at the moment."

"Where's he gonna go? He's come over from Hong Kong. He's hardly likely to fly home for a week, surely?"

I was torn on this. I didn't want any harm to come to Stevie, but it did seem like a good opportunity to get another look at the station. He might just see something that I didn't. "Ok. If you go, how long will you go for?" I asked him.

"Just for a night out and long enough to get a look around the station," he said. "Let me give Callum a call now and see what he says. I'm sure he'll jump at the chance of a few beers and time to catch up. I promise you I'll be no longer than one night."

And off he went, out to reception.

I turned and looked at Beth.

"What do you think?" I asked her.

She rested her chin in her palm, her elbow on the table and looked back at me. "Well it is just for one night," she said.

One night... I didn't even make it that long.

I didn't say that out loud though.

TWENTY

Despite everything that was on my mind, I had another wonderful night's sleep. The alcohol had anaesthetised me sufficiently and though I have no idea of the exact time that we called it a night, I am sure that it wasn't too late. We were all bushed and had just come to the decision that it was the end of the show.

Stevie had spoken to his friend Callum, who was in Akron, having decided to stay on for research during the break. He was overjoyed at the chance of hooking up with Stevie. Apparently they hadn't been that close in Hong Kong, but had frequented the same bar on a regular basis, while Stevie had been there exploring for month or so. They'd been on a boozy trip to Macau together, which had been run by the bar, an Irish tavern, and when Stevie had left he'd swapped details with Callum, as he had with many people he'd met on his travels. Callum had been in Akron for the past month or so and had just settled into his apartment on campus. There was room there for Stevie to crash, so he'd made plans to set out the next morning and meet him up there around lunchtime.

I'd offered to keep an eye on the Inn while he was away and Beth had made plans to come around before Stevie took off, so that she could show me the ropes.

I was very stiff when I awoke, which was to be expected I suppose and I'd had to pop a painkiller before venturing downstairs. After battling to get my clothes on without screaming out loud, I had a quick wash and cleaned the old teeth. Then I hobbled down into reception to find Stevie sat at the desk with a whole load of paperwork in front of him.

"Morning Stevie," I said.

"Hey," he replied, not looking up from his work. "How are the aches and pains this morning?"

"Oh not bad," I lied. "You mind if I get myself some coffee?"

"Go right ahead man. Do you know where everything is?"

"No, but that's half the fun. You want one?" I asked.

"No thanks, I just put one out," he said. "If you need anything just holler."

I just put one out... very amusing... I must remember that one.

I wandered into the kitchen and spent the next five minutes opening every door in there. There was clearly an agreement that everybody had their own storage space. When I came across the fourth cupboard with coffee in it I decided that I would need to ask which one I was ok to use and made a mental note that I needed to go shopping for provisions today.

"You having problems?" asked a female voice from behind me.

I turned around to face Beth, who was a sight for sore eyes most of the time, but this morning was wearing some figure hugging jeans that stopped at her hips, revealing a good two inches of waist before her t-shirt began. She was filling her t-shirt quite well also and I decided that I must be feeling better, as I couldn't possibly have been entertaining thoughts like this twenty four hours previously.

I guess I was staring at her like some dumb college student, because I didn't get to reply before she reached past me, opened a cupboard door behind me and said, "Ta-da!"

I took full advantage of the situation by grabbing hold of her round her waist and pulling her towards me. I then smiled down into her face and got a smile back in return. "Morning," I said.

"Morning," she replied, raising an eyebrow and we kissed.

This kiss was a little longer and fuller than the one the day before and I was still stood there enjoying it for a couple of seconds after she had finished, grabbed some things out of the cupboard behind me and was headed over to a coffee percolator which I remembered from yesterday, but had forgotten existed.

"You feeling ok this morning?" she asked, as she busied herself making coffee.

"I am now," I answered. "I was a little stiff and achy first thing, but that's cleared right up."

She turned momentarily and smiled at me, then returned to the task at hand.

Yeesh!

No idea what it means, but it just came to mind and it's vaguely onomatopoeic.

At that moment, the moment of 'yeesh', Stevie walked in and caught me leering at his sister's figure.

Oh well… busted!

"I'm on my way guys," he said, seemingly unfazed at what could be going on under his own roof, with his own sister.

Did I tell you how much I liked this guy?

"Please do me a favour Stevie," I implored him. "Keep in touch with us and keep your wits about you."

"I've travelled around areas of Asia where they didn't look like they'd ever seen a westerner, Mike. I think I may be ok in the next state."

I took that as a rebuke.

"Sorry man. When are you planning to visit the railway station?" I asked him.

"Not sure yet," he replied. "I'll play it by ear I think, but I'll let you know. I may even ring you from there!" he threatened, smiling.

Beth was stood with her arms crossed and I could see that she'd changed personalities again. Stevie turned to face her and I watched his face change.

"Don't sweat it," he offered. "I'm a big boy."

And with that, he turned on his heel and headed back out to reception. Beth followed him and I heard her telling him to … "At least drive safely! … And don't forget to call when you get there."

My feelings about this girl were mixed to say the least. Let's just say I had a mild concern about how much I was liking her, whilst also realising that there could be a danger of her becoming irritating. Best to leave the jury out for the time being, I thought.

Stevie headed out and we drank coffee, without exchanging any more intimacy. Then we got down to the work at hand in reception, which was basically none. There was no one checking in and no one checking out. The rooms were all paid up front and they held a bond for each 'visitor'. The cleaner had already arrived and had started upstairs before I had come down.

She would then leave the laundry for the laundry service, having put fresh bedclothes on the beds while cleaning.

All I had to do was check her time slip, pay her for her time and keep the laundry behind reception out of the way in case of fire, where it would be available for the laundry guy who generally came mid to late afternoon. Aside from that I was to deal with any requests from the 'visitors', none of who were in town, having departed Pittsburgh for the weeks break. So we drank more coffee and chatted a bit, but about nothing exciting that I would bore you with here, just general talk about the area and where I could buy provisions.

I decided that I would go out to the local market/deli place to stock up and to buy us both a sandwich for lunch. This was also going to be a good excuse to see how I went on with walking like a normal person thirty six hours after being nobbled by a thug.

The walking was surprisingly easy and the fresh air was especially welcoming. I found the store with no problems, literally one block down on the same street and spent an enjoyable half hour just browsing the items on display.

I always enjoy shopping, even at supermarkets! I think I must be strange. I can't even really tell you why I enjoy it so much. I just do. But I enjoy it even more when I'm in a different country, just to look at the different things on offer. Or variations of the same things back home. The USA don't really ever seem to have got their shit together when it comes to crisps, or 'chips' as they call them. Salt and vinegar are incredibly difficult to find. You would have thought that Walkers would make a killing out here! Everything seems to be cheesy, or barbeque, or mesquite. Not too imaginative really. I never really understood what mesquite was and up to this stage of my life can't remember asking anybody. I'll add this to my list of things to find out.

After all that, I bought some 'chips', mesquite flavour just for the hell of it and some coffee and tea – at least I think it was tea that I bought. I then wandered to the deli counter and bought us a couple of subs, stacked high with all kinds of tasty morsels, which probably shouldn't go together in the same sandwich. I also liked the look of the salad, so I bought a couple of containers of various salads. Finally I got a large pack of bottles of water and figured that this would all last until this evening at the worst. Then maybe I'd suggest we go out for something to eat.

I hauled my swag back to the inn, which took a little longer and was a little more painful than the outward leg and returned to find Beth in the midst of detective work, staring at the computer screen with the index cards spread out in front of her, pen poised in her hand above a yellow lined legal pad and the printer buzzing, and ticking away next to her.

A kind of hot Miss Marple, if you will.

I began to ask her what she was on to, but got a palm in the air as way of reply, so took the hint that she was in mid thought and went straight into the kitchen, returning with lunch served on a large silver tray which I had discovered and looked like it should have been the ladies runner up prize at Wimbledon.

Beth looked at me, like the cat that had got the cream, desperate to tell me what she had found out, but also a little smug with herself at finding whatever it was and I guessed, needing a little congratulating.

"Go on then, clever girl, what have you come up with?" I asked.

She was silent for a moment, milking it for all she was worth. "You… won't believe what I've found out while you've been out," she began.

"I've only been gone ten minutes," I said.

"What? Ten minutes? Try more than an hour," she said. "I would have thought you'd gone the wrong way, if I hadn't seen you turn right with my own eyes."

Over an hour! Boy that was some good shopping!

"Well it was good shopping," I said, "I wanted to get you a nice sandwich for lunch. It was the least that I could do."

She looked down at her sub and lifted the top layer gingerly, "What flavour is this exactly," she asked, screwing her nose up ever so slightly.

"Try it… you'll love it trust me," I said. "Anyway go on then I can't wait, what did you find out?"

"Well…" she began… drum roll, "… I was thinking that there must be newspaper reports of the armed robbery and the newspapers now have most of their archives on the net, so I went on-line to see what I could find."

She paused here. Maybe for dramatic effect or maybe the sandwich was too good to resist. She took a bite and again looked at me with a puzzled look and her nose a little screwed up as she chewed slowly, tentatively.

I was loving mine! In case you are interested I got spicy salami with salad, mayo and lettuce, then on top I couldn't resist some jalapeno peppers. Mmmm!

"I checked websites for the Cleveland Sun and the Akron Beacon Journal…" she began, "… and they lead me onto a whole host of interesting sites."

Another pause and another tentative bite of the sandwich.

I'd nearly finished mine and was looking at the salads now… the fresh air must have given me an appetite.

"Anyway… I found a robbery that took place on a security van seven years ago in Cleveland and there's a whole host of stories about it. I printed some of them off."

She picked up a pile of about twenty pieces of paper off of the printer and made as if she was going to pass them to me, then stopped and pulled them back, clearly enjoying this moment and not wanting me to be distracted.

She put the pages back onto the printer and continued… "Your friend Anthony Woolf, spelt 'W-O-O-L-F' by the way, is mentioned in all of these pieces. It seems he was part of a gang, if not the ringleader, that lead a bodged attempt to make off with the contents of this security van."

"Why bodged?" I asked, jumping in during another pause.

"Well it looks as if they blew themselves and the van up by mistake whilst trying to get into it. Two of the four gang members died in the explosion, which also injured the security guard who was in the back of the van and the driver who was locked in the cab."

"So what happened to Woolf, why wasn't he injured?" I asked.

"The newspaper reports say that he was probably in a nearby vehicle, which is how he fled the scene. The fourth gang member was captured by police in the area, while he was trying to hide out."

"I wonder why he didn't leave with Woolf?" I half asked, half pondered aloud.

"This is the part you're going to love!" she said, dangling again, with eyes wide open staring at me.

"Well go on then," I urged, "spit it out."

"The fourth gang member was named Nat Schulman. Ever heard of him?" she asked.

"No, should I have?"

"His brother, Rich, was one of the gang members who died in the explosion and he later sang to the police, which was how Woolf came to be picked up. The papers say that he was incarcerated too, but out of state and was given a shorter sentence in exchange for the information."

I took a moment to mull and process this information and looked back at Beth, who was positively bursting.

"So I'm thinking that he MUST have been the person that attacked you in Akron." She looked at me for a response.

Logically she had to be right, but this lead onto another questions…

"Ok, so let's say you're right and I think you are by the way… What was in the van? And why does our friend Mr Schulman think it's still at large if the van was blown up?"

Beth smiled. She obviously had an answer prepared for this also. "I can't find any clear information on that. The official police line in the report said that the entire load of the security van was destroyed in the ensuing fire."

She was still smiling. There was clearly more.

"But? …" I prodded.

"Nat Schulman was knocked unconscious by the blast and when he came round, it's his testimony that the security guard who had been in the back of the van was laying out on the sidewalk nearby. He was in no fit state to have got there under his own steam, so it would appear that Woolf must have climbed into the van and dragged him out before fleeing.

Schulman can neither confirm nor deny this, so all we can go on is what Woolf said in court, which is that he did indeed rescue the guard before driving away. And this went a long way to lightening his sentence."

"So if Woolf was in the van," I began…

"… He could have made off with whatever they had intended to steal," she finished.

"And…" I added, "Nat Schulman, or whatever his name is now, plainly believes that this is exactly what he did."

"Right!" said Beth.

"You clever girl," I said.

"Thank you."

"No, I really mean it," I said, "… now we just have to figure out what Carrie-Ann and Akron Railway Station have to do with all of this."

TWENTY ONE

After the burst of excitement that accompanied all of this new information came the mundane task of dealing with the laundry service.

Two guys arrived in matching overalls and Beth let me go ahead and deal with them. This was not especially taxing and only really involved pointing out the sacks of bedclothes that the cleaner had brought down and signing a chitty which gave the name and address of the Inn, and the number of bags.

When they had gone and I'd received plaudits for my first dealings with the laundry, I suggested to Beth that we ring Stevie and give him an update. She readily agreed as it gave her a chance to check that he was in Akron safe. It was also an opportunity for us to push him on when he was going to the railway station.

While Beth was punching Stevie's number into the phone I took over at the computer terminal, which was still online, with the intention of searching for some information about

Akron station. I didn't have much luck to begin with. They clearly did not have their own website, or if they did, it wasn't linked to any of the search engines. I tried Amtrak and was rewarded with a link for 'trains and destinations', which then took me to 'Midwest' and a listing for 'Akron, OH'. While I was waiting for this page to upload, Beth was leaving a message on Stevie's voicemail and looking at me quizzically. I mouthed "what?" at her and lifted my head. She hung up the phone and said, "He's not picking up, do you think he's ok?"

How do you answer a question like that?

Reassuringly.

"Sure he's ok. He only left here a few hours ago. Maybe he's just arrived at Callum's home and he's saying 'Hi', or perhaps he's at a gas station and he's filling up? He'll ring back, don't worry."

She looked worried.

"I am worried," she said, frowning. "What if he's run into Nat Schulman at the railway station?"

"First of all," I answered, "how in the hell would Nat Schulman know who he is? Do you think he's lying in wait and questioning everybody who tries to catch a train?"

A touch sarcastic and probably not very helpful, but she had to realise that the likelihood of getting into trouble within hours of arriving in Akron was slim.

Wait a minute… scratch that last part.

Mercifully at that moment the phone rang. I prayed it was Stevie and went back to the computer screen. My prayers were answered, as Beth started to give whoever was on the other end of the phone grief for not picking up his cell phone when he got out of the car.

The page that I was looking at said very little that I didn't already know about Akron Railway Station. Apparently there was a 'Taxi Service Available' and an 'Enclosed Waiting Room', which I hadn't seen. I tried to cast my mind back and envisage the station interior. It seemed a long time ago now and there wasn't much that stood out. I remembered that it had struck me as odd that there was the long stretch of wall with posters stuck up on it. As far as I could make out, the only waiting area was where I had stood, unless it was out on the trackside?

I listened as Beth filled her brother in on her detective work and decided that I'd interrupt her once she got onto his visit to the station and ask him to look for an enclosed waiting room, in the hope that this would help.

There didn't seem to be anything more that this page could offer me, there wasn't even a telephone number to call. The address was the same, '96 E.Bowery St.'

Except... Wait a minute...

I grabbed at the index cards, which were scattered in front of me and tried to find the envelope, which Carrie-Ann had given to me with her cell phone number and the addresses on it.

It wasn't here.

Where was it?

It must have been still upstairs in my rucksack. I took off across reception as quickly as my bruises would let me and up the stairs, with Beth calling after me.

As I entered my room, I saw the rucksack next to the bed where I had left it and tried to bend down next to it. This hurt. A lot. I gritted my teeth and let out a scream as quietly as possible, then went down into a kneeling position next to the rucksack. I picked it up and emptied it onto the bed in front of me. Fortunately the envelope was one of the first things out so I grabbed it and stood up again with as little movement in the waist and lower chest as I could manage. This still hurt, so while I was here, I ducked into the bathroom and picked up the painkillers off the sink where I had left them. I then headed back out of the bedroom and down the stairs into reception where Beth was still on the phone, but looking over at me with a concerned look on her face. I waved at her in my best 'don't worry I'm fine wave' – I think this is a standard wave? I'm sure you know it. It's the one where you simply hold the palm of your hand up towards the person you wish to convey the message to, while making a facial expression consistent with the theme. A different facial expression can give the wave a whole different meaning, as I'm sure you are finding out whilst reading this and simultaneously holding a hand up to an imaginary colleague. I hope that you aren't reading this on a train, or in a crowded room.

"Are you ok?" asked Beth, with a hand over the phone.

"Sure. I'm fine thanks, I just needed to get this from upstairs," I said, waving the envelope at her.

She returned to the conversation and began to explain to Stevie what was going on at our end as I put the envelope on the reception desk and looked at the address for 'Mr Lewis Pine'.

'96 E.Bowery St., Akron, OH' as per the website. But the zip code…

The envelope read '22510', whilst the screen in front of me read '44308'.

Ok… what did this mean?

I thought quickly…

"Beth, ask Stevie if he's with Callum now," I said interrupting her.

"Sorry Stevie, Mike's asking something," she said into the phone, then to me, "What's going on Mike? What have you got?"

"Just ask Stevie if he's with Callum now… please," I added. She looked at me with a mild irritation creeping into her expression and spoke back into the phone, "Mike wants to know if you are with Callum at the moment." She nodded at me, whilst listening to Stevie, who was clearly also asking why I wanted to know this information.

"Can you ask him to ask Callum what his zip code is please," I said to her.

She frowned at me and said "What? Why? What are you talking about?"

This was getting frustrating now. I could also hear Stevie asking questions through the receiver in her hand.

"Beth please, just trust me, all with be revealed, I just need to know Callum's zip code. Please?"

She began to speak into the phone, "He needs to... yes..."

And then to me, "He's asking him. Why do you need to know this Mike?"

And then back to the phone, "Ok... 3 – 2 – 0... got it. Hang on."

Back to me...

"It's 4 – 4 – 3 – 2 – 0. Why?"

Wow... what did this mean?

I just stared at Beth for a moment with my mouth open without realising it, which must have really wound her up because before I knew it she had her hand back over the receiver again and was talking to me with more than a hint of impatience.

I missed everything that she said though, because all that I could think was 'What on earth is 2-2-5-1-0?' I knew that I had found something relevant here, but what did it mean?

"Mike!"

I snapped out of it and came back to earth. Just in time by the look of it. Beth's face was bright red and looked like it was about to go off! Another point worth noting for future reference!

"Sorry... what?" I asked, absent-mindedly, as I clearly knew what she was wanting to know, but was giving myself breathing space while the cogs in my head were turning.

This brought a sound that was half frustration, half growl in the back of Beth's throat. She told Stevie that she'd call him back and hung up, staring at me.

"What?" I asked her.

Again, I knew that this was dumb but couldn't help myself. Perhaps I was expecting some flash of inspiration, which would answer my question. 'What was 2-2-5-1-0 all about?' Maybe I was enjoying winding her up.

"Mike... hello? Are you still with us?" she asked in a voice that was barely a decibel down from a shout.

"Yes… sorry, I was just lost in thought," I answered.

There was silence again while Beth waited for me to go on. I was probably looking for another question and one did come after another few seconds.

"Well?"

"2-2-5-1-0," I answered.

This was greeted with another expression of the hand variety. You know the one where both palms are placed flat out dramatically in front of you. It's kind of like 'what!' or 'and?'

"Mike, you are making no sense whatsoever and I'm gonna inflict more damage on you if you don't get a hold of yourself and tell me what is going on!"

All in one breath!

Time to tell her I guess… I think the suspense was a little overplayed.

"Callum's zip code is 4-4-3-2-0 and the zip code on the address for Akron Railway Station here on the net is 4-4-3-0-8, but…" I dangled, and received more hand gestures, "… the zip code of the address on the envelope which Carrie-Ann gave to me reads 2-2-5-1-0."

Beth stared at me.

"So what does that mean?"

"A great question, Beth. That's what I've been trying to figure out in the last two minutes, which is why I was a little hard to get hold of," I replied.

She went silent for a moment, which was a relief I have to say.

Don't get me wrong, I really like this girl, but she had some edges that were a little too sharp. I hoped that I had what it takes to smooth them out. I was going to have to think some about this.

But back to the code… wait a minute… maybe that was exactly what it was!

"A Code!"

I said it out loud to see how it sounded.

"What?" asked Beth looking at me.

"Maybe it's a code of some sort?" I mulled aloud.

"A code for what though?" she asked.

"I don't know Beth. Get Stevie back on the phone. Tell him that 2-2-5-1-0 is a code and ask him to look out for something in the station that it could relate to."

She was already pressing redial.

"Tell him," I continued, "to look for an enclosed waiting room. Maybe there are some lockers or something in there. Wait!"

Things were clicking into place now.

Hold the front page!

"Can I have the phone please Beth? I want to speak to him," I asked.

"Sure," she said, probably relieved not to be caught up between us again.

She passed me the phone. The line was open, and Stevie was talking, "Hello? Anybody? What's going on there?"

"Hey Stevie, it's Mike, sorry for the confusion. Normal service has been resumed buddy."

He laughed, "What's the story Mike? I'm heading to the station right now," he said.

"Okay. The zip code that was written on the envelope that Carrie-Ann gave to me is incorrect. In fact it's miles out and I think this was done on purpose. I think the number we have is some kind of code for something. When you walk into the railway station you'll see there is a long stretch of wall in front of you on your left. You have to walk past it to get to the restrooms, you can't miss it."

"Okay," he said.

I took a deep breath.

"I think that there used to be some lockers against this wall. I read somewhere that after 9/11 lockers in airports and railway stations were deemed to be a possible terrorist target so they were removed."

"That's true," Beth interrupted, "they did that at the University as well."

"So…" I continued, "I think that what we are looking for may have been stashed in a locker there, which now may have been relocated. Exactly how you go about finding out where the contents are I don't know, Stevie. But I do remember seeing flyers and posters all over that wall, so maybe you'll get lucky."

Beth was nodding her head, and smiling. Mood change!

"Great thinking Mike," said Stevie, "I'm on it. I'll ring you back when I've checked the place out."

And with that, he hung up.

I stood up and did an exaggerated stretch. It was a reflex action, and despite the pain in my ribs, it felt like it had done some good. I walked over to where Beth was stood and put a hand on either one of her shoulders.

"Sorry for being an arse. I just couldn't think fast and operate at the same time. I'm still new at this amateur sleuthing."

She smiled up at me and shook her head.

"You don't need to be sorry. I was just trying to understand what you were saying, while explaining to Stevie what was going on. It just got a bit manic for a while that's all."

I removed my right hand from her shoulder and used my thumb and index finger to lift her chin up towards me, then leaned in to give her a kiss.

This was reciprocated.

"So do you think Stevie knows that something is going on?" I asked her.

"Oh yeah, he's not stupid. He won't get involved though, unless he disapproves," she replied.

"So that's a good sign then?" I asked.

"Well..." she began, and stopped abruptly.

"Well what?"

"If he asked what was going on, I don't really know what I'd say anyway."

Alert! Alert! Some difficult questions were looming. I tried delaying tactics.

"Let's try not to put any labels on anything just yet, eh?"

She smiled, and then narrowed her eyes to look at me with suspicion.

What did she say that she was studying? Psychology? Psychoanalysis? Hmm...

TWENTY TWO

It was over an hour until we heard back from Stevie.

In the meantime we did all that we could to avoid each other. We'd reached a stage in this 'thing' where we knew what the logical next step was and both of us were holding back. I think that we were both going through the infatuation stage, but there was also the 'Akron' thing going on which was jumbling our feelings. I certainly felt like I needed some cuddling and warm words after what had gone on and I think Beth had some kind of need for love and maybe the safety/security side that a new relationship dangles in front of you. All of this was pulling us together so dramatically that it was all that we could do to keep our clothes on as soon as everybody else left the room. I was sure that Beth felt this too. I could feel it in the air like electricity.

Thankfully I was old enough to know better and Beth had more wit (or 'smarts'). Either that or the emotional upsets of her past had strengthened her resolve to tread carefully when opening up her feelings to possible upset and damage.

Whatever... what will be will be I suppose and maybe there's a case for saying 'fuck it' and just getting it over with before it becomes too big a thing for us to handle?

Stevie was more excited than I had heard him up to this point when he rang back. I took the call from reception, where I was keeping my nerve by playing Freecell on the pc.

"Mike, we hit the jackpot, buddy," he said.

"Excellent. Tell me what you found."

Beth walked back through from the kitchen at this stage with two cups. I determined that I should keep her involved so I told her that Stevie was on the phone and he had some good news. She placed the drink in front of me and I thanked her.

"Sorry Stevie, just letting Beth know you're safe, go ahead."

"I was hoping that you were going to be taking that mantel off of me Mike, but I guess she's gonna worry about me until one of us kills the other." He laughed at this and I laughed along, though I must admit, I didn't totally understand what he meant and consigned the sentence to memory for review later.

He went on, "So I found the enclosed waiting area Mike, but there was nothing there. Just a couple of long benches and two vending machines… that was it. The only other place that there was anything worth looking at was exactly where you described. And we're in luck. There did used to be lockers along that wall until recently. I found a formal letter addressed to anybody who may have items stored away, with instructions on how to go about getting them back."

I broke in at this stage to ask if he had noticed anybody watching him or simply anybody strange hanging about and he replied in the negative, saying that in the whole time that he had been in the station only two people had entered and both of those had been to use the bathroom, then they had departed without so much as a glance in his direction.

The letter had given an address to write to, enclosing the locker key and a nominal fee for administration charges. Seeing as we did not have the key we all assumed that this part had already been taken care of and Stevie thought that the best idea was to ring the telephone number given on the letter, a '216' code which, like the address, was in Cleveland. I took the number down and thanked Stevie for his labours. He said that was going to go out with his friend for a few beers and would check in with us later. I advised him to stay away from the Emerald Grill.

After I put the phone down Beth and I debated the next telephone conversation. We knew that it had to be done and the sooner the better. In the end we agreed that it should be Beth that made the call. My accent would only stand out if anybody was looking out for anything strange and sometimes a female voice can get more information than a male's can. That's just the way it is!

Beth dialled the number and I waited, looking for something to do, trying not to add pressure to her task.

"Hi, I wondered if you could help me please," she began, "I need some items which I believe you have in storage and I wanted to know how I go about retrieving them."

So far, so good…

Listening to one side of a conversation is incredibly frustrating. You can only guess what the person at the other end is saying, so you end up wanting to ask questions yourself, which is soooooo annoying to the person making the call. I had already decided that I would say nothing.

"Well I have a five digit code number, does that help?"

Fingers crossed.

"Two two five one zero."

It was at this stage when I realised that they may need a name, or a contact number and this was not something that we had discussed. I grabbed one of the index cards, turned it over and wrote on the back, 'Give your real name if they ask' then put it in front of Beth.

"Elizabeth Deskin," she said into the phone and gave me thumbs up.

'Deskin?' I thought. I couldn't believe that up until this point I had no idea that their surname was Deskin. She was listening intently to whatever she was being told. I prayed that they would not need any further information from our side.

"The name it was taken out under?" she said, with a look of horror on her face.

Quick as a flash I grabbed the envelope that Carrie-Ann had given to me and put it in front of her with the now famous railway station address facing up and pointed at the name. She nodded and without missing a beat said, "That would be my uncle Lou, so it will be under Lewis Pine."

I crossed my fingers and closed my eyes.

"Yes, the locker address was '96, East Bowery Street, Akron, Ohio'".

Beth was listening again, not giving anything away facially.

"Okay that's great. Where are you located please?" she said and then took up the pen and started writing an address on the same index card.

'Thank God!' I thought.

When she had finished writing down the address she asked about the opening hours and jotted these down also. Then she thanked the person at the other end of the phone and hung up.

Halleluiah!

"Nice work, Miss Deskin." I said to her.

"You think? I'm drained!" she said.

"So what did it play out like?" I asked.

"If he had any suspicions that this was out of the ordinary then he didn't give it away. All I need to do is show up with I.D. and the code number and I can take my 'possessions' as he called them. There is nothing else to pay, as whoever sent the key back to them took care of that."

"Do you think that was Sarah Woolf?" I mulled aloud.

"It must have been, surely. Then maybe she mailed the letter to London to Carrie-Ann and destroyed everything else that led to whatever it is that's in storage and left it at that."

"So the person or persons who killed Sarah Woolf were after this information?"

She put a hand to her mouth, "Yes. And that's why it looked like a burglary gone wrong. Because they were searching for the locker key, or anything that gave them access to it."

"But how did 'they' know about the locker in the first place? This must be Nat Schulman that we are talking about here, either operating on his own, or with somebody else. But how did he know about the locker?"

We both sat in silence for a short time, wheels turning. Eventually Beth stood up.

"I think we should go to Cleveland," she said.

Oh fuck!

"Yeah me too," I admitted begrudgingly, "but I just didn't want to be the one to say it first. And to be honest Beth, I think we should go now. Before whoever it is that is going around killing people, gets wind of our phone call and decides to sit in wait."

"Okay. Here's what we'll do. You go and grab whatever you need while I call Gerry and ask him if he can fill in. We can leave the place empty tonight and put the alarm on, but there will need to be someone here in the morning. I'll go home, and grab some things and we'll lock up and go, so we can be there first thing in the morning when they open at eight thirty."

"Great. Let's do it," I agreed. "We can ring Stevie on the way and meet him there."

So… that's what we did and without so much as a break in the rush, we packed and locked up. Beth set the alarm and we shut the gates, then we jumped in the Durango and before you could say Moses Cleaveland I was back on the road north, which I knew so well.

Fortunately Izzy was still in the CD player and even though Beth had never heard of him, she seemed to be enjoying. Other than the CD there was not much in the way of distraction and I found myself thinking back to the last time I'd driven up here, only two days before.

I didn't recognise any of the scenery from then. My mind must have been a mess. In fact my mind was due a well-earned break when all of this was over. I needed a holiday! Wait… didn't all of this start out as a holiday? Perhaps I needed a real job? Then a career? Maybe a wife and some kids? A dog? Responsibilities to fill my life to prevent me from wandering off and getting into trouble, was that what I needed?

I wondered what Beth wanted out of life? She was still young and had plenty of time to worry about that. I turned to look at her. Her skin had a porcelain-like quality to it: pale, with no visible blemishes and fragile in a way, like she could break if she wasn't handled correctly. Her profile was soft, no straight lines, but she was deep in thought and her face was tensed up around her eyes. Her eyebrows, like her hair, were amazingly blond, almost to the point where they were invisible.

She caught me looking and her features relaxed as she broke into a soft smile. She then turned to face me, bringing up one leg as she leant her head into the seat. I thought she was going to start purring at any moment. For two pins I could have picked her up and carried her off to somewhere, where we could be alone for a while.

As I was thinking this, her smile curled up wickedly almost on cue and again I was sure we were on the same page again.

"Where are you taking me, Mr Huntingden?"

It was a fair question. I had only been to Cleveland once, on the ill-fated trip with Graham where I had been ill. We had arrived in Cleveland in early February and Lake Erie was frozen over. I had no patience for hotel hunting and I think Graham knew this. Bless him, he'd seen the Ritz Carlton and walked right in there. Next thing I knew, he was coming back outside with a bellhop and we were residents. I remember that the beds had been the most comfortable that I ever had the pleasure of lying in, but I was so ill that I couldn't sleep for sweating and lying freezing cold tucked up tight. Now was a good time to get the most out of the beds.

"I'm taking you where any gentleman would take a lady on a visit to Cleveland. The Ritz-Carlton," I said.

She sat up for a second. "Are you sure?"

"Well I figure that you and your brother are giving me a roof over my head without cost at the moment, so it's the least that I can do."

She curled up again and wrapped her hand around my arm. I turned to face her and she was looking at me, this time without a smile and I could almost see the conflict in her head, as she battled with herself for some sort of clarity.

"Don't worry," I said, turning back to the road, "I'll get us a couple of rooms and then there's no pressure."

"Thanks," she said.

"I'm not saying that we have to use them both. But they are there just in case."

She laughed.

I think she napped for a while then because she closed her eyes and was quiet. The next time she stirred we were entering the Buckeye State.

"Morning!" I said.

She stretched next to me and rubbed her eyes.

"Where are we?"

"Ohio. The Buckeye State," I said. "Do you know why it's called the Buckeye State?"

"Are you going to tell me?" she asked.

"No, I was wondering if you knew."

"It's to do with the trees I think," she answered. "Buckeye trees grow around here. I think they get their name because of the knot in the wood. It's supposed to look like a Buck's eye. How's that?"

"Excellent! Thank you. Could you tell me the name for the piece of furniture which you find in hotel rooms that is used to sit your bag on top of?"

"Excuse me?"

"You know the thing. Sometimes it's a table with rubber pads running along the top, or sometimes it's folded away in the wardrobe and can be opened up."

"I know what you mean Mike, but I have no idea what it's called. How long have you been wondering about that?"

"Oh quite a while. I have more if you're interested?"

She was and she clearly thought I was mad, but it amused her. We didn't resolve anymore though, not definitively. She was fairly sure that 'airplane' is American English, whereas 'Aeroplane' was used in England, as the 'aero' part of it came from French, or Latin. She's probably on the right lines with that.

We rang Stevie then, but his phone was on divert to his message service, so we decided to try again when we got checked in, then we could give him room numbers.

I took the '80', when the '76' split. There probably wasn't much in it, but I wanted to avoid driving past Akron. It wasn't somewhere that I really needed to see for a while. We were speeding through the countryside, with not a great deal of traffic on the roads and pretty soon the city sneaked up on us. Not in the dramatic way that Pittsburgh had done when I'd been driving back from Akron. Cleveland was a steady growth of urbanity, with no collection of glass and steel skyscrapers. It's a lovely place, but in desperate need of a lot of money throwing at it. There are shiny new sports facilities and lakefront museums, like the Rock n Roll Hall of Fame, but the rest of the city is tired and old, and looks like it needs pulling down and rebuilding. I remembered the layout from my last visit and using the Gund Arena as a landmark, I found the Ritz-Carlton quite easily. It's set back about ten blocks from the lake, right next to a shopping mall, with a Hard Rock Café. I pulled up to the front of the hotel and immediately Beth's door was opened by a liveried young man who bade us a "Good afternoon and welcome."

We caught the elevator up to the beautiful luxurious reception. All polished metals, gold and brass with large floral decorations everywhere you looked. A heavy tread, thick carpet that you could almost lie down and hide in led us up to the reception desk, where I was treated like visiting royalty and nothing was too much trouble. We checked in and took the elevator up to the eighth floor.

I got the bellboy to open the connecting doors so that we could walk through both rooms and I pretended to be taking it all in my stride while Beth 'oohed', and 'aahed' her way around. I suppose there is a fair amount of professional curiosity for her when she's in a hotel. Maybe she was looking for little touches that she could export to the Inn, but she was evidently very happy with her first stay here and I was secretly excited about what was in store while we were here.

"I'm just going to try Stevie again," she said, as I headed to the bathroom.

Evidently he didn't pick up, as I heard her leaving a message to tell him that we were staying in the Ritz-Carlton in Cleveland if he wished to get hold of us. She said it in her best English royal family accent and I couldn't help but laugh.

While I was in the bathroom, I decided to take a quick shower. The tractor beam was too strong. It pulled me in.

I had just begun to carefully wash my war wounds when the shower curtain moved in the draft from the bathroom door being opened. I stood still for a moment, listening hard over the jet from the shower. Hoping it was Beth, but somehow expecting somebody else. Then I heard Beth's voice… "Do you need any help in there?" she asked.

Bruises? What bruises?

TWENTY THREE

Now I know that I've gone on and on about the virtues of a bath, but I'm here to tell you... showers can be good too!

In the tradition that gentlemen never brag about sexual encounters and that you please try to see me as a gentleman, I will simply volunteer that things were far better than I could have imagined in my wildest dreams. This may seem a little over exuberant, but – trust me – if you were in my position and all of a sudden a beautiful, nubile, young, athletic, pert... you get the picture. I felt ever so slightly blessed and more than a little thankful to whomever I should be thanking.

That out of the way, I was also extremely relieved, to use a pun, to get 'it' out of the way and so was Beth. This may seem a tad unusual after all I've just said, but it was getting so that it was looming large in front of us and we were both worried about it happening and when it was going to happen and where. It was becoming a bigger thing than it should have been. Or so I had thought!

I wonder how people went on years ago, when – allegedly – people met, courted (whatever that means), then got married after a reasonable period, before any sexual encounter had taken place. Do we believe any of this? Did people not experience sexual tension and magnetism?

I am fairly sure that our ancestors in the caves didn't have such manners, so where and when did this restraint take place? I feel sure that religion will have some place in this somewhere. But anyway… it's hogwash. Sure, people would like others to see them as pure, innocent and following impeccable morals, but we all have needs and these are generally triggered off when we least expect them by contact with another human being. And we all love it, no matter how much we deny it.

I won't labour over this any further, except to say that immediately following our exploits we both became much more relaxed. This was evident in our post coital conversation, where we both admitted that we had been looking forward to getting sexually entwined, but at the same time we had both had trepidation and had worried about the consequences. I can honestly say that the consequences were of little concern to either of us at that particular point. But a lot of smiling was going on if that tells you anything.

So… moving on. We agreed that food was probably now a good idea, so got showered – again – this time separately and dressed. I suggested the Hard Rock and Beth agreed.

We took the elevator down and walked from the hotel directly into, and through the shopping mall into the Hard Rock, hand in hand, like young lovers. Horrible stuff! Quite sickly!

In order to celebrate our union we decided on a pitcher of frozen margarita and went at it in fine style.

We ordered food and chatted. I won't bore you with the drivel that we were coming out with, I'm sure that you've been in this situation. It was fun though. I felt like I was twenty one again and the horrors of the past few days were forgotten for the time being.

I say 'for the time being', as it was ironic just how close they were at that moment.

We ate and drank a beer each with the meal then I decided to pay a call, my first of the evening I may add! I remembered that the toilet was on a lower floor and was accessed via an elevator to the left hand side of the bar, so I wandered over and pressed the button, staring at pictures of Sid Vicious prior to his demise while I waited. Finally the doors opened and I walked in.

This elevator was not to be used in case of fire! There was room for two people at a squeeze and the speed that it operated was pretty close to stop. I pressed '1', knowing that I was on '2' and tried to work out what the song was that was playing over the elevator speaker.

Then, just before the doors began to close I realised that right in front of me, twenty yards away, sat at a table in the same restaurant that we were eating, was my friend with the long black hair in a pony tail!

Talk about a mood dampener!!

Why did I always see this guy from the inside of elevators? Was this going to be a recurring event for the rest of my life?

He wasn't wearing his trademark red and black shirt, but it was definitely him. He was sat on his own, facing out of the restaurant, so that he was sideways on to me and he didn't seem to notice me, on account of the fact that he was working hard on his teeth with a toothpick.

I couldn't move! I just waited for the doors to close on this ancient elevator, which seemed to be taking forever. He was clearly deep in concentration, so maybe he'd had the ribs?

Unfortunately I just kept on staring and if you pressed me, I'm fairly sure that my mouth was open.

The doors were slowly but surely closing and when they had finally closed all the way I breathed a sigh of relief. He hadn't turned to face me at any time and so, as far as I knew, he wasn't aware that I was there.

But had we walked past him when we had arrived?

I didn't think so, but then again would I have noticed? I had other things in mind at that point. He seemed to be alone, so maybe he'd walked in after we had and was taking a quick early evening snack.

This wasn't good news!

The elevator had now reached the lower level and the doors opened lethargically. I had lost all intention of using the facilities, but I got out anyway and walked into the men's room.

What was he doing here? He HAD to be here because of us. He must have been tipped off by someone at the storage place! It was too much of a coincidence to run into the guy in three cities within five days! We were rumbled! I needed to speak to Beth and to Stevie.

I washed my hands, dried them on a couple of paper towels and headed back to the elevator. I pushed the button and was rewarded by the door opening immediately. The other bonus was that there was no surprise guest waiting behind it.

As I stood for an interminable amount of time while we rose up one solitary floor I thought about what actions I would take when I got there. I came to the conclusion that it would be best to do exactly what I had done in the hotel in Pittsburgh. I would act as if there was no problem, simply walk out and back to the table.

We had stopped and the big polished brass door was sliding open at a snail's pace. I tried to get as far to the right as possible, making it hard for anybody to see me until I exited. When the door had run its course I walked right out, facing the direction that I was heading.

You know what it's like when you don't want to look at someone, or something, but you can't help but take a sneak peak? It was impossible to resist a quick glance to see if he was looking my way and to see whether he showed any recognition. So at the last second, before I walked behind a pillar and into the other side of the restaurant, I turned my head to his table, to see an empty chair pulled back and a member of staff picking up the tip tray.

He had gone.

I made it back to the table whilst furtively looking around to make sure that he wasn't still lurking somewhere close by. Beth plainly saw that something was up and as I sat down to face her asked, "What is it Mike? What's happened?"

"We need to get out of here and back to the room as quickly as possible Beth. The guy from the airport and the Marriott in Pittsburgh was just here!"

Her mouth dropped.

I caught our waitress's eye and motioned for the check.

"Are you sure that it was him?"

"Positive. I was staring at him for an absolute age while the elevator doors closed. I can't believe that he didn't see me."

Beth swigged the rest of her beer down in one, as the waitress arrived and handed me the bill in the usual black wallet that you see in every restaurant.

She made some remark about hoping that everything had been just fine for us both in a last ditch attempt to get the tip percentage raised and turned to leave. I caught her before she could go and handed her my credit card. She then trotted away and I imagined her copying it fourteen times and running off fraudulent payments.

Ignore the last remark. I was in a very untrustworthy and unhappy state of mind. I shouldn't take it out on those nice people at the Hard Rock. 'One planet, one love, etc etc.'

"Do you think that he noticed you?" asked Beth.

"You know, I don't think that he did. I don't know what he would have done if he had noticed me, but I just got the feeling that he was here by coincidence. That might be naïve of me, who knows?"

The lovely girl who served us returned and I tipped her handsomely. We then stood and made a wary exit back into the huge shopping mall where anybody could have been watching us from any number of places without us possibly noticing.

We held hands again, as we made our retreat back into the opulence of the Ritz Carlton, but this was more out of making sure that we were both together and no-one was being left behind, than any romance that remained in the evening.

We got back to the room, or rooms and I decided it could be a good idea to order some alcohol to calm the shock. I'm not convinced that Beth was entirely in agreement on this as she wasn't saying a great deal. In fact neither of us said very much at all until the room service guy had been and gone, and we had taken a couple of mouthfuls of beer. I had taken the liberty of ordering six bottles and an ice bucket, and I was expecting to have to call them again.

While we'd been not saying much I had been mulling and had come up with a few things that I now felt ready to say out loud. I was sat on a sofa in the single room with my feet up on the table and Beth was slouched on the bed, knees up, holding on to her beer with both hands.

"I was thinking," I began, "... when I first saw this guy in Philadelphia, we never made eye contact. He never saw me unless he looked at me when I walked by him in the bar, but that was a split second thing. Then when I saw him in the hotel he had already passed me getting out of the elevator and only turned to look at me at the last minute. I don't think that at any time I have ever shown that I knew who he was."

Beth frowned, "I don't know what that means."

"Sorry," I said, realising how it must have sounded. "I'm assuming that our friend is here in Cleveland because of me. He was at the hotel in Pittsburgh which means logically that he still wants to talk to me about Carrie-Ann's murder."

I looked at her and saw that she was nodding with understanding, "And you think that you could now be in more trouble for running?" she asked.

"Yes, but he never saw me running away, or acting like I was escaping, or scared, so as far as he knows I could have simply been leaving the hotel oblivious to whatever he was doing there. Maybe I now get in touch with him and apologise, but say that I had decided to move hotels and forgot to leave a message with the Marriott? I could say that I'd only just remembered our conversation of four in the morning because I was jet lagged straight off of a plane. He could just believe me when I say that I'm still in Pittsburgh, but I'm leaving tomorrow lunchtime if he still needs to talk to me."

"And you are thinking that this may prompt him to go back to Pittsburgh tomorrow morning?" asked Beth.

"Maybe. It might be worth an attempt. It would at least give him something else to think about. The only flaw is that I don't know where he works. That and the fact that we are assuming that he is Lieutenant Saxton and not some murderer who is in cahoots with Nat Schulman and just wants to kill me to get his hands on the swag."

"Well anything is worth a try and it will certainly be better than doing nothing. Why don't you try Akron first, seeing as that's where Carrie-Ann is from, AND where the robbery took place," said Beth.

"It would make sense wouldn't it?" I replied, and picked up a hotel pad and pen to actually use instead of flinging it in my bag to take home.

I dialled operator assistance and got the number for Akron Police Headquarters, then rang them before I talked myself out of it. The phone was picked up almost straightaway by a friendly sounding female.

"Lieutenant Saxton, please," I said without a hint of question in my tone.

"One moment Sir and I'll connect you," she replied.

Excellent!

Of course this now opened up a few possibilities, ones that thankfully I'd also been thinking about in the last hour.

First, the phone is picked up by the real Lieutenant Saxton, who has been trying to reach me at the Marriott, in Pittsburgh. Second the phone is picked up by the real Lieutenant Saxton, who has no idea who I am, because his name has been used by another person. And third, Lieutenant Saxton is not there because he's out of town eating ribs, picking his teeth and working on a case.

I'm hoping for the third option.

After a short delay, during which I thought about buying cigarettes, the phone was picked up and a voice said, "Boyd, homicide."

I leapt into action. "Hi, I'm trying to get hold of Lieutenant Saxton please."

"I'm afraid he's not here at the moment. Is it Lieutenant Saxton that you need specifically, or can I help you? I'm Lieutenant Boyd. I'm in the same department."

He sounded helpful enough, a little young maybe, but voices can be deceiving. "Well it was Lieutenant Saxton that I was wanting to speak to really. Can I leave a message for him?"

"Sure. Hang on while I grab a pen."

I hung on, while Boyd grabbed a pen.

"Okay, fire away," he said, jauntily.

"Great. If you could tell him that Mike Huntingden called from Pittsburgh. He may have been trying to get hold of me, but I'm over here on vacation and I just realised that I had switched my phone off."

"Can I tell him what this is in connection with?" he asked.

"Erm," I said, thinking quickly. "He'll know what it's about."

"And he knows where to get hold of you?"

"Yes, he has my cell phone number. Tell him that I said I'll try again later tonight if he doesn't reach me."

Boyd promised to pass all of this on and I hung up.

I had thrown the last part in, about ringing back on purpose. Saxton hadn't told me where he worked for a reason. He didn't want me ringing in. Why, I didn't know, but there must be something behind it.

I explained all of this to Beth, with my theory that Saxton would ring me back as soon as he could and I took my old phone out of my rucksack and switched it on so that Saxton wouldn't have problems getting though. The more I thought about it, the more I was sure that he would have tried my phone several times, certainly before he made the call to Rachel. But he hadn't left a message because he didn't want to leave any tracks behind him.

I had a scent for this now and was getting juiced up. I opened a second beer and offered one to Beth. She accepted, so I opened it for her and went to sit on the side of the bed next to her.

"Are you okay with being dragged into all of this?" I asked her.

"Yeah. I mean, it's a bit tense at times, but it's exciting. Plus I get taken to fancy hotels by handsome foreigners as part of the deal so I cope."

I leant over and kissed her.

"We need to concentrate on what's gonna happen Beth, cos it feels like it could be dangerous. Can you ring Stevie and tell him to get here early tomorrow morning?"

"Sure. What time?" she asked reaching for her phone from her bag.

"Well according to what you wrote down the storage place opens at eight thirty, right?"

"Yes, that's right, that's what the guy told me."

"I reckon we should be there before they've had time to get their coffee and settle down. So ask Stevie to get here for seven, earlier if possible."

"That shouldn't be a problem for him," she said. "He's always up at the crack of dawn anyway, rain or shine."

She hit a couple of keys on her phone and put it to her ear.

I walked over to the window. It was getting dark now. Almost eight o'clock and the lights were on to my right towards Lake Erie. The city seemed very still, nothing moving at all. I pulled the curtains shut, then walked to the room next door and did the same routine, as Beth left a message on Stevie's voice mail asking him to ring us.

There were so many loose ends in my head that needed tying up.

Where was Schulman? Was he with Saxton? Who killed Carrie-Ann? Was Tony Woolf in Cleveland too?

The first time I had stayed in this hotel I had not slept a wink. It looked like this stay would be similar.

TWENTY FOUR

We were on our final two bottles of beer when the phone rang. Beth was matching me without any problem. I remembered that this had been the case on Sunday also. Maybe it was bar work that did it? Maybe it was the genes? Nature versus nurture? Go figure...

As is the case these days, we both picked up our phones at the same time before we worked out that it was my phone that was ringing.

I knew that Beth was worrying about her brother. Truth is I was looking forward to hearing from him also. It would be good to know that he was ok.

But it wasn't Stevie, it was my old phone that was ringing, which meant that it had to be our friend, the Lieutenant calling and it was time to go to 'code red'.

We'd had a bit of a chat about what should, or should not be said to Saxton. Because of our pressing engagement tomorrow morning Beth had proposed that I tell him I had a flight home booked for early in the afternoon. This way, he'd either have to drop everything and go back to Pittsburgh to speak to me in the morning, or deny me my right to leave town and therefore the country, and this surely would mean that he'd have to involve a third party, such as Boyd, or a routine cop, in having me watched, or brought in. He had so far seemed unwilling to leave a trail, so we agreed that he would probably go for the former. In addition we had agreed that, following my earlier thoughts about whether I had registered any recognition when I had seen him in the hotel, I should not mention the incident at all and if asked about it, pretend that I didn't know what he was talking about and say that I simply moved hotels to cut costs.

We had ruminated about the fact that the person in the hotel in Pittsburgh was Mike Huntingden, the person who was in Akron was John Adams and the person who had called the storage place here in Cleveland was Elizabeth Deskin. This lack of a connection would hopefully confuse anybody who was plugged in to everything that was going on and be another factor helping us out. But at the same time, we knew that an Elizabeth Deskin did exist somewhere on record and whilst there had to be a plethora of them across the Mid West, it would not take much manpower to find out which one was sitting in a hotel in Cleveland if the right people wanted to know. This had troubled us somewhat, especially in relation to what would happen should we walk away with ill-gotten gains from a heist that dangerous people were trying to get their hands on. Beth didn't want to have to give up her home on return and didn't want to be frightened to live there.

After a bit of upset, we had decided that we either went home now, or we take things step by step from here. Beth had relented and pointed out that the damage was done anyway now, as she had already given her name and even if we didn't go to the storage place tomorrow, somebody would come looking for her to find out the code. I was well aware that I had been the one who had told her to give her own name and I knew that she wished that she could go back and change that. But the fact of the matter was, what was done was done and we had to get on with things and deal with the consequences.

My phone rang a full twenty seconds before I had composed myself enough to answer it, "Hello, Mike Huntingden."

"Mike, this is Lieutenant Saxton returning your call," said the voice and I pictured him sat in some darkened motel room toothpick in hand, red neon light blinking on and off through the window.

"Hi Lieutenant. Thanks for returning my call. I was trying to get hold of you regarding the homicide which we spoke about."

"Yes?" he replied.

He clearly wanted me to show my hand before he volunteered anything. For all I knew at this point, this was the 'real' Lieutenant Saxton and the person that had called me and Rachel had been an impostor. He could be clueless as to what I was calling about, but interested. I decided that I would take a similar line.

"You were wanting to speak to me?" I countered.

He was silent a moment, thinking about his next card.

"Where are you now, Mr Huntingden?"

"I'm in Pittsburgh," I lied.

"Ok, if you'll give me the address, then I'll send somebody over to take a statement in the next day or so."

"Well that's the thing," I said, starting to go into my pre-prepared lines, "I actually fly home to the UK tomorrow and I'm leaving Pittsburgh late in the morning. I was wanting to get this over with before I left."

Again a pause, while he considered his options and then, "To be honest Mr.Huntingden we have leads now and we only wanted to speak to you in order to eliminate you from the investigation, so to speak. So we have no real need to keep you here in the US. If you'll give me your address in the UK then we'll contact you there should we need anything further."

This was not something that we had foreseen. I looked up at Beth, who was trying to follow the conversation from my side, but was now powerless to intercede. She shrugged at me in response to my look. I would have to 'go dark'.

"The truth is, Lieutenant Saxton," I began, then halted a second for dramatic effect.

"Yes?" he prompted.

"Well… I did see something that I only thought about after our conversation and I've been a bit worried about it."

Beth stood up off of the bed and raised her hands to her face in a pose reminiscent of 'The Scream'.

"What was it that you saw?" he asked.

How much to lie, how much to tell the truth? I decided I'd not lied to him yet and I'd try to continue on that tack.

"I don't really want to say over the phone and when you hadn't got in touch, I thought I'd better ring you. But I could really do with meeting you tomorrow morning, before I leave. Is that possible?"

Much shuffling and sound effects came from the other end of the phone. He must have been wondering what on earth I'd seen. Maybe he was wondering if I'd seen what happened in the airport in Philadelphia and now he'd have to find out for sure.

I hoped so.

"Well then we'd better set something up," he said. "Are you still at the same address?"

¿Que? Was he double bluffing me?

"Yes, I am," I lied.

"Ok then, what time will you be available Mr. Huntingden, as I have a lot of business to sort out tomorrow."

I'm sure you do, I thought with a wry smile.

"I'll be waiting for you around 8:30 if that's ok with you?" I said.

After I had put the phone down, I made it a priority to order more beer from room service.

I then explained the other side of the conversation to Beth and we both tried to work out what had gone on. I wondered out loud whether Saxton had been concentrating his efforts on what was happening in Akron and trying to trace the money there. We agreed that the introduction of Beth into the equation, with her ringing the storage firm in Cleveland had probably been the catalyst for him deciding that I was no longer necessary in his quest, especially as I was 'going home'.

He had now come to Cleveland as it was where the game was ending. I suspected that he was going to be in Pittsburgh early doors, with the intention of wrapping up me, or the story, before high tailing it straight back here.

Exactly where Nat Schulman fit into this scenario we weren't sure, but we expected that if they were in cahoots, he was the muscle that would be left behind up here to keep an eye on things. Why they weren't together in the Hard Rock was another thing though. I suspected that he was still in Akron, but didn't dare voice that opinion as Beth had her cell phone on the bed in front of her at all times, willing it to ring.

The arrival of room service with more supplies was a welcome distraction and thankfully, as we opened two fresh bottles, Beth's phone did ring and it was Stevie.

His news was, he was quite merry, having a great time and he threw in a cryptic comment to Beth about how he hoped that we were too. Nudge nudge, wink wink.

We both spoke to him and filled him in on the dramas aside Lake Erie. He wasn't so merry that he didn't totally understand the situation and promised to be knocking on the bedroom door between seven and seven fifteen in the morning. He asked that we order breakfast on his behalf and bade us both a good night.

This seemed to take care of business for the day and we both admitted to being worn out. Not too worn out that I couldn't clean my teeth though. I headed into the bathroom, beer in hand and looked at myself in the mirror.

Carrie-Ann had been buried today. It had been at the back of my mind on a couple of occasions, but I'd held it there on purpose. I wondered what I'd be doing now if I hadn't had the fortune to be seated across the aisle from her. Pointless thinking about it I supposed. I silently toasted her in the mirror and drained the beer. I then cleaned my teeth and snuggled up in bed next to Beth who was already fast on and fell asleep almost straight away with no further thought of Carrie-Ann.

Beth was already stirring when I woke up on Tuesday morning. I collected my thoughts and checked the clock. It was just after six.

Reading my mind and hearing that I was awake, Beth asked me what the time was in an ever so cutesie sleepy voice. I turned over in bed to face her, feeling her warm body next to me in the comfiest bed in the world and looking down into her face, suggested that it was "Morning sex time"?

This got a tiny giggle and an 'mmm' kind of noise in response, so I took that as a sign of approval and proceeded with caution.

I shall use the same manners as before. You're possibly not interested anyway by now. There are, after all, more exciting things about to happen.

As I showered afterwards I started to turn my mind to what was about to go off, but I couldn't seem to get my thoughts to click into place and decided to leave things for now. I had the beginnings of a cunning plan, but it would have to wait until I had food inside me. I contented myself with the thought that a day with such a good beginning couldn't possibly turn out badly and decided that this would be my mantra to get me through whatever was coming.

My chest was still very tender and dressing wasn't getting much easier. I had been forced into returning to my usual attire of t-shirts and had still not found an easy way of either putting one on, or taking it off. I had a feeling that another consultation with speed doctor Robert could be a good idea when we got back to Pittsburgh.

We had ordered breakfast in the room the night before, by filling out one of those cards which hang on the outside of the bedroom door handle, making sure that there was enough for three people. I am always a little wary of this way of ordering something as important as breakfast, convinced that some late night reveller will decide to take it, or alter it in a fit of drunken giggles. Perhaps I'm judging other people by my own wicked standards? This was the Ritz Carlton after all.

Beth had busied herself with making sure that the single bed looked like it had been slept in. This was obviously an important task, by the way in which she was going about it and repeatedly stepping back to admire her handiwork. I stopped for a while in the doorway to watch her.

I still had no real ideas on what was going to happen between us, but maybe things would start to look clearer when all of this was over with, then we could talk things out. She sensed me watching her and turned to face me.

"What?"

I just shook my head in response and smiled at her.

I knew that she wanted to pout in return and give me a spirited defence of her actions, but it was hopeless, she knew it and burst out laughing.

Then there was a knock at the door. We both stopped what we were doing and looked at each other in the hope that one of us would make a decision for the other. I looked at the clock behind Beth at the side of the bed, which told me it was just after seven and I tried to be confident that it was either Stevie, or room service.

I approached the door with Beth right behind me and checked the spy/peephole. Thankfully I was greeted with an out of focus Stevie staring up at me. I exhaled with gusto and opened the door.

"Morning all," he said jauntily as he strode into the room, taking off a denim jacket and flinging it onto a chair back. "Is breakfast here yet? I'm starving."

"Not yet, no," I replied, as Beth threw her arms around her brother in a manner that suggested he'd been tracking Shackleton across some frozen tundra.

"Morning sis, sleep well?" he asked, with more than hint of something in his voice.

Or was that just guilt I was feeling?

TWENTY FIVE

Breakfast duly arrived and we all tucked in, nobody mentioning what was to happen today until the last of the coffee had been finished and we were all slumped in luxurious overstuffed chairs.

Then Stevie began, "Ok, I've been thinking the whole way up here and here's how I see it."

He brushed a lock of hair out of his face and behind his ear, before continuing, "You can't go today Mike. Too many people know you."

This was something that I had wondered about, but kept putting off bringing up. I was the one who got everybody else into this and it would be unfair of me to expect them to walk into trouble while I sat in the Ritz Carlton drinking coffee. I decided not to protest and kept quiet for the moment while I allowed him to explain what he had worked out.

"Beth has to go because it is her ID that will be needed in order to get access. I think we're all agreed on that. Obviously she can't go in alone, so I'll go with her. If we take the

Dodge it can't be traced, as it's a hire car, so we park right outside the storage place and go in and out as quickly as possible. Maybe then we should meet you somewhere other than the hotel when we get back, so that we don't bring anyone back here?"

"How about the mall next door?" volunteered Beth.

"That sounds perfect," Stevie agreed.

"I know there's an entrance to the mall at the other side of the block," I said. "And from there you can't even see the hotel. I could be waiting there, at that entrance for you to arrive and you could do a hand off?"

"Great and then you just walk back through the mall and into the hotel," said Beth.

"Mmm… Sounds too easy though," said Stevie, beginning to doubt his own plan. "What if somebody does follow us and they get out and give chase? There's no guarantee with these guys that they'll act like gentlemen simply because you are in a mall. Or they could just follow you into the hotel."

We all sat in silence for a moment.

I had the bones of a different version of the same plan, which could make things easier…

"How about if…" I said, still working on my idea as I was talking, "somebody is waiting INSIDE the mall to watch out for anyone following and if they are, then we make another switch?"

"But then we need an extra person," said Beth.

"Not necessarily," I replied.

"Well how would that work," asked Stevie, "if there are two of us in the Dodge and you on the pavement?"

"Give me a minute," I asked, standing up and walking over to the window. I had had the beginnings of this idea in the shower this morning. It was only slightly different to Stevie's but would offer more chance of success.

I cleared my head, as I looked out over the city morning laid out in front of me. There was smoke rising from several buildings in downtown Cleveland, as factories and businesses began to start their operations. I don't pretend to know what the smoke was, machinery? It looked like the kind of smoke that you see rising out of the subways in New York City.

The weather looked chilly out for the first time since I had arrived, but maybe it was just the fresh air coming in off of the lake. Maybe it wasn't even cold at all. Why was I worried about the weather? We weren't going fishing!

Whatever went down today had to work. We needed to cover every option. There was potential danger everywhere in this. I turned to face them both. They both looked up at me from their seats expectantly. I felt like we were back at the Inn, sat in the kitchen and wished that we were. I decided to say what I was thinking out loud and see what response I got.

I cleared my throat and began, "The way I see it is that even if you both go in to the storage place it could be dangerous. There could be six guys in there waiting for you. The more of us that turn up there, the more it potentially provokes the situation. All being well, Saxton should be out of the way, but we don't know about Schulman and we don't know if he has other helpers. He's obviously got somebody working on the inside for him. I think it would be better if Beth arrived alone in the Dodge, parked outside and walked in by herself."

Beth started to protest, but I stopped her by holding up a hand, "Hear me out Beth, please," I said and Beth immediately started to look annoyed, and a little worried. "If you can think of something better afterwards then I'm happy to work with it, but give this a chance and see what you think. Please," I added again for emphasis.

I turned to face Stevie. "Stevie, how about you take your own car. Wait at a distance for Beth to walk in the building, then pull up and walk in, pretending that you are another customer and you two have never seen each other before. They won't know. You two don't exactly look alike, so why would they suspect anything? And they are less likely to do something to Beth in front of some guy who's a potential customer than in front of her brother."

Stevie started to nod his head slowly, as if he was taking this in and understanding my point.

"This could just be a good enough ruse for them to decide that they'll follow her when she leaves, rather than doing whatever they were planning to do, there in the storage depot."

I was addressing Stevie totally now, instead of both of them, as he seemed the most receptive to my idea. I think Beth was still a little unsure at this point and I knew that if I sold Stevie on the plan, then the two of us would have a better chance of persuading her.

"You just make out you are someone who is looking for storage and ask them loads of dumb questions. But not too dumb, we don't want them to suspect anything."

"So what do I do when I get out of there?" asked Beth in a way that sounded like, 'I bet you haven't thought of this HAVE you?'

I turned and sat back down in the chair next to her, "You get straight in the Dodge. Lock the doors. Throw whatever you got out of the storage onto the back seat. There can't be much, because we know it fit into a locker in Akron Railway Station. Hopefully it will be in a bag of some kind. Don't go directly to the hotel, or the mall. Drive around the city, staying on busy roads. It'll be rush hour and there will be cars all over the place."

This didn't seem to have filled her with a burst of enthusiasm, as her expression didn't change at all, so I turned back to Stevie.

"At the same time Stevie, you leave the storage place when you think it looks right. Not immediately, as it'll be too obvious, but don't leave it too long. Then head straight back to the hotel. Pull up outside the hotel and leave your car with the valet to park, then head into the hotel lobby where I'll be waiting for you. I won't go anywhere till you get there. Then when we walk into the mall, you stand near the hotel entrance to the mall, at a place where you can see the door that I am going to take out into the street. That way you will be able to see if anybody is following me back in when I return."

I had a roll going here and the plan was clear in my head. It seemed even better out loud.

"Beth, I'll show you the doors that I'm talking about before you leave. I'll ring you when I'm on my way out from meeting Stevie. Don't stop there if I'm not outside, just drive on by and do another loop. When you do see me just pull up and unlock the doors from the drivers override. I'll open the back door, grab the bag, shut the door again and walk right back in the mall. Then you take off and do maybe a couple more loops through traffic before going back to the hotel, give the keys to the valet and come back up here to the room."

That seemed to make Beth a little happier now, as she was nodding herself.

"So what happens if somebody follows you in?" asked Stevie, should I give you a signal or something?"

"Yeah, I'll just walk towards you and if there's anyone coming up behind me, just lift an arm up to your head or something, make it look like you're pushing your hair back behind your ears like you do all the time."

He smiled, "Right. Otherwise I'll leave my arms by my side and you just walk right by me into the hotel.

"Exactly."

"But what happens if somebody IS following you?" asked Beth.

"Good question," I answered. "Anyone?"

Nobody answered that one.

The last question remained unanswered and we left it hanging. An unspoken vote of confidence that we were not going to get into that position. I hoped that I was the only one who had reservations.

But my plan had passed muster and not been criticised half as much as I had expected when I was reviewing it in my head, so I felt quite buoyed by the morning. The only addition to it was that we were all to keep our phones close at hand and ring in at each stage of the proceedings.

Beth suggested that they leave now, even though it was still before eight. She thought that it was important to find the place, get accustomed to the surrounding streets and the route to and from the hotel. This was good common sense and didn't get any arguments from either me, or Stevie.

I accompanied them down into the lobby and we took a walk into the mall, to look at the logistics of the plan in that location. We checked out the doorway from the mall into the street and everybody seemed to be as happy as could be with their role.

They departed, while I went back upstairs to try to kill some time in the room before heading back down to the mall. I hadn't said anything to them while we were down there, but had been a tad nattered when we found the mall empty. I didn't expect that it would be open yet anyway, but had not considered the fact that it may not even be open when they got back. Don't malls open around ten normally? This was worrying! A potential hole right in the middle of my big plan!

I put the TV on and tried to find something to watch, but couldn't concentrate, so I gave that up as a bad job. I looked around for something to do and even thought about taking another shower, but that would have been plain stupid. In the end, with the opening times of the mall still at the forefront of my mind I left the room at eight fifteen, sporting my purple LSU baseball cap, and caught the elevator down to the lobby.

The mall was still deserted, except for the cleaners and security people. It is quite a large space, probably the size of a football field, with shops down either side and at one end. The other end to my right, which faces away from the Lake, has tall glass windows, which lets the light flood in. From above the floor plan is in the shape of an '8' with the floor in the middle being open giving you a view of the lower floors. The centre section of the '8' is where you get access to the escalators. Shops are only down the outside walls, so the inside is open, with just a glass wall and a rail preventing a nasty fall into the lower level. I suppose that sets up a particularly grisly death later in the story, but that would be predictable and real life doesn't often go there. The floors and walls are in a polished marble effect and everything is either a shade of white, or glass. The overall effect is one of space and elegance, which sits very nicely with the Ritz Carlton thank you, but I'm not sure about the Hard Rock Café opposite.

The only part of the mall that seemed to be alive at this time was the food hall on the lower level, so I took the escalator down to wander amongst the people stocking up on coffee and carbs before they began the days slog. I noticed some movement behind the windows of a few of the stores on my way down and several people stood at storefront grills laden with trays of coffee, whilst colleagues opened up for them.

There was no way that I could eat or drink anything, but I didn't want to be seen strolling by myself staring at expensive retail outlets whilst security guards were patrolling, that was not needed here today. I had to blend in, not be recognised in a lineout, so I queued for a coffee and took a seat at a table facing into the mall.

Time, predictably, was passing very slowly at that moment. Either that or my watch was broken. Isn't it funny how quickly we start to doubt a piece of equipment that we rely on from day to day. I found myself imagining that Stevie and Beth had already left the storage and I wasn't ready for them when they returned. What a nightmare! It was still not even eight twenty five. The storage place wouldn't even have opened up yet. And Beth would ring in when she was on her way, as she had promised.

A businessman in a suit who had been sat at the next table stood up to leave, without taking his newspaper with him. I waited until he had gone far enough that he wasn't coming back and I leaned over to pick up his paper. After a few moments of rearranging it into a position where I could turn the pages – don't you hate it when people fold newspapers in places other than the fold? – I began to flick through with impatience, trying desperately to find something, anything, that was worthy of a few moments of my attention.

Of course there was nothing…

Before checking my watch for the thirty seventh time that minute, I made an effort to slowly pick up my coffee and to lean back and take a long leisurely drink. This done and another twelve seconds gone, I looked at my watch. Eight, twenty six, or maybe seven, depending on the angle that you looked at it.

Sheesh!

I heard the sound of another grill being lifted on a store somewhere behind me and to the left. I turned to see a guy going through his morning opening up ritual. This looked hopeful!

Quite what I would do with flowers at this time of day was anybody's guess. But still, it did look like he was heading for an eight thirty opening and if he was, then maybe others were too?

The flower guy was now doing his best to arrange flowers and plants tastefully outside his store, in the hope that he could attract passing trade from the food court. He looked to be in his fifties, slightly balding, but of a cheerful disposition and I made the snap decision that I would buy flowers for Beth. I certainly had the time to take them back to the room if needs be.

I abandoned my weak coffee and my neighbours' weak newspaper, and strolled over to the flower shop.

As I approached, the guy disappeared back into the store, so I hung about outside, looking at his display, trying to find something that would be presentable to a beautiful girl who had just risked her life for some hair-brained scheme, dreamed up by a foreigner who she'd known less than a week.

"Can I help you, sir?"

No rhetorical pleasantry! What a refreshing start to the transaction. I turned to face the shopkeeper, who was now resplendent in a green apron and had his hands linked together in front of his chest expectantly, with a welcoming grin on his face.

What a nice bloke!

"Ah, yes please. I'd like some flowers to give to a beautiful girl, who is out in the big wide world, risking life and limb to make me rich. Do you have anything in that line?"

Honesty is usually the best way forward.

He laughed in an infectious manner, like an uncle, or your grandfather and I found myself laughing along with him, partly out of nerves I suppose.

Five minutes later I left the shop richer for having made his acquaintance, poorer by thirty bucks and laden with flowers.

TWENTY SIX

I paid a quick visit to the room to deposit the flowers and pay a call to the little boy's room, before heading back downstairs and out of the front entrance of the hotel for some fresh air and a walk. I was bade a cheery good morning by two more members of the hotel staff on the way and was offered a cab at the front. Very nice gesture chaps, but not today thank you.

This was my first proper visit outdoors, having only stepped outside earlier, when we had all checked out the mall entrance. The temperature had dropped, so my earlier suspicion had been correct. It wasn't quite pullover weather yet, but I suspected that this time was fast approaching.

I wondered at pros and cons of phoning Rachel. There were still some unresolved issues that needed attention. Whilst I was sure that the relationship was over, it now seemed churlish of me to assume that I had the right to end it by simply running away. We'd had a lot of good times and I owed it to both of us to make things right. It probably wouldn't be good form to be ringing her now, when it was three thirty in the morning back in the UK, but I resolved to make the call soon and suggest we talk things to an amicable conclusion. I mulled as I walked and before I knew where I was, the time had rattled neatly along to eight fifty.

I wondered how long they would take?

I couldn't really do anything at all except wait. A cigarette would be just the ticket and I thought seriously about buying a pack, but was afraid of what the dizzy spell, which had accompanied my last cigarette, would do to my already frayed nerves.

Why hadn't anybody called me yet?

Surely it shouldn't take this long to sort out! I began to wonder about what was going on, letting my imagination run riot. What would I do if I didn't hear anything from either of them again?

Should I call the police? Yes, I'd have to do that. I couldn't just leave them to be beaten up, or strangled by some psychopath. But how would I explain our actions to the police? Would we be in trouble for our part in all of this?

It didn't matter. The safety of Beth and Stevie was more important than getting into trouble with the law. We could deal with that later.

So it was decided. I'd call the police if I had to.

But when?

How long should I give them? At nine thirty they would have been incommunicado for more than one hour. Was that a reasonable time?

Maybe that was too long! It would surely take the police ten to fifteen minutes to find the place. Perhaps I should make the call at nine fifteen?

I was starting to sweat now. I made a promise to whoever was listening that I would NEVER, under any circumstances attempt to do anything as stupid as this ever again, if only we could all get out of this safe. I wasn't bothered about the money. I just wanted to be back at the Inn, in Pittsburgh, eating pizza, and drinking Yuengling.

At that moment, my phone rang. I was across the street from the front entrance of the hotel and decided that this was a good place to take the call, away from eavesdropping doormen.

I fumbled around in my jeans pocket for my phone and managed to get it out without dropping it… just.

"Hello?" I said, answering the call.

"Mike, it's Beth," she sounded breathless, and tense. "I'm out and on my way."

Oh, thank god!

"What happened? Did you get the stuff? Was anyone suspicious? Is Stevie ok?"

I realised I was throwing a lot at her at once, but at least she was doing something. I was going mad here, with no idea what was happening!

"Uh, yes. To all of that… except for anyone being suspicious. There was only one guy there and he was real friendly. He asked Stevie to wait while he showed me where the lockup was and then when I came out he was answering questions and showing Stevie a price list or something. He seemed fine."

"What was in the lockup?" I asked.

"It's just a bag… a green bag," she answered. "A bit bulky maybe, awkward to carry, but not too heavy. It's on the back seat just as you asked."

Thank god! Thank god! Thank god!

"Don't forget to lock the car doors and keep them locked until you pull up outside the mall."

"Don't worry, I won't!"

She was more relaxed now, I could tell because she was snapping at me. I must admit, I felt a lot better just for speaking to her and hearing her voice. I would never put her in this kind of situation again. Honest!

I realised that I should get off as Stevie would be trying to ring in soon.

"Beth, I'm gonna have to go now, I don't want to tie up the line if Stevie is trying to get in touch," I said.

"Yeah ok, will you call me when you hear from him Mike?" she asked.

"Sure I will," I said. "Are you ok Beth?"

"I'm fine, thanks. Just a little pumped. It's quite exciting, but I can't wait until it's all over and we can have a beer to celebrate."

"Never mind beer. I'll get you the best champagne money can buy," I said.

We said our goodbyes and I promised again to ring her as soon as Stevie checked in.

Fucking fantastic! The first part of the plan had worked. All we need now is for Stevie to get himself back here and we were… no… I'd better not start thinking like that. It was probably better to be a little tense and full of adrenaline. Don't want to be too relaxed and forget to do something.

The two guys working outside the front of the hotel were taking it in turns to whistle cabs around for hotel guests and getting their fair share of tips. Not many people were dropping cars off at this hour and I guessed that people would probably be leaving either first thing, before nine am, or around midday, check out time.

My phone began to ring again. I was still holding it tightly in my sweaty palm.

"Hello?"

"Mike, it's Stevie. Piece of cake. I'll be back with you in five minutes buddy."

Oh yeah baby!! Things were just fine.

"Great! No sign of anyone following you?" I asked.

"Not a chance. The roads are quiet around here until you get back into the centre of the city, there's nobody behind me. Is Beth ok?"

"She's happy and on her way back also Stevie. I promised to ring her when you checked in, so I'll see you just inside the hotel lobby real soon."

"You got it pal," he replied, and hung up.

This was such a sweet plan. I had a whole new career waiting for me here!

I rang Beth's phone and she picked up straightaway.

"Hi?" she said.

"Hey Beth, your brother checked in. He says that all is fine and he will be back here in the next five minutes," I told her.

"Thank god. I forgot to ask you Mike are you ok?"

Aah… aint that nice. She's thinking about me.

"I'm fine Beth, thanks. Like you I can't wait until this is all over with. I'll see you very soon. Ok?"

"Great. Seeya," she replied.

I could picture her saying it. She really was having fun.

Odd? I dunno? I wasn't having any fun at all!

I took a deep cleansing breath and crossed the street. The two guys out front were having a conversation with each other that was causing one of them to laugh out loud. Why did I think they were laughing at me?

They both bade me a cheery 'good morning' even though they'd just done that already and one of them held the door open for me. I thanked him and stepped inside to the warmth and comfort of this lovely, lovely hotel.

While I waited for Stevie to return, I peeked into the mall and was relieved to find that there were quite a few shoppers milling about now. It didn't seem like all of the shops were open yet, but at least it had picked up.

I turned back into the hotel lobby to a position where I could see out into the street, so that I would see Stevie arrive.

At this point I realised that I had absolutely no idea what car he drove. I had never seen him in it. I had to stop myself from calling him to ask him this question. He had more important things on his mind. He didn't need me ringing him while he was negotiating the city streets whilst keeping his eye out for bad guys.

I looked at my watch. Again.

It was just after nine. I wondered how long it was since I'd spoken to Stevie. Three minutes? Four?

I spent the next interminable time period wandering in and out of the mall, just to keep myself busy. When Stevie finally arrived and walked into the lobby I was returning from my sixth or seventh mall run and he almost reached me before I spotted him.

"Stevie, thank god! I was starting to wonder what had happened."

He shrugged his shoulders and frowned. "Just a little delay with the valet. Nothing to worry about man."

Without another word I put the call through to Beth and left Stevie standing at the entrance to the mall, heading across towards the exit while I waited for her to pick up.

"Hi", she answered.

"Hi back, it's me," I said. "Stevie is here and I'm on my way out."

"Great, I'll be there in two minutes, I'm only around the corner," she replied.

This was really going well! So why couldn't I breathe?

I was, however, glad that I finally got to play a part other than co-ordinator. It was much easier doing something rather than waiting around for other people to do their thing.

Within moments I was at the exit. There were four glass doors in a line with chrome handles that lead into an in-between entrance / exit, no mans land type of area, which I guess people use as somewhere to put on their coats, or put up their umbrellas before walking out through the second set of four doors. From inside the mall this, again looked like a large window and allowed the light to flood in. I walked through the first set of glass doors and looked out into the street. Two cars were driving by, but there wasn't any sign of life other than that.

I pulled open the door and walked out into the street, feeling the cool air hit me again. As I edged up to the kerbside, looking to my left I could see a dark blue Dodge Durango turning the corner and heading down the street towards me. Timing really is everything you know!

Beth pulled up to the kerb next to me with the precision of Dale Junior hitting his pit box and I wasted no time in opening the rear door. Right in front of me was the green holdall, as promised. It was probably a couple of feet long, by a foot wide and looked full of something by the way it bulged out.

"Everything ok?" I asked Beth, who was still facing forward and looking at me through her rear view mirror.

"Yep," she replied. "I'll just do another loop and I'll be right with you guys."

"Great. Take care. See you upstairs."

I pulled the bag out of the car and shut the door, then, without looking at anything, not wanting to risk any distractions, I turned around and headed straight back through the first set of glass doors.

Almost there! I pushed open the second doors into the mall.

The whole time that this had all happened I had not seen one solitary person. I don't know whether this was because I was concentrating so much on what I was doing, or whether there really was nobody else about at that moment. Either way I was happy with it.

The mall, however, seemed to have suddenly got busy. It was as if a bus trip had just pulled in! I could only catch fleeting glances of Stevie as I started back across towards him and couldn't see if he was making any signals or not. Finally I escaped the melee, which seemed to have congregated outside one certain store. I had no idea what that was about, but wasn't hanging around to find out.

Stevie was stood, casually, with his hands down by his side as I approached and he stayed that way as I walked slowly past him and back into the lobby of the hotel. He turned and fell into step with me as we got to the elevators. I wasted no time in pressing the button and the doors began to open. Neither of us said a word, as we entered the elevator and I leaned against a sidewall as Stevie pressed the button to take us up the one floor to the reception area. This short journey was only punctuated by heavy breathing and my heart beating so loud that I was amazed that Stevie didn't mention it. The doors to the reception level opened and we stepped out.

Directly opposite were the elevators to the guest floors and people were just filing out of one, so we crossed to it and walked right in.

How well things were going? What could go wrong?

I pressed the button for eight and stepped back. The doors were just beginning to close when there was a shout and a large hand grabbed at the side of the door nearest to me, causing the automatic mechanism to stop and the doors began to open again.

I turned to Stevie, who had one hand up to his head, running it through his hair.

TWENTY SEVEN

Three extremely tall gentlemen; two young black men and one an older white guy stepped into the elevator and resumed a conversation that they had clearly been having in the reception area.

The gist of it was that they were heading out to training shortly, which caused my mind to leap back to my previous visit here with Graham. We had been fortunate enough to have shared an elevator with the basketball commentator and ex-player Bill Walton, and his son Luke, who played for the LA Lakers. This hotel was evidently a favourite with visiting NBA teams.

I decided a little conversation would lighten the mood at this time.

"Excuse me… Are you guys playing at the Gund tonight?" I asked, referring to the Gund Arena, home of the Cleveland Cavaliers.

They stopped talking, and all turned to face me. One of the black guys, the REALLY tall one, who I recognised, but couldn't remember his name, smiled at me and replied, "Yeah. It's an exhibition match. Pre season, you know?"

"Are there still tickets available?" asked Stevie jumping in.

The two younger men, turned to the third, older individual, who must have been a coach, or part of the coaching staff. He saw that he was being looked upon as the font of all knowledge and seemed happy to be useful, as he answered, "I don't think it'll be a sell out, it never usually is at this stage, so you should be able to get tickets on the door fairly easily if you want to come."

We looked at each other. I quite fancied a basketball game. "We may just do that," I said.

The elevator had stopped and the doors were opening. This wasn't our stop. It was the sixth floor.

We said a cheery goodbye to our tall friends and I noticed a 'Spurs' motif on one of the bags that they were carrying.

On any other day I would have loved to have gone to see San Antonio play against the Cavs, but I am sure that I wasn't the only one desperate to get out of Ohio as soon as possible.

We alighted at eight and found our room. As soon as the door was closed behind us, I dropped the bag on one of the beds and let out a huge sigh of relief. Stevie following me in began to laugh.

I turned to him in amazement, but found that I was laughing along with him. He was soon guffawing like a good one. Some kind of nervous laugh I suppose. Whatever it was it continued for a good five minutes until we both realised that we weren't laughing at anything at all. We ended up shaking hands and staring at each other big stupid grins.

"How was your morning?" he asked me.

"Oh, you know, same old same old," I replied.

We both chuckled a little more and turned to face the bag, lying on the bed, staring back at us with those big... zips!

"Nice bag Mike".

"Thanks".

"What you got in it?"

This was the big question. What was in the bag?

"I dunno, but I hope it's worth all of the emotion and pain of the last five days, that's all I can say".

We both stared at it some more.

Then Stevie asked, "Should we open it, or should we wait for Beth?"

Was he kidding me?

"I think we should really wait for Beth you know? She'll go fucking mental if we open it without her Stevie. Jeez!"

He laughed again. The same guffaw. Again I tried not to, but again I couldn't help joining in.

"You've really got to know my little sis haven't you?" he asked.

Where was this going?

Was he referring to the temper and the mood swings, or was this some veiled attempt at discovering if I was doing the honourable thing, or just boinking her for the laugh?

I went for the former, with a touch of the latter thrown in for good measure. "She's sure got a bit of a twist in her temperament I'll say that. But it's quite endearing really, as long as you can ride it out."

We looked at each other again and I tried to read his thoughts. Had I said the right thing? Should I follow it up? Nah, he knew what I meant.

"She's been through a lot you know? … For someone so young. She's been forced to grow up a lot quicker than most and accept life's harsh realities."

He had a kind of a melancholic look to him. Like he was about to drag a guitar out of a cupboard and start singing a ballad. I shouldn't take the piss here, I know. But it was as if he was feeling sorry for himself. Maybe that was it. Perhaps he felt he was partly to blame? Beth had said that he was in the Far East when their parents had died. I wouldn't have bet against Beth telling him what she thought of him for not being there when she needed him. Or, on second thoughts, it was more likely that she hadn't and those words had gone unsaid. But she'd made it obvious hadn't she. That's how she was. Poor girl. I wondered if she'd ever spoken to anyone about it all? She'd opened up to me a bit that night back at the Inn. Maybe I was the one who could help? I felt kind of warm with that thought.

Maybe I could do something here. Perhaps all of this was going to be good for all of us. There was too much going on at the moment to start pondering at fate. Why I had felt like I had to leave England and everything I had, knowing that I wanted to come to the US, but not knowing where. Ending up in Harry's bar by chance and hooking up with these two people. But it got me thinking and I knew I'd be doing a bit more of that when I got chance.

"She's got a lot that she needs to work out still. I can see that Stevie and if I can be the person that helps her in that then I'm happy. I certainly am not just here for the bollockings and the mood swings mate… I hope that I can be part of things for a while yet."

I hoped that came out right.

It seemed to do, cos he had dropped the melancholic look and was looking at me like and approving father now.

"I think you could be just what she needs, Mike. Somebody new, who doesn't know and approach her as someone to feel sorry for, like a couple of the guys she's known. She only ends up walking all over them and that doesn't help her out at all. You're a good guy and I hope you'll stick around too."

It was manly hug time.

We did the manly hug and the requisite three pats on the back, which show that whilst you can express yourself, you are still a man. I always think of the scene in 'Planes, Trains, and Automobiles' when I hug blokes. You remember? Where John Candy and Steve Martin end up doing spoons in bed and when they realise they both jump up out of bed and one of them says, "Did you see that Bears game at the weekend?" and the other says "Yeah!" both in deep gruff voices. Very amusing. Not that I hug a lot of blokes you understand. I don't mind doing it, but there has to be a time, a place and a good reason. This fell into the category.

Where was Beth anyway?

"Where is Beth anyway?" I asked out loud.

"Good question," answered Stevie. "What did she tell you?"

What DID she tell me? Hadn't she said she was just doing one more loop and then seeing us up here? She couldn't be far away surely.

"She's probably just having 'valet problems' like you did," I ventured, but I hadn't convinced either of us and a slight nag was creeping into my head.

We both looked at the bag again.

"I'll ring her," I said.

"Good idea," said Stevie.

I grabbed my cell phone and punched in her number. I really did need to sort out the address book! I heard two rings and the line connected, but then I got a muffled sound, like when somebody rings you by mistake because they haven't put the lock on their phone and all you get is the noise from inside of someone's bag, or pocket. I heard Beth say something, but couldn't tell what.

"BETH?" I said, in a loud speaking voice. Not quite a shout.

"What is it?" asked Stevie.

I looked at him, still listening to the static and background noise from the phone. "It's like she's answered it by mistake and it's in her bag or something."

This is when I usually start to whistle down the phone, but I could definitely hear her talking to someone. Maybe it was the valet? I kept listening.

Suddenly there was a lot more static, like she was lifting the phone out of her bag, or pocket and the line came clear.

"Beth?" I said.

"No... not Beth", said a male voice! A voice that I'd never heard before. It was macho sounding, almost Sylvester Stallone. In fact that's exactly what it sounded like.

I must have looked shocked or confused and Stevie read it in my face.

"What?" he began.

I held my hand up to stop him.

"Who is that?" I asked, "Where's Beth?"

"Beth's right here with me. You needn't worry Tiger."

Tiger? What the fuck was going on?

"Can I speak..." was all I got out before he interrupted me.

"You have something that we want. We have something you want." This guy was straight down to business. I wasn't liking the sound of this at all.

"The obvious solution would seem to be... an exchange."

He emphasised 'exchange' making the word last twice the normal length, pronouncing every syllable precisely, leaving me with no doubt as to what he meant.

Stevie had his hands up to his head and was staring at me, whilst rubbing his temples. I don't know if he thought that this tuned him into the conversation or if he just didn't know what to do, but he didn't look as happy as he had two minutes before, when he had told me that I could be just what Beth needed.

I don't think he was so sure of that anymore.

I guessed that it was my turn to speak, as everything was silent from the other end. How to deal with this guy?

"Look, you're going to get no problems from me mate. We can sort anything out that you want. Just please don't harm Beth at all…"

Silence.

"Promise me you won't."

I didn't seem to be getting anywhere.

"If you…" I began, but again he interrupted me.

"I'm going to give you a bit of time to think about how you would like to go about making the exchange," again with the stress on 'exchange', what was with this guy?

"From this morning's display, you seem to be good at planning little capers. Try and put your thoughts towards planning this."

Planning what? Where were we going to meet? Did this guy think that I did this for a living? Or was he playing with me? I needed to try to assert myself, show him that I had something that he wanted too.

"I want to speak to Beth," I said.

"Easy, tiger. You'll get plenty of time for that when you've figured out how we're going to get together. I'll be in touch."

And with that hung up.

"Hello? HELLO?"

No, he really had hung up.

"WHAT IS GOING ON?" demanded Stevie. How was I going to explain this?

Shit! Maybe my big plan wasn't so great after all. Fuck!

"MIKE!"

I explained to Stevie exactly what the guy had just said to me, told him that I was sure that I had heard Beth's voice in the background right before he came on the phone and tried to reassure him, and me, that all was going to be ok.

He didn't look reassured.

I felt like this was all my fault and it was… to an extent. But, and I know this is a cliché, we really did need to concentrate on what we were going to do now.

I reasoned with Stevie that we had the bag, we had something that they clearly wanted badly and that surely they wouldn't jeopardise things by doing anything stupid.

Would they?

When I thought about it, they, whoever they were, had a history of killing people, women, who it looked like they needed. I was sure that Stevie wasn't so stupid that he didn't realise this also, but I wasn't going to talk about it right now. They'd given me, us, a chance to arrange an exchange so we needed to think about things and we needed to do it soon. They could be ringing back anytime.

"We need to do this somewhere public," Stevie said, after he had sat in silence for a few minutes. He wasn't looking at me while he was talking, which wasn't a good sign.

"Stevie," I said and he turned to look at me.

"Yes."

"We need to be together on this. I don't care what you think of me, or this whole set up, at the moment we really need to put our heads together. It's too important not to."

He turned away from me again.

Then my phone rang.

Not my new one... my old one...

Shit! Saxton!

"Oh fuck!" I said out loud.

"What? What is it now?" asked Stevie jumping out of his chair again.

I walked over to where I had left my phone on the table in the other room and picked it up.

Saxton hadn't been here in Cleveland. He was in Pittsburgh. He couldn't be involved. Could he? It certainly wasn't his voice on the phone just then.

I was suddenly struck with another idea, that we needed some help here and Saxton could be the one.

I turned back towards Stevie before answering my phone. We hadn't filled him in on the Saxton angle this morning. He didn't know anything about it.

"Stevie, this is going to be the Lieutenant I told you about. Beth and I came up with an idea to send him on a wild goose chase to Pittsburgh. You gotta trust me here, this guy could help us."

I looked him in the face, willing him to give me his blessing.

"Go for it. Anything is worth trying," he said.

I pressed the phone answer button.

"Hello?"

"What the hell's going on Huntingden?" said the voice at the other end.

It was Saxton.

TWENTY EIGHT

"Ok, first of all let me start by apologising," I said to Saxton. "I lied to you. But I had to. I needed to see if I could trust you."

A bit of improvisation there, but after the experiences on the last phone call, I needed to start out on the offense otherwise I was gonna get nowhere fast."

"Trust *me*? That's a hoot."

This was gonna be a hard sell. I kept quiet.

There was a big sigh at the other end of the line.

"Okay I'll buy it. I know that you're not here in Pittsburgh and you're giving me the runaround. So why don't you do us both a favour and try being honest with me, THEN we'll see if I can't trust you."

Where to start?

"I need you to know that I didn't kill anybody. Not Carrie-Ann Novitski, not her Aunt, nobody."

If he was surprised that I knew about the aunt, he didn't show it.

"Do you really think that if you were a suspect in either of those murders I'd be letting you walk around right now?" he said. "I know that you sound like you've got yourself mixed up in something that you don't belong in, otherwise you wouldn't be playing games, but I gotta tell ya, Huntingden, the people that you are getting involved with don't play. They are for real. You are in over your head here sonny and you're gonna be adding yourself to the list of casualties if you don't level with me."

He sounded very convincing and he had a very good point. We were in over our heads. We shouldn't be doing this, I knew that. I wasn't exactly having fun here. I needed to speak to Stevie though. We needed to work out a story first. I felt scared. For me, for Stevie and especially for Beth. "Is there a number that I can reach you on, Lieutenant?" I asked him.

"Why?"

"Because I need some time to think about what is going on here. There's not just me involved. I have other people to consider. You have my word that I will be back to you in half an hour tops. You have to trust me. Please."

I thought I sounded convincing.

"I guess I don't have much of an option now do I?" he replied.

I took his number down, thanked him for his understanding and hung up.

Stevie had followed me into the single room, which Beth had redesigned so effectively. I walked over to the bed, which she'd distressed only this morning and sat upon the edge of it.

"DO you trust him?" asked Stevie.

Without looking up I replied, "I don't know who I trust anymore Stevie. To my mind there are only two people that I could say for sure and I've let one of those down."

He slumped into the chair by the window facing me.

"It's not your fault Mike," he said. "And I'm sorry if it seems like I'm mad. I am mad, but not with you."

Huh?

"I'm the one who's supposed to look out for her and I guess I just let her down again."

Great. Melancholy again. We didn't need this and that was for sure. "Stevie, you know what, you can't be responsible for everything your sister does. She wanted to do this. You guys both wanted to do this. Otherwise I wouldn't have let you talk me into getting back involved. Now before you say anything, I'm not trying to pass the blame, I'm simply illustrating that Beth has her own mind. Do you think that if you'd told her that this morning's little stunt was too dangerous and you wouldn't let her go, that she would have agreed?"

He smiled wryly.

"Hell, no, she wouldn't have let you dictate what she was gonna do. We've got to get past this and come up with an idea how we're gonna get out of it. To my mind, Saxton could help us. He's in Pittsburgh now, which means he's not here and maybe he's not involved. We can't do everything by ourselves. We're gonna need some help."

I'd pitched my case and couldn't say anymore. I lay back on the bed and stared at the ceiling. I just hoped that Beth was going to be safe. Please let her be safe.

Stevie stood up again and walked back towards the connecting door, then stopped.

"Well then, I think we'd better take a look at what we have that is so important that someone has to kidnap my sister.

You coming?"

Now he was talking.

Stevie was already unzipping the green bag when I joined him.

The bag that Beth had retrieved from the storage.

The bag that Tony Woolf had filled with things stolen from an armoured car and hidden away in a locker in Akron Railway station.

I held my breath.

Your wildest dreams would expect this bag, bursting at the seams, to be stuffed with bundles of cash, wouldn't it?

Bingo!

I watched, mouth gaping, as Stevie pulled bundle after bundle of dollar bills out from the bag and placed them on the bed. God knows how many bundles there were, but it was more than a few.

I inched closer and picked up one of the bundles up in my hand. Wow! Andrew Jackson frowned up at me. This was for real.

"How much do you think there is here?" I asked Stevie.

Stevie turned to me and exhaled in disbelief.

"I dunno," he said, "but it sure looks like a lot."

"I wonder if it's traceable?"

He stopped what he was doing and looked at the bundle in his hand, examining the money closely, as if this would reveal the answer.

"There's only one way to find out," he said and with that he pulled the little paper sleeve off of the bundle, and grabbing his denim jacket off of the chair, tucked the money into an inside pocket and put the jacket on.

"Where are you going?" I asked him.

"Well, the way I see it, we're gonna need to keep these two rooms for another night. I'm going to go see reception and tell them that we're checking out early tomorrow, if not late night tonight and I want to settle up now… in cash."

I thought about protesting, but he seemed hell bent to test his theory out and I was fascinated to see what would happen. Let's face it, the worst thing that could happen would be for the police to be called. We were already on the brink of notifying them anyway, so I'm sure that this could be explained away.

The door shut behind him as he headed off on his crusade and I walked over to the open bag, peering in to see just how much more there was in this magic porridge pot.

There was a lot more. But just how much money could there be?

I did a quick bit of mental arithmetic, while picking out the next few bundles. Each bundle was about an inch or so thick and each note surely had to be about a millimetre, so let's say there's twenty five notes in a bundle and each one is a twenty dollar bill. That would make five hundred dollars in a bundle. Okay this is where it gets confusing… a million would be two thousand bundles to my reckoning. I looked at the bed, and the bag. There couldn't be that many bundles, surely?

I picked another bundle out of the bag and my hand felt something else in there. What was this?

It seemed like whatever it was, it was leather and as I moved bundles aside to get at it, it became clear that it was an envelope or folder of some kind.

I managed to extract it from the bag and looked at it closely. It was made from soft brown leather and looked to be like a kind of professional document carrier, like a slim satchel, which was held shut by a simple brass clasp. I pulled the clasp apart and opened it up.

Inside was a stack of paper certificates… Bearer Bonds!

These were what everybody so desperately wanted to get their hands on, not the money. I'm no banker and don't know too much about money at all, but I understand what a Bearer Bond is from years of watching films and reading thrillers. These were unregistered methods of payment, which meant that in anybody's hands they would be worth the money stated on them, as the bearer, currently 'me', was the owner. I didn't know where you could change them, I'm sure that you couldn't use them at Ihop, but banks must be a reasonable place to start. I flicked through the ones at the top. They all seemed to be worth one hundred thousand dollars and there were A LOT here!

Jeez! This really was a haul! I wondered where these had come from? The big rubber companies in Akron maybe? Somebody had to be really pissed that these went missing! There had to be lots of people hunting for them. No wonder people were dying!

Beth! We needed to speak to Saxton!

Where was Stevie?

At that moment, there was a knock at the door. I put the leather folder on top of the TV console and walked to the door, looking through the spyhole.

It was Stevie. Thank God!

I opened the door and without speaking beckoned him in, shutting the door and locking it behind him.

"I had a great idea!" he said as he marched past me towards the bed.

"Did anybody think that it was odd that you showed up with a stash of clean pressed twenties?" I asked him, interrupting his flow.

"No, not at all," he said. "Maybe it's normal at the Ritz Carlton? Anyway, why should they care, it's money to them isn't it?"

Adrenaline was driving him on. I let him continue.

"So… while I was in the elevator I saw two more basketball players and I thought, 'why not get tickets for the game?' So I got the concierge to sort it out."

Wait! What? Had he lost his mind?

You hear stories about people who behave totally irrationally when they get handed large sums of money.

He must have seen the look on my face and he pressed on, "Think about it Mike. Thousands of people in one place at one time. It's a perfect place for us to meet up with this guy and get Beth back. It couldn't be safer!"

Ah! I see. He had a point. It was a good idea.

But I could see a flaw, "It's a great idea Stevie, but how would we get the money in?

You saw the bag. You can't get anywhere near a place like that without going through checkpoints where they search your bag. We'd be hauled away for sure."

They had got a good club shop at the Gund Arena, but I couldn't see them buying the idea that we were on a shopping spree. I'd burst his bubble now. His excitement had drained away. Great… what an arse I was.

Wait!

"Stevie, check this out!" I said to him, grabbing the brown leather envelope off the top of the TV and handing it to him.

"What is it?" he asked, perking up again.

"Open it."

I watched him open it up and saw the realisation dawn on him, as it had on me.

"Think about it Stevie. Realistically there can't be as much as a million bucks in cash here. Now don't get me wrong, that's a whole lot to you and me. But… enough to kill two people and kidnap a third? I don't think so. I think this," I said, pointing at the open folder in his hands, "is what they are all after. This is what they want back so desperately."

He put the folder down on the bed, took off his jacket and sat in a chair, leaning forward with his hands up to his face. This was plainly 'deep thought' position.

"I wonder, Stevie," I said, interrupting his mulling, "if they even knew that the money was there?"

We stared at each other, neither blinking, for what seemed an age, each trying to draw on the other's thought process and hoping that we could work this conundrum out.

"How about we just take the Bonds then?" he said finally.

"And leave the money here in the room?" I asked.

"Yeah," he said sitting upright and running his hand through his hair, tucking bits behind his ears. "That way it can be used as a trump card if necessary, you know if they decide that they are gonna kill one of us anyway. We can dangle the money as incentive to keep us alive.

What do you think?"

It was definitely the easiest way to get into the Gund and was a good backup plan in case we needed it. I had another idea.

"Ok, but how about this? Nobody knows that you are here. Hopefully they don't know you exist. How about we go to the game, but as strangers? It worked before at the storage place. You stick nearby, hang back and wait for an opportunity to grab Beth if possible?"

He looked at me, one hand cupping his chin, thinking, "But what about you? Where does it leave you if Beth is gone? They'll kill you!"

"No they won't. I have the bonds."

We had the making of another good plan here and we spent some time working out ifs and buts, then I rang Saxton.

We'd decided that we still weren't going to fill him in on everything. This was a purely 'need to know' basis, as they say in all the best spy movies. I told him that I had involved a girl that I had met and that together we had worked out that Carrie-Ann had come back to the US to pick up something that her uncle had stolen from an armoured car. I left out the whole Akron episode and didn't tell him how I'd worked it all out. He didn't seem interested anyway, just wanted to know the facts. I told him that we had come to Cleveland and retrieved the stolen goods. That my lady friend, Beth, had been snatched and I had been contacted about doing a little swap. I laid it on thick that I was really worried and that I knew that I had done wrong getting involved, but that I hadn't actually committed any crimes, I was just curious about the whole buried treasure thing.

He seemed to buy my story and asked me where I was, and when I was going to be speaking to Beth's captor(s) again. I told him that I was in Cleveland, but I didn't want to tell him where exactly at this stage. He wasn't very happy with this, but I told him that was how it was gonna be, that I didn't want the police coming in and getting Beth killed. I kept Stevie out of the story and Saxton never asked me about anybody else being involved. I finished the call by saying that I planned to meet them at the Gund Arena tonight and that I would ring him back when I had spoken to them.

Saxton said that he was on his way to Cleveland now and that I had to keep him informed on anything that happened. He told me to try to get to speak to Beth personally so that we would know that she was ok and still with them. He also stressed the importance that I make sure the actual timing of the meeting was left undecided until everybody was actually at the Gund itself. To suggest that I call them when I was there and arrange the meeting point inside the stadium. That way everybody would be contactable at the game and Saxton would have time to work out the best area for it to go down. This seemed like a very sensible idea and I was glad that we had decided to involve him. Somehow I felt like it legitimised what we were doing.

We ordered room service while we were waiting to hear back from Sly Stallone. Not that either of us was hungry at all, but time was passing and we needed to eat. I suggested a couple of club sandwiches and some iced water, and Stevie agreed. We could certainly afford the tip!

We packed up all of the cash into the green bag, zipped it up and put it in the wardrobe of the single room, then decided that we would go to the mall and buy a backpack to put the folder in for the trip to the game.

The food came. We picked at it and put the tray back outside the door.

We then made a trip to the mall and managed to get hold of a kid's backpack in the colours of the Cleveland Cavaliers, with a number '23' it. This really was about all that we needed to do.

It had reached three in the afternoon by the time my phone finally rang and we both looked at each other before I picked it up as kind of a way of asserting our team spirit.

I was ready for this, we were ready for it. After the 'mishap' this morning, we had prepped for every single thing that could happen and I knew exactly how I was gonna handle this call.

"Hello?" I said, in as non-committal a voice as I could muster for a guy who'd been waiting five hours for this call.

"Hey, tiger," the same voice replied. Tiger again! What was with this guy?

"Did you come up with a plan yet?"

He sounded as uninterested as I was trying to be. Like he was doing something else at the same time as speaking to me and I was getting in his way! "Yes I did."

"Well?" he prompted.

"I'll see you at the Gund. The Cavs are playing a pre season friendly against the Spurs. Bring Beth along, I'll bring your goodies and we'll do a little 'exchanging'." I emphasised the last word as much as he had before.

Silence for a second. Then, "The Gund, eh? Good idea, lots of people about. Nice work, my friend. How do you know you can get tickets?"

"I have a ticket already. It's up to you how you get them, but if you want what I have then I'm sure you'll manage somehow."

"Listen kid, don't get uppity with me. I'm in charge here. What I say goes. In fact I don't think I want to go to the Gund tonight…"

I took a deep breath and dived in, headfirst.

"I don't give a shit what you think, my friend, I don't need this crap." I took another breath, my heart was beating like a racehorse. Stevie was sat opposite me with his eyes closed. I continued… "If you're going to kill Beth, then just do it. I've only known her for three days, I'll get over it. I'll put this phone down now, throw your fucking bag in the river and catch a plane home. See if I care!"

"HEY!" he shouted, "CALM THE FUCK DOWN, ok?"

Now I was holding my breath. I hoped that I hadn't blown everything.

"You're smart. You'll do what's right," he began. "Bring the bag to the game, but we'll contact you there."

Phew BIG time!!

"Let me talk to Beth!" I demanded.

Everything went quiet.

I heard a squeal, like a door being opened and then…

"Hello?"

It was Beth. Oh thank god!

"Beth! Oh fuck, I'm so sorry for getting you into this. Are you ok?"

"Yes I'm fine," she managed between sobs. "It was my fault Mike, I forgot to lock the car door. I'm sorry."

"Don't be sorry. I'm going to sort this out Beth. We'll be together again sooner that you think."

I wasn't talking to anyone though. The phone was dead.

We had game to go to!

TWENTY NINE

The Gund Arena is a relatively new building, about two blocks from the Ritz-Carlton near the banks of the Cuyahoga and the railroad tracks. It's got everything necessary for a successful sports facility, a railway station underneath, ample car parking, which can be accessed by overhead walkways, bars and restaurants in the complex itself, and a BIG star.

That's probably THE most important asset.

When LeBron James put his name in ink in 2003, businessmen all around the Cleveland area must have rubbed their hands together. Now was the time to build. It was about time too. Cleveland looked like it needed a facelift from what I'd seen of it. I'm sure that the arrival of 'King James' had a lot of people wondering whether it could have the same effect on their town as Michael Jordan had done with Chicago. The Gund Arena gave them as good a place as any to start with. In LeBron's first season he had more than lived up to expectations and would only get better. All that was necessary for a shot at the playoffs was a team built around his considerable talents. It was hoped that the draft would deliver that in the next few years and with some clever free agent shenanigans too Cleveland could possibly be the jewel on the lake in years to come. But… many a slip twixt cup and a lip as they say… whoever 'they' actually are.

I've never met 'em.

The hotel concierge had sent somebody over here for tickets after Stevie spoke to him earlier and we had lucked out with Row 1 in the upper tier. Section 213 wherever that was. I was seat 9 and Stevie had seat 10. Stevie had paid in cash, naturally, and tipped heavily for the service.

We had decided that we would walk over separately, but close enough to each other that we could respond to any emergency and I was heading into one of the entrances now, with my Cavs backpack slung casually over one shoulder.

I had called Lieutenant Saxton back to tell him that the plan was in operation after speaking to Beth and he had pointed me to an entrance on Huron Road, next to the NorthWest ticket office. He had a buddy who worked on the security at the entrance there who was keeping an eye out for me and wouldn't give me a hard time about a leather wallet in my backpack containing millions of dollars worth of Bearer Bonds. This was the theory anyway. I had put on my purple LSU baseball cap (as it had been such a lucky mascot so far!) and was wearing this as way of a signpost. Unfortunately I knew nothing about this guy who was supposedly looking out for me other than he wore glasses and was a man. I didn't need to know however, as when I entered he spotted me straight away and signalled me over to join the line in front of him. He was a thin guy with a beer belly hanging over his belted trousers, wearing the regulation security garb and game face. I put him at mid fifties, grey, but with a full head of hair and clean-shaven. He either owed Saxton a favour, or was putting one in the bank, either way worked for me.

There were seven other lines of people waiting to have their bags checked, but the process was a quick one and I was soon stood in front of Saxton's 'buddy', who made short work of looking into my backpack before handing it back to me, then saying, "Enjoy the game, Tiger."

Again with the Tiger!

What was this about?

Suddenly I realised… stupid boy! Shit! Shit! Shit!

I followed the signs leading me up the escalators to the upper level and headed in a counter clockwise direction until I reached my section, '213'. I had no reason to hang around so I went directly to my seat and found Stevie was there ahead of me.

"Stevie, please tell me that LSU's football team isn't called the Tigers," I said as I sat down.

Stevie looked around, as if this was some kind of code word, then looking forward, instead of directly at me, answered, "Ok, but I'd be lying."

Shit! Shit! Shit!

Stevie was clearly trying to make it seem like he wasn't with me, but I had more important things on my mind. Besides, even if Beth and her captor were there, he had no idea where we were sitting.

"Stevie, the guy who has Beth called me 'Tiger' on the phone. At first I thought that he was just using some kind of nickname, but clearly he wasn't."

Stevie looked at me now.

"Shit!" was all he could manage.

Perhaps a thesaurus would have been a useful addition to the club shop?

"Exactly," I said. "Which means that he must have seen me taking the bag from the car. The green bag. The very bulky green bag. The very bulky green bag that looks absolutely nothing like the backpack that I am now carrying."

"You'll just have to make something up Mike. Tell him that it was stuffed with newspaper."

Oh come on! I looked at him, incredulously.

"He is NEVER going to buy that," I replied.

"Well ok, I don't know, be honest then. Tell him that you are bringing him millions of dollars worth of Bearer Bonds and you are keeping the cash as you have earned it. Try it on. You never know, he might actually respect you for it."

Hmm…

"Well it's worth a try, it's all we can do now anyway," I said.

"Of course there is always the chance that he'll decide to blow you away, but I doubt it." He was smiling now. We needed a bit of humour here, no doubt about it. We were both wound so tightly at the moment that one of us was liable to go off.

"Well if he does," I replied, "you'll be one rich puppy."

"Hmm. I guess. I'd be able to buy a box here then."

I laughed and looked out at the arena in front of me. US sports venues never bore me. They are so way more equipped for the public and for ease of use than the English counterparts. The atmosphere is always so tangible too. Like it was when you were a kid and went to a rock concert, or a sports event. The expectation hangs there and you're ready to leap out of your seat and cheer. I sometimes wonder if this is the 'sugar coated' syndrome and if I lived here would it get boring and regular? Probably… but it's best not to dwell on that and enjoy while I have chance. And anyway… you can drink beer here while watching the game – so there!

The fact was though, I wasn't here to enjoy and once the sound of the laugh had died in my throat, everything came back to me in a rush.

I wondered if Beth was already here?

The clock on the jumbotron read six minutes and was counting down.

When would I get to see her again? I was dreading meeting up with the guy, whoever he was and finding that he had come alone. Stevie and I had discussed this in our list of possibilities and eventualities and come up with the definitive action, which was to turn and walk away. He had to believe that I was serious in what I had said on the phone, that I wasn't that attached to Beth really. I had assured Stevie that I WAS that attached to Beth and he had told me that he didn't need to hear that, it was obvious. This had made me happier.

But I was still feeling an incredible amount of dread. I suppose that this was inevitable.

Then my phone rang.

SHIT! Here we go…

"Hello?"

"Huntingden, it's Saxton." When would this guy ever call me Mike? Probably never.

"I spoke to Dreyfuss and he said you had already arrived."

Dreyfuss… yep, that one fit the face.

"Yes, I'm in my seat now, trying to relax before the action starts," I told him.

Right at that moment, somebody came and sat in the seat next to me.

Up until that point there was nobody between me and the aisle seat, but now two girls had sat down and were chatting away. They were mid teens and looked to be alone. Hopefully they would be absorbed in the game and the athletes, and talk of Brad Pitt, or whoever was the 'in' guy at the moment and be too preoccupied to notice two middle-aged fidgeting wrecks next to them.

I switched the cell to my other ear, nearest to Stevie just in case they were undercover spies.

"I found the perfect spot," continued Saxton. "There's a food court right outside areas 107 – 110. It's a big area and will have people hanging around, going in and out of the washrooms all through the game."

107 to 110 was back downstairs. I wasn't sure of my geography, but surely 113 would be right underneath where I was sat, so I was guessing that the food court was right near the escalators, which I had used.

"Okay I'll try and persuade him that we should meet there," I said.

"Great, just let me know if there is any change. And when you hear from him and get a time, ring me straightaway."

"Will do."

I filled Stevie in on the plan and waited for the next call. Would he call before the game began, or would he try to play a few mind games and leave it a while? If he rang while the game was on, would I hear him?

I kept my phone out and checked it every ten seconds.

The game began right on schedule. No word from my friend Stallone. I tried to get absorbed in the game, but couldn't. I was too concerned about my phone, and what was about to happen.

I went through the motions of clapping when the Cavs scored and couldn't help being amazed at a dunk that LeBron did over Tim Duncan, especially given the size difference, but overall I was on tenterhooks.

The first quarter ended with the score 22 – 19 in favour of the Spurs and Stevie and I shared a look, which needed no translation.

What was the delay? Was this really going to happen? For the millionth time I hoped that Beth was ok.

Just as the second quarter was about to begin, my phone rang.

"Hello?" I answered.

"Hey Tiger, you ready for action?" came the same voice.

This was it! Game on!

The noise level was raising in the arena as they were about to 'tip off', so I made my apologies and eased past the two girls next to me, heading out onto the concourse where I knew that I would be able to hear better. I didn't turn around to check whether Stevie was following me, but I was sure that he would be. There was no way that he would leave me now.

As soon as I got through the doorway, I spoke into the phone, "Hi. Sorry about that, the noise made it impossible to hear you," I said.

"Enjoying the game?"

"Oh yes, superb thanks. We're getting together for beers after if you're about?"

Two could be sarcastic.

"Let's get to it. Where are you?" he asked.

I was standing outside section 213, but I wasn't about to share that with him. I noticed that Stevie had walked past me and was now pretending to look at a poster a little way ahead of me, waiting for my next move. I started walking towards him and the escalator.

"I'm heading down to the food court right outside sections 107 to 110. It's a nice big area where we won't attract any attention. See you there in five minutes?"

"You got a date," he replied and hung up.

Great… despite all of the thought that Stevie and I had put into what I was going to say and do in the next ten minutes of my life, I was a nervous wreck! I had a struggle just getting to the escalator and that was right in front of me.

I had already passed Stevie and was just concentrating on putting one foot in front of the other. I was breaking out in a sweat, I could feel it and I was very, very frightened. I really didn't want to do this. Was there another way?

No… there wasn't, I knew that and I also knew that Beth must be more frightened that I was. My thoughts jumped back to the Tiger reference and the tiny backpack that I carried. This was bound to cause a problem.

I was almost at the foot of the escalator now and looking over the side to my right I could still see people queuing for that last minute beer, or pretzel before they went back to their seat.

I wondered if there was anyway that the kidnappers could have smuggled a gun in here? I didn't recall any metal detectors at the entrance.

Oh no! I hadn't called Saxton!

In the midst of this panic attack that I was going through I had clear forgotten one of the most important things that I had to do!

I stepped off the escalator and reached into my pocket for my phone, but then stopped… what if they were already here and watching me? I couldn't risk making a call. It could jeopardise everything. I was going to have to head back upstairs to ring him. Surely I had time.

Whilst I was wrestling with this I spotted a face in the crowd in front of me that I recognised. I lost him almost as soon as I had seen him and moved my head to look between the people dashing back inside for the game. There he was again! It was Donnie Novitski!!

This was perfect. In a split second I made another decision. I didn't need Saxton! Nobody would fuck with me in the presence of Donnie Novitski! I made a dash towards where I had seen him, before he too disappeared back to his seat. This was the best luck that I could have had here. For all I knew I could end up leaving here with Beth AND the backpack!

Looking back on this … none of it made sense. Maybe I was just desperate not to be alone in this? Maybe I needed my hand holding? If I'd stopped and thought for a moment I am sure that I could have worked out what was going on… but I didn't.

As I got to within ten yards of where Donnie was, with his back to me, I noticed that he was with two people. As he turned around and clocked me, I realised that one of the two was Beth and the other had long black hair in a pony-tail.

"Well if it isn't our second President," said Donnie Novitski with a big smile on his face.

"What happened to your face? You get in a fight?"

The game was up. We were all fucked!

THIRTY

I just had not expected this at all. I really don't know what I had expected, but it wasn't this.

"I don't think you've actually been introduced to my brother Leo, have you?" asked Donnie.

His brother!

Man this was getting worse. My brain was trying to unravel untruths and ravel new ones.

Leo was Sylvester Stallone! He was the brother from the East Coast. The one who was going to be 'getting in for the funeral.'

So, here I was, stood with Akron's version of the Kray twins and aside from Stevie, I had no back up. Just great Mike! Way to go!

I stretched out my hand to Leo, no sense in being impolite. He took it and made it into a show of his strength. I made a concerted effort not to let him know that he was breaking my hand. I managed… barely.

"Hi Leo, I hope you made it back to Akron in time for your cousin's funeral," I said, with no trace of humour or sarcasm in my voice at all, then looked directly at Donnie Novitski, the man who, it seemed, had killed his cousin for cash and bearer bonds. I had made an error of judgement with this guy. I knew that he was some big shady character that people were frightened of, but I'd had a grudging kind of respect for him at the same time. Weren't all mob figures supposed to be looking out for the family? The tears that he had cried in front of me that night in Akron, had they all been for show? I hadn't thought so. It seemed I'd been fooled and he had been playing me all along.

"Don't smart mouth us kid!" he threatened. "Just cause there are a few people around, don't think we won't put a cap in your ass."

I tried to show indifference to this comment, whilst registering the fact that, more than likely, they did have guns with them.

Great! The odds just got even better then!

I hadn't looked Beth in the face as yet. Stevie had suggested to me that I should avoid any contact with her at all. Any show of emotion would be a weakness that would be exploited. He was right. I could feel her eyes on me, desperate for my attention. I was bursting to return her gaze and show in my face that I cared and was there to rescue her, but I knew that I would betray too much to others. I needed to make the Novitski brothers believe that I cared more for my own ass than for Beth. This HAD to work.

"It was real clever what you did, I have to tell you," Donnie said. We were standing about ten feet away from a store selling hot dogs and tortilla chips and there were people still making last minute purchases before they took their seats for the second quarter. They were walking right by us, oblivious to our situation.

"I gotta be honest with you and say that you surprised me."

I wasn't sure whether I was supposed to be grateful about these compliments, so I threw a compliment of my own in return. "Yeah, well you surprised me too," I said, and kept staring right at him.

"Yeah, how's that?"

"Well, you seemed genuinely upset about your cousin's death and here you are still trying to get hold of some bearer bonds which seem to be the reason that she died in the first place."

He took half a step back at this, as if to compose himself and twisted his head around while shrugging his shoulders. Some serious stress knots there! At the same time as he was doing this, he let go of Beth's arm. In the corner of my eye I saw movement from Leo, as he stepped in straightaway in case Beth got any ideas about running. Donnie avoided my gaze for a second, but I kept on looking into his face, not giving an inch. When he turned back to face me he had thrown the momentary anger off and was ready for more. I had seen a chink in the armour, but just what would I gain by continuing in this vein? A mistake by them maybe, but one that could be potentially life threatening to Beth!

"You really want to be careful what you are saying here," said Donnie, in a very low voice. "You think we care about security in a place like this? You think Leo here is gonna be worried about pulling out a gun and blowing a hole through this pretty girl's head?"

The truth was: yes I did actually. I thought he was bluffing. Whether he was or not didn't matter really. For us all to get away safe, I was gonna have to carry on pushing up the stakes. I had nothing to lose at this point.

"I'm sure you don't care," I said. "Anyone who could be so cold as to kill his own cousin can't really have much in the way of morals."

He seemed to have acquired a small twitch around his eye now. I was really getting under his skin. He had killed his cousin and it was causing him all kinds of issues with grief and probably self-loathing. Check me out… psych major! For a moment I'd forgotten the position that I was in and was pretty happy with myself.

"What? What did you say?" his voice was getting louder and he did seem genuinely surprised. But then again, he'd seemed genuinely upset at the Emerald Grill.

"You think I killed my fuckin cousin?" he asked. Again this was great acting.

"Well you, or your brother yes."

He stepped back again and made a gesture of slapping his palm against his forehead, as if in disbelief.

"You gotta be fuckin kidding me, right? You think I killed Carrie? Why the fuck would I do that?"

"To get your hands on these bonds. I would have thought that was kind of obvious," I said.

He was upset and angry, but I had thrown him a curveball here, I could see that. Either he hadn't expected me to call him on this, or he really hadn't killed her. Either way, I suspected that most people didn't get away with talking to Donnie Novitski like this and was well aware that I was on the edge.

"But she was my little cousin," he almost pleaded with me, with more than a little feeling, like he was reaching out for understanding. I could still go either way on this, but there were questions that needed answering. I needed to work out for myself what had gone on.

"She was Leo's little cousin too, but she didn't exactly look thrilled to see him in Philadelphia airport!" I spat out with more feeling than I expected.

I was still staring right at him and everything that was going on around us now was irrelevant. I had my poker face on – even though I'm useless at poker – but Donnie Novitski didn't know that. I couldn't even see Leo or Beth now. I was in the zone man!

Donnie, on the other hand, was on the back foot.

"I can't believe this. I can't believe what you are saying to me. Leo went to Philly to pick Carrie up, to bring her back. Why am I explaining this to you?"

"Because it makes no sense and you're trying to make it seem plausible," I countered. "If Carrie-Ann was meeting her cousin then why did she seem like she was shocked and frightened by him?"

"Jeez!" Donnie was stepping backwards and forwards. He was off balance and not comfortable with how things were going.

"Look!" He said, pointing his finger at me, still speaking in a raised voice. "Listen to me!" Then he suddenly quietened down to a conspiritual tone, "Carrie wasn't exactly expecting Leo ok? She didn't know that her Uncle had told us about the stash. That's why she was surprised to see him. She didn't know whether to believe us at first. Leo was bringing her back to Akron so that her Uncle could tell her the truth."

I was incredulous. But at the same time, the thought came into my head about why she had given me the envelope when she did. Maybe she had expected a welcoming committee?

"The truth?" I replied, shaking my head, "And what was the truth?"

"That this is family money. That Tony approached me and asked me to recover it, before anybody else got their hands on it. Carrie was out of the country when Tony got out and she didn't know that we were in on this."

This kind of made sense, but I still didn't totally believe him. I stick to my original comment about Carrie-Ann looking like she was under the power of Leo Novitski. Surely a cousin, even a made guy like Leo, would not cause such fear? Plus she was dead...

"So how come she winds up dead, when the last person she was with was your brother?" I asked him.

"I don't have to defend my brother's innocence to you. I'm trying to do is recover our family's rightful possession here. In the process two members of our family have died." He sighed, and continued, "Carrie was pulled out by security when the plane landed in Akron. Leo had to leave her there. Somebody else was on the trail and still is as far as we know. I have an idea who this is, but not where he is. I can tell you this much, he's a dead man when I catch up with him."

He had the same look on his face now as he did when he had said something similar that night in the Emerald Grill, and it entered my head that he actually might be telling the truth. Why would he care what I thought? Why was he explaining all of this to me? He could have simply taken the bonds and left. There were still some things that didn't add up though.

"Why did you have me beaten up when I left the bar?" I asked him.

He studied me for a moment.

"So that's what happened huh? You got a beating? Well, I can tell ya, it had nothing to do with me? You must have caught someone else's attention."

"Really. So what were you and Tony Woolf talking about right before I left and why did he question me in the toilets?"

Donnie actually laughed now.

"He's just come out of the joint. You don't expect him to be suspicious? He's like most ex-cons, wary around everybody new that they meet. Especially when there's money involved. He asked me if I thought you were in on all of this and I'll be honest with you I didn't think you were at the time and told him so."

But what about the phone calls? It may have been early in the morning, but I was sure that it had been Saxton that I had spoken to. Was he in on this too then? I didn't think so, but I'd been wrong before.

"Why did you ring my ex-girlfriend in England pretending to be police?" I asked him, still trying to eliminate parts of the puzzle.

"You gave Leo the slip in Pittsburgh and you were our only lead at that point, what did you expect us to do?"

"But how did you know where I was staying?"

"What, you don't think we have people inside the police?" he asked, looking at me like I was an amateur – which I kept forgetting – I was.

"Once we lost Carrie we had to rely on other sources and we knew that the police were looking at a guy in a hotel in Pittsburgh in connection with this. Leo went down to try and find out what you knew, but that was some good work you did."

He smiled. He had that paternal look in his eyes again. Like he was proud of me, or something. "You surprised me Johnny, or Mike, or whatever the hell you are called. That's what I was trying to tell you earlier."

Now I was rocked back. He WAS telling the truth.

I'd totally forgotten all about the other guy in all of this.

"Now play the game and give us the bag, and we'll let you guys go, as agreed. Nobody gets hurt."

I wasn't listening.

Who was the guy who had beaten me up in the alley? In all of this excitement I'd forgotten his name. The reintroduction of Donnie Novitski and his brother, Leo, who *wasn't* Lieutenant Saxton, had thrown my brain into confusion.

Leo was trying to take the backpack from my grasp and in my zombie-like state I was hanging on to it. Not intentionally you understand. I could feel him trying to take it from me, but I had other fish to fry.

What was his name?

Somebody else said something, but I'm not sure who, or what they said. It sounded like it came from another part of the food court, as it was distant, but louder and it was at this point, according to what I was told later, that Leo let go of Beth completely in order to wrestle the bag off of me.

And all shit went down!

Apparently Beth had already noticed Stevie nearby and he had made a couple of signals for her to make a break for it. She'd plucked up the courage and decided that she was going to do just this at the next opportunity and here it was presenting itself to her.

Meanwhile I was still in dreamland, trying to get my thirty five year old brain to work. It was Nate something…

Leo finally snatched the bag away from me and I looked up as Donnie stepped across me obviously trying to grab at Beth as she escaped.

Then I remembered.

Schulman… that was it, "Nate Schulman!"

I think that maybe I said this out loud, as I remember the look in Donnie Novitski's eyes, confirming that he agreed with my thoughts.

Everything was now happening in slow motion around me. It all seemed amplified, as my senses were working overtime. I was looking at Donnie, but my eyes were refocusing on something going on over his shoulder, which was catching my attention. The huge frame of Nate Schulman himself was heading right towards me! I was rooted to the spot.

Schulman was approaching from right behind Donnie Novitski and was clearly visible as he was more than a foot taller. He had his left arm outstretched in front of him and in his hand was a gun, which was pointed right at Donnie Novitski's back.

I saw the flash before I heard the bang and the bang wasn't at all what I expected. More of a 'crack' really.

Up until this point I don't think that I had ever heard a gun go off, I'd certainly not been involved in a gunfight. It all seemed a bit surreal to be honest. Nothing like you expect from seeing it in the movies. I definitely wouldn't want to experience it again.

Ironically it must have been the gunshot that triggered my self-defence mechanism into throwing me to the floor.

Even before I dropped though I knew that Donnie had been hit. He was facing me at the time and hadn't seen Schulman approach. His whole face changed in the split second after the shot rang out and it was clear that he knew exactly what had happened.

As I went down I saw Leo Novitski spinning and moving, his red and black jacket a flash memory imprinted in my mind.

Next I heard two quick shots in succession, different sounding to the first one that had hit Donnie and then there was a final bang which seemed to come from away to my right hand side.

I was listening to all of this with my eyes closed, but then a softer plopping sound which came from nearby caused me to open my eyes briefly and I saw the backpack had fallen about an arms length out in front of me. To my right I could see the familiar red and black pattern of Leo Novitskis jacket and a haphazard splatter of another red substance. I closed my eyes again.

There seemed to be a long period of silence. I am sure that this is exaggerated in my mind, but it was so quiet that I began to wonder whether the gunshots being so close had deafened me, or worse… had I been shot? I dismissed that straightaway, as I was sure that I would have felt it if I'd been shot, but all was still and it was like the world was a DVD that had been put on pause.

As quickly as it started the silence ended and was replaced by screaming.

Screaming all around me.

And the sound of panic. People running, feet pounding against the floor.

I screwed my eyes up as tight as I could and tried to shut it all out.

THIRTY ONE

It was midday when I made it downstairs to the kitchen the next day. I was back at the inn.

The horror/nightmare/adventure – call it what you will, I still hadn't decided - was over. The only emergency at the moment was the fact that I had no toiletries bag, so I couldn't clean my teeth and you know how I am about my teeth!

When we had finally arrived back during the early hours of the morning, despite our pleading, Beth had insisted on going back to her house. She had taken off in Stevie's car and we had only realised after she had gone that she had our bags aboard. Ah, well… we didn't have the energy to care at that stage. The sheer fact that we were all back in da Burgh safe and sound was enough.

My aches and pains were not nearly as bad, despite the exertions that I had encountered in Cleveland. I still had considerable bruising on my chest and around my eye, but when I contemplated just how close I'd come to a bullet the day before I was fairly happy with the outcome. As for my mind, the trauma of it all was something that I recognised that I may have to deal with down the line, but as it stood I felt reasonably good about how I'd handled the pressures. Maybe there really was a future for me in this industry?

Mmm... maybe not.

There seemed to be nobody up at the Inn... Quiet ruled, which was nice.

I don't think I'd spent too much time by myself in the building up to this point and the peace and quiet of my own company was luxurious.

I made coffee and sat at the kitchen table sipping a cup, reflecting on what life had dealt me recently. It was not a short reflection, as you can imagine. A lot had gone on. There were still roads to cross in the upcoming weeks, but I felt like I was on the right page of the map.

I had come to the USA in search of a new life, fulfilment, a purpose and a better me. I was happy that I had found a place where I fitted in and people that I could trust. I was confident that fate had brought me here and was anxious to make the best of the opportunity. It hadn't been easy so far, but I'd not run away from anything. I was fighting for something - that much was clear.

I had come through a gunfight! How much chance was there of that happening back in the UK? I didn't feel any compulsion to go back and face another episode like that but I had the experience tucked away. I also felt very happy with myself for not backing down against a character like Donnie Novitski. Ok, so he hadn't murdered Carrie-Ann, as I had incorrectly suspected for a short time, but he hadn't been a pussycat. Him and his brother Leo were big players according to Lieutenant Saxton. They had evaded the law for a long time by various underhand means, including corruption, violence and blackmail. I had played a big part in bringing the family business to a halt.

Saxton had been extremely generous in his praise and very helpful in the whole mess afterwards.

It had only been when he walked up to me afterwards and introduced himself that I had realised that I'd never actually met him before. We'd spoken on the phone, but that was all. My first impression was that he looked quite distinguished. He was an older guy, with short grey hair combed neatly into place and wore a suit with a shirt and tie. He looked like he belonged in another era and had clearly been a cop his whole life. He had a friendly, open demeanour, but I couldn't help getting the feeling that this was his work face. I was too tired to think too much about it at the time, but there seemed to be more to Saxton.

We had been helped into police cars and taken to the police headquarters in Cleveland, where Saxton had very kindly walked us through all of the paperwork. He told us that he understood what we'd been through and was doing his best to make it as painless as possible. He offered to let us come back and do this when we had got over the ordeal, but at the same time pointed out that it was probably best to get it out of the way while it was fresh in our memories. For my part I just wanted to get it all over with and get away.

When we had finally finished a squad car had taken us back to the hotel to pick up the luggage and Stevie had driven us back. I think I'd slept the whole way. The Cleveland PD had picked up the Dodge from a parking lot at the Gund and were keeping it to go over for evidence. They said they'd square it all with the rental company and were going to return anything that I had left inside. All that I could think was that my Izzy Stradlin CD was aboard. We'd spent some time together, that CD and me. I didn't intend to give it up!

When I had eventually finished my first coffee and felt up to it, I fetched both of my phones from the bedroom and returned to the kitchen for a fresh cup of coffee. Then I made some calls.

First I rang my mother and had a ten minute conversation, which went a heck of a lot better than I ever expected. She neither lectured me, nor asked me when I was coming back to Blighty, instead she patiently asked how I was and where I was. I lied to her on the first part, as people often do with their parents and gave her my new address on the second. I got the low down on family to-ings and fro-ings of the past week and promised to ring her again soon, then said goodbye.

Next I rang Rachel, but got her answer phone. This meant she was either still in bed, or early at work. Probably the latter. I left a brief, but friendly message giving her my location and telling her that all was sorted out on the homicide front. I said that I hoped she was well and promised to ring her soon also. It sounded right at the time.

Finally I rang my mate Graham. I had not heard back from him since I sent him the text message from the hotel. But that was Graham for you. Dependable. I had said that I would be in touch soon and he had read that and left me to it, knowing that I would be in touch when I had the time. You can't buy friends like this! I spend a good twenty minutes on the phone with Graham, making a third cup of coffee while we were talking. I didn't tell him about the dramas, but I told him everything else, about the Inn, Stevie and Beth, going to Akron and Cleveland again, and staying at the Ritz Carlton. He could read me like a book and asked me more about Beth. I told him I'd tell him more when I'd worked it out for myself. We made a loose arrangement that he would come out to stay when I was settled and left it at that.

As I was saying goodbye to Graham, Stevie appeared from the stairwell at the other side of the kitchen, the one that came directly from his room in the attic.

"How you doing?" he asked as he headed for the coffee.

"Surprisingly well thanks," I replied, as I put my phone down on the table top, "You?" He filled his cup and joined me at the table.

"I'm good, slept like the dead," he said.

Irony anyone? It didn't seem intentional, so I ignored it and continued the conversation.

"I'm not surprised after driving back all of that way. You must have been shattered. Thanks for that."

"No worries man."

"Have you heard from Beth this morning?" I enquired.

"No. I was just about to ask you the same thing. I'm sure she'll be round here when she's up and about," he said. Then he looked at his watch and seemed to change his mind. "I'll give her a call."

That was good. Apart from anything else I needed to clean my teeth. Priorities, ok? Of course I wanted to see Beth as well. Shit we had a lot to talk about. That conversation was looming big time.

Stevie suggested that we should all go out for lunch. I agreed heartily, not having eaten anything since the club sandwiches the previous day, which we had only picked at. He left the kitchen to call Beth and I went back upstairs to check on exactly how many items of clothing I now owned that were clean. I needed a washing machine, surely Stevie had one. I couldn't be sending t-shirts covered in blood away with the laundry service. I'd throw them away first.

When I got back downstairs Beth was just arriving. Both Stevie and I went outside to grab our bags from the car. Beth was stood next to Stevie's car, with a huge grin across her face.

"What's up, smiler?" asked Stevie as we approached.

"Who packed the car?" asked Beth in reply.

She got blank faces in response to that question. I couldn't remember anything about the packing. I remember going back to the hotel in an unmarked squad car, Saxton had insisted on that, but other than that I thought that the valet brought the car around and the bellhop loaded it. I'd been 'encouraged' to make myself comfortable in the back and I'd willingly followed orders. As I said, I'd slept most of the way back, waking only as we arrived back, to find Beth snuggled up against me. I remembered the feeling of warmth and comfort. Thinking, 'we're home'.

I came back to the real world as Beth popped open the rear window and lowered the tailgate, allowing us a view of our bags... which included a bulky green canvas affair!

Hello?

We all stared at each other.

Stevie looked as shocked as I felt, but was the first one to speak. "Well I didn't even go up to the room with you guys," he said. "My bag was already in the car, so I stayed downstairs waiting for the valet to bring it around."

Beth crossed her arms and leant up against the tailgate, "I think the bellhop must have got it out of the wardrobe and loaded it," she said. "I just flung my things into my bag and I'm pretty sure that you did the same Mike. The bellhop arrived while we were doing the packing and you gave him some money, then we left him to it and caught the elevator back downstairs."

I reached forward and unzipped the bag slightly. Piles of money stared back at me from inside it.

My heart sank. This could not be good, surely. I looked at the two of them again.

Beth was grinning. "I guess lunch will be good then," she said.

Shit! I really didn't know whether this was a good thing or a terrible thing. It wasn't over was it?

Stevie made the decision for all of us and, reaching past me, picked up the bag, along with his own and walked back to the Inn.

I grabbed my trusty rucksack and turned to look at Beth, who was looking right back at me. Man she was beautiful! She could make me forget about everything that was going on. And to think I'd nearly lost her, before we even got started!

I dropped my bag again and giving way to impulse, wrapped my arms around her.

Neither of us spoke a word. We just held each other, tightly. I think enough was said in the action itself. We could talk later.

Stevie stashed the bag in his attic apartment and I gave my teeth a deserved clean, while Beth stood in the bathroom doorway and filled me in on the action at the Gund from her point of view. Somewhere during the narration – my teeth needed a good clean, ok? – Stevie joined us and sat himself down on the bed. He jumped in occasionally, adding things from his recollection.

It became clear that the shout that I had heard before the shooting started had come from Schulman, who Stevie had seen walking towards us, while Beth was making her escape. He hadn't known who Schulman was, but it was not difficult to see that he was danger, as he walked towards us with his gun drawn. Before Stevie could raise the alarm Schulman had put a bullet in Donnie's back.

Beth added that the shot had caused her to hit the deck and she had looked up to see Leo getting the two shots off that I had heard next.

These two shots had stopped Schulman literally dead in his tracks. One of them had been a headshot according to Stevie and had made a hell of a mess.

Stevie and Beth had retreated a safe distance, but not too far that Leo Novitski didn't know where they were and after he had shot Schulman he had turned to face them. Beth said that she was convinced by the look on his face that he was going to shoot us all and then turn the gun on himself.

That was the moment when Saxton arrived, with the cavalry in the shape of uniformed officers and he had taken out Leo with one shot before anything else could happen. This was obviously the last noise that I had heard, before the backpack had dropped in front of me.

"I'm so sorry for getting you both into this," I said, finally coming out of the bathroom, after washing and shaving (I hadn't JUST cleaned my teeth).

They both made noises about how it had been their fault because of this and that and the other, and how they had persuaded me to get back into it.

In the end we agreed to differ.

"What are we going to do about the money?" I asked, looking at Stevie. I don't know why I chose to direct this question at him, perhaps because he was the one who had been the most decisive with it before, perhaps because it was in his apartment.

"What can we do with it?" he countered. "We can't just hand it in now, can we? There will be all kinds of new questions to answer and I don't really feel like I need any fresh angst, do you?"

Stevie pointed out that the police had never asked about it while we were all being 'processed' at the station in Cleveland. They had taken the bearer bonds and asked questions about them, but they had never even shown any interest as to whether there was anything else. "They must have thought that we wouldn't be so bold as to hold out on the Novitski brothers," suggested Beth. I wasn't so sure. He was right though. I certainly didn't need any more hassle, but at the same time I had this feeling in the pit of my stomach that just wouldn't go away. Surely no good could come from this?

"Look," said Beth, "we all need time to think about everything that has gone on. Let's just leave the money upstairs for the time being. We know where it is, but we're not spending it. We couldn't possibly be held responsible for this. No jury in the world would convict us. Unusual conditions made us act irrationally."

I wasn't sure. I needed food.

I suggested that we take Stevie's advice and go out to eat. We had a unanimous decision on that, so at least that was good.

We had lunch at a local Denny's and Beth picked up the tab. Nobody argued.

I had picked up a copy of USA Today at the counter in Denny's. It reported that the Spurs Cavs preseason friendly at the Gund Arena had been interrupted then abandoned by a shooting incident in the concourse area which claimed the lives of three Akron men. According to local police, this appeared to be the result of a long running feud, involving well-known underground figures. No further information was given.

A couple of other things still bothered me slightly. I wanted to ask them out loud, but now wasn't the time. I don't think that any of us wanted to be the one who brought it up again at the moment. We'd done enough detective work for the time being. Besides that, I couldn't put my finger on what it was that was bothering me, but something just didn't sit right in my mind. Saxton had got all of the information that he needed from us apparently and had said that, because there was nobody to be prosecuted it was an open and shut case. Why wasn't anybody concerned about what else there may have been in the locker? Why so quick to trust us? I wondered who would benefit from the recovered Bearer Bonds? Surely they had been insured originally, so the insurance companies would be the recipients?

But, as I said… later…

THIRTY TWO

Nine o' clock that night found Beth and I lying together on my bed at the Inn.

Stevie was winding down by giving his record collection an airing and was clearly untroubled by playing his music as loud as he desired tonight. We were being treated to Exodus by Bob Marley, which was fine by me. I suspected that the music was his way of making sure that he was unable to hear anything from us, as much as for him to chill out and relax.

Beth was having a hard time with the whole sex under her parents' roof routine, despite the fact that her parents were both dead and she was one of the owners of the Inn. After abandoning my fruitless quest, I quelled all animal instincts and decided to swing the conversation around to how she was feeling given the events of the past few days.

I found her to be unusually open and she began to volunteer things that I thought I'd be wondering about for months. She told me that Leo and Donnie had treated her very well throughout her ordeal. They had taken her to somebody's home in the Cleveland area. She wasn't clear on the address, as she'd told the police, but she was sure that it was owned by 'a friend'. Somebody who Donnie had felt able to call upon in such a circumstance without fear of recrimination. The Novitski network was clearly a wide one. Beth had never been openly threatened and she had been made to understand that she was not in any danger at all unless she tried to do anything stupid. She was offered food and drinks, and was left alone on a sofa, in a room with a TV. Someone she didn't know came to check in on her every so often to ask if she needed anything, or wanted to use the bathroom. She said that she had never felt in trouble and the only thing that she was upset about was that she had let us down by making a silly mistake.

I tried to reassure her that each of us had reasons to feel that way and gave her mine. I didn't think that this was going to be the last time that we spoke about what went on in Cleveland and wanted to suggest that she may need to seek some professional help, but I was impressed with her ability to discuss it with me. Maybe we could work this out together? I hoped so. Besides I think you know Beth well enough yourself now to know that, as I had told Stevie, she is a big girl with her own mind and well capable of making decisions for herself. I fully intended to be around should she need any help making them.

From here, the conversation led onto our relationship and we were both honest about our feelings. We were both keen to see things progress at a leisurely pace and keep talking about 'everything'. This was more than I could have hoped for at any time over the past day or so and I have to say that I am optimistic about our futures together, even if I have no idea what I am going to do about staying in the US when the time comes. This was something else that I was shelving for now. The time would come when this too could be discussed.

We talked for so long that before we knew it, it had reached eleven thirty and Beth started to make noises about going home. I had decided that I wasn't going to plead with her to stay here, instead I offered to accompany her and stay at her place, but she politely declined.

I'm not sure about how I viewed this. In a way I was offended as a male that I wasn't irresistible and that she was immune to my charms. Also I think I was concerned that so soon after a traumatic experience Beth was going to be alone (and so was I!). But at the same time I think I was glad that we weren't going too far, too fast down a street with no visible exits.

Does that make sense? I hope so... I think it's just one of the characteristics of the new me.

My consolation prize was the pleasure of escorting Beth to her door. It was literally a five minute walk and quite a pleasant one at that, hand in hand, on what was quite a warm night in da Burgh. I won't wax lyrical about birds tweeting and lights sparkling, but it was one of those occasions that you could walk for hours and every passing building seems to be welcoming. I was truly looking at my surroundings with rose tinted spectacles and as long as Beth was beside me nothing could go wrong.

Now you could be critical here and point to one of seventy things that had gone on in the previous days but come on... give me my moment in the sun!

Beth's house wasn't what I expected. For a start it was big. Not big as in the size of the Inn, but a little too big for one person to be rattling around in and I couldn't help but wonder at the memories that must be contained inside the walls. I had pictured her living in a small house with a porch. Painted wood and climbing flowers. Don't ask me where I got the impression, we weren't exactly on Cape Cod here. Instead I was face to face with a two storey stone built detached house, with a small garden at the side and a smaller one at the front. The gardens were separated from the roadside and next door by a wall just the right size for perching on without sitting down. The presence of a tree in the side garden was welcoming as its branches hung over the wall, making a curved edge to the abundance of straight lines. Everything about the place said 'well-off professional family'. I wondered how Beth found time to keep up to the garden and clean a house of this size, as well as her studies, the Inn and her bar job. Maybe this family just bred workers? All of the evidence so far would point to them being brought up to understand the value of hard labour and the fruits that were possible from it. I briefly considered how she would deal with it when she realised that she was dating a lazy English slob? Another bridge to cross at some stage…

She made it clear that I wasn't going to be coming in for a nightcap, despite my hints and I found myself troubled with thoughts of Beth still sleeping in her old bedroom and her parent's room being almost preserved, like a room at Graceland. I hoped that I was wrong and that this wasn't the reason that she didn't want me to see the inside, but I had a very strong feeling that I wasn't far off the mark.

I contented myself with a long lingering goodnight kiss on the doorstep and looked forward to the trials and tribulations of our future together.

I waited at the garden wall for Beth to close and lock the door behind her then I turned back towards the Inn, smiling like any other sixteen year old after walking his young beau home for the first time.

When I reached the front of the Inn, I could see the lights from Stevie's windows and hear the music playing. We had moved on to Tom Petty now.

At that moment something switched inside of me and I found myself suddenly alert and cautious. This could have simply come from singing along to 'American Girl' before my arrival in Akron, but there had been a very definite change in the air and as I opened the front door to the Inn I hung back before entering.

I was aware that up until this point, the Inn had been almost a place of sanctuary to me, somewhere that I had been relieved to be.

The mood had altered. It was like there was a presence here that was uninvited, like something out of a horror film, but it was there. I wasn't imagining it.

I realise that with what I had faced in the last week, anyone would sympathise with me getting the willies here, but I'd also like to think that my experiences had heightened my sense of awareness. Perhaps I was more able to pick up on things?

Perhaps I'm talking bollocks? But I wasn't taking any chances.

Nobody was in the entrance hall that was for sure. All of the lights were on, as they had been when I had left. I stuck my head into the back office and turned off the light in there shutting the door on my way out. If I had to go around the whole building eliminating rooms, so be it, but I had a hunch that eventually I would come across one with the 3 bears in it.

Next I headed for the kitchen, which was also lit. I guessed that Stevie would be coming down here to check on things before he turned in for the night, so I wasn't worried about this. The only sounds that I could hear were from the top floor and were coming down the main stairs at me, as well as from the back of the kitchen, where the other staircase was.

Of course! I could bypass the other rooms and go direct to Stevie's room from here then we could check for intruders together. Strength in numbers!

I paused for a moment to consider this. Maybe Stevie would think I had lost my mind? No sense in involving him if this was just me reacting to my trials. But what if he was in trouble? If I could use the back stairs, so could the intruder!

I looked into the kitchen from the hallway, but couldn't see anything out of the ordinary. I edged closer to the open doorway keeping my eyes peeled for any movement, but saw nothing. Finally when I was almost in full view of the door I burst into the centre of the room and did a complete 360 degree turn whilst stood in some kind of defensive crouch. The kind that you would see on Charlie's Angels.

I'm quite sure that anybody who had been lying in wait would have been perfectly able to break through my fortress of courage and simply kick me over, but the manoeuvre made me feel safer for some reason.

All irrelevant though, as there was nobody here.

The door to the back stairs was closed. I grabbed the handle and turned. It was locked! This wasn't good. I hadn't known him to lock it before. I don't suppose that I'd ever tried it before, but it did seem odd that he would lock it, when the front door to the Inn was constantly unlocked and the alarm system was hardly ever in use.

I tried it again, just to be sure. No… idiot… It was definitely locked! Shit!

I checked the downstairs bathroom. It was empty, as was the dining room, so I shut all the downstairs doors and, the ground floor checked, began to climb the stairs… slowly.

I knew that all of the rooms which were taken would be locked until their occupants got back from their breaks and the one empty room was kept locked anyway.

This left my room and the top floor: Stevie's apartment, as the only two rooms which could be accessed without vandalism.

My room was nearer, so logic dictated that my search would begin there. I was at the top of the stone staircase now, peering up and down the hallways. They ran in an 'L' shape, one leg heading off to my left, and one which ran straight in front of me. The lights weren't on up here, but it wasn't too dark that I couldn't see that there was nobody about.

Again, I wanted to believe that I was wrong, that I was being paranoid, but I knew that I wasn't. I was more certain now than when I had first got back.

My bedroom door up ahead on the right was ajar. The darkness behind it punctured by my bedside lamp, which was very weak and had given Beth and I such a romantic setting earlier. Now it was throwing shadows around the door, into the corridor and looked anything but that. I walked slowly down towards the doorway, careful to keep an eye on it, in case someone in a hockey mask should leap out at me.

I realised that the noise from above was loud enough that I didn't need to be creeping about, as no potential murderer hiding behind my bedroom door would be able to hear my Nikes on carpet above the sound of Tom Petty. But at the exact moment that I reached the end of the hallway and my bedroom door, the song playing in Stevie' apartment above me finished abruptly, leaving the inn in total silence.

The silence took me right back to lying on the floor at the Gund Arena, the same feeling of expectation, knowing that something was about to happen and having no control over it.

I had to fight myself to snap out of it. For the moment I stood outside my bedroom door, not daring to breathe. I did have control here! I was the offense, not the defense. I had the advantage of surprise on my side.

As the opening chords of 'Mary Jane's Last Dance' rang out, I held my breath, as if I was diving off a boat into unknown waters, flung the door back and strode into the room keeping my back to the wall, and facing the bed.

The half light which wasn't from my bedside lamp, as I had suspected, but from the bathroom revealed the figure of a man sat waiting patiently on my bed. I flicked on the light switch, reaching out without averting my gaze. Nothing happened.

"I removed the bulb," said the voice casually, as the figure moved to stand up. And as he stepped towards me and his face passed through the light shining from the bathroom I realised that it was none other than our friend Lieutenant Saxton.

THIRTY THREE

I tried to step back, but I was already up against the wall. Saxton walked casually towards me, like he had all the time in the world and I looked at the open door. Surely I could make a run for it if I moved now. He anticipated this and placed his foot against the bottom of the door, pushing it shut.

My instinct was to move away from him, whilst knowing fully that I was moving away from my point of escape, unless I was willing to leap out of a window, which I most certainly wasn't – yet. I crossed the room, passing the window and stood beside my bed facing back at him.

I was starting to get used to these situations. They were becoming almost commonplace and I was finding that I was adapting to thinking on my feet at the required moment.

Now plainly I was aware that Saxton was a trained police Lieutenant and in the line of duty had surely been thrown into tense situations many times. Indeed I was sure that he had been trained to handle them, but I felt that, having outwitted Donnie Novitski in similar circumstances, I was no longer an amateur. I wasn't going to fold, or back down and if I was about to lose my life, I was sure as dammit going to find out what the hell was going on and get all the answers to my questions if it was the last thing that I did.

"What are *you* doing here?" I demanded.

Saxton leant back against the wall and chuckled.

"I wanted to see how you were holding up. You've been a busy boy since you first got here and seemed a bit out of sorts last night, so I thought I'd better come down and check up on you."

"Great. You guys make house calls in the dead of night now do you? Breaking in and making yourself comfortable is part of the training, huh?"

"The door was unlocked. I called out hello, but nobody answered, so I figured that I'd wait until you got back from walking your lady friend home. I hope you don't mind?"

He didn't seem to be too outwitted thus far and I wondered if the mention of my lady friend was a deliberate thing. A veiled warning maybe?

The music was still playing away upstairs. I hoped that Stevie was ok. I had no way of knowing just how long this guy had been in the house. I hadn't seen Stevie since earlier this evening and I realised that he could have been murdered before I left with Beth. But that would mean that Saxton changed the music and he wasn't the Tom Petty type. Plus I wasn't going to give Saxton the satisfaction of showing that I was concerned. If he thought he was scaring me with his tactics, he might well be right, but he was going to have to try very hard if he wanted me to display any emotion. I was going to throw a few pitches at him and see what he hit back.

"So why did you kill Carrie-Ann?" I asked him, getting right down to it.

"I didn't," he replied, with considerable calm. "That was down to that knucklehead Schulman. Most regrettable. He was supposed to be finding out where the money was and got carried away with all the excitement," he said.

"Like he did with her Aunt?" I fished.

"Hey, you're good, you know that? You should be on the force! Yeah. Exactly like he did with her Aunt. I knew the guy wasn't going to be Mr.Reliable, but he was the tool that I needed to get what I wanted."

Well that solved the murders anyway. Saxton seemed happy with the space between us and the fact that he was controlling the exit. He was so at ease with everything that this was obviously not the first time he had stepped outside the law. As he stood, leant with one shoulder up against the wall next to the door, he could have been chatting in a local bar, or at a party.

My eyes had adjusted to the light a little now and I found myself marvelling at how I'd not noticed that he was so short. Not a pygmy, don't get me wrong, but if there was a minimum height for the police out here, then he must have been it. He was certainly more than a head height smaller than I am. I was sure that he more than compensated for this in some kind of boxing skills or karate, but it still gave me a feeling that I had the edge. I couldn't tell how old he was, but my previous memory of him was that he looked 'older', maybe ready for retirement and looking for his last payoff?

"So the Novitskis were another 'tool' to get what you wanted and then you decided to blow them away, conveniently leaving you with the money?"

"No, I was never working with the Novitski's. I may have thrown them a few crumbs when the case was looking lost and I needed a few stones turning over. But you gotta understand time was of the essence." He paused and checked his pockets, looking for something. A gun? A knife? Then he continued, "I couldn't risk Schulman getting excited and killing anybody else, especially not in another city. The last thing I wanted was an intercity tie up, especially with a city like Pittsburgh." He stood up straight now, gesturing in a sweeping arm movement. That must have been him referring to Pittsburgh. Then he put a hand, almost absent-mindedly into his inside pocket, still searching for something, as he carried on with his explanation, "I wouldn't be able to control it all here. So I released a little info through the right channels and it got you running to Akron where that was possible. Clever huh?"

He was bragging now. Trying to show me just what a master of crime he was.

This was all leading to the scene where I was killed. I knew too much now, it was hardly likely that he was going to trust me to be quiet, or escort me to my gate at the airport.

Saxton hadn't mentioned the money yet and presumably that is what he had come for, unless he was just here to silence us. But how could he know that there was any money? Was he gambling here? He must have planned all along to walk away with everything and he had lost it all when Cleveland police got involved.

I hadn't been able to ruffle him at all, even with direct questions and was running out of ideas. I couldn't get out of the room unless I was willing to take him on. I didn't have a phone and the music upstairs was so loud that Stevie wouldn't be able to hear me, if he hadn't already been killed. I decided it was worth trying to antagonise him a little more. If nothing else, at least it may prolong the exchange until I saw a way out of here.

"So you didn't answer my question… What are you doing here? Are we really that dangerous to you? Did you think we'd start asking questions?"

He glanced nonchalantly at me and finally pulled something from the inside of his jacket. "I don't care to be honest. You think you could cause ME problems up in Akron? I don't think so."

I couldn't tell what it was he had in his hand, but he was giving it a clean now, rolling it on his jacket sleeve. It seemed to be black and cylindrical in shape, like a small torch?

"So you're just pissed because after all of this work, your payday has gone to the Cleveland PD? Won't they share it with you?" I asked.

He was reaching behind his back now, underneath his jacket and when he pulled out a gun I realised that the cylindrical object was a silencer. What did that mean? I detached myself from my predicament and thought about this. Was Stevie still alive? Was Saxton trying to keep the noise down here? Maybe if he killed the out of town English boy it wouldn't be such a big deal as if he killed a local boy?

He interrupted my thoughts. "I know that there was money in the holdall and that you have it. Schulman was at the storage place, he watched your girlfriend take the bag. I'm going to ask you where it is and if you don't tell me I'm going to kill you. Then I'm going to kill your friend upstairs. Anybody could have broken in here and murdered you two in a robbery. It happens."

It was all so 'matter of fact'. So much so, that I had trouble believing that it was all happening. I certainly didn't feel scared. Not like I had done in previous encounters. Maybe I was becoming battle hardened? Getting used to it all? Had one gunfight turned me into a cold ruthless professional? Hardly… I guess I just didn't believe that it was happening.

I leant back on the wall behind me, as if to demonstrate my new carefree nature and straight away felt something that got my heart beating and my hopes rising.

If you lean on a wall in your house/flat/ apartment and get somebody in another room to close a door you will feel the vibration, but if that door is connected to the same wall that you are up against then you will REALLY feel it. In that split second, as I felt the wall pulsing into my back I realised that directly behind me were the stairs, which led from the kitchen to Stevie's bedroom and that I had felt a door closing. The door in question had to be either Stevie's bedroom, or the kitchen. The music was still playing above me and as I looked over at Saxton, who was carefully threading the silencer onto his gun, I decided to make my move.

I began to swing my right foot, making it appear from the far side of the room that it was in keeping with my relaxed stance and each time that I drew it back I kicked against the wall behind me as hard as I dare. Whilst I engaged in this I continued with my line of questioning, "So, let me get this straight, you don't think that the murder of two guys who were just involved in a gangland shooting the night before is going to look suspicious?"

Saxton smiled back. If he had noticed my ploy, he showed no sign, so I kept swinging my foot. I could only hope that Stevie was inside the passageway at this moment and had not just left it going back into his bedroom, or into the kitchen. It also struck me that this repetitive banging against the wall, while I could be shut in my bedroom with his sister doing God knows what, could cause him to turn the music up, so I tried to vary my beat.

Saxton had finished his preparations now and began his approach.

He ignored my previous question and got right down to it, "So I'll ask you one time… where is the money?"

He was walking very slowly across the room towards me. This reminded me of the closing scene of 'Flash Gordon' when I was a child. You remember? When the drama was stretched out beyond what seemed possible. The laser was inches from his head, creeping towards him and certain death. Then in the next shot it was further away, but still edging nearer to frying his skull. The trouble was, I wasn't Flash Gordon and he was way too small to be the Emperor Ming. Thoughts of Flash Gordon weren't going to save me and Stevie hadn't broken down the door yet, so I had to decide whether he was bluffing, or whether I was going to give up the money.

I didn't think he was bluffing.

In fact, I was sure that he was going to kill both me and Stevie. He'd already told me how he was going to make it look to whoever found us, probably Beth.

I decided that, no matter what, I wasn't going to let that happen. Stevie hadn't heard my foot calls. I was on my own. I was going to have to actually fight with somebody! Well… I'd done just about everything else this week, so maybe it was time I learnt!

Saxton was less than six feet from me now, with the gun raised, pointing at my head, which, given his height, meant that I couldn't see his face for the gun and his hand. It was impossible to read his thoughts.

And him mine.

Now was as good a time as any. As quickly as I could move, I dived underneath his outstretched arm and headfirst into his chest. The surprise of the movement causing his arm to lift high and he released the gun from his grip. Cardinal sin for a cop, surely! This only gave me more reason for optimism. I heard the gun clatter against the wall behind him as he brought his elbow down hard into my back.

As this was happening, the bedroom door was thrown open and light flooded into the room.

The cavalry were here!

I powered forward with fresh impetus and knocking him over, fell on top of him. Saxton tried desperately to wriggle out from underneath me, but I was the heavier of the two of us and I managed to make my weight pay surprisingly easily pinning him to the floor until I heard Stevie's raised voice telling Saxton to "Freeze!"

Saxton quit struggling underneath me and I rolled off of him, onto my back.

Hey, what do you know… I won a fight! Ok… so I needed the Americans to come in at the last minute to help out. Wait why does that sound familiar? Who cares?

When I looked up I saw Stevie pointing the gun directly at the body of Saxton, lying, beaten on the floor next to me.

The adventure really had ended now, or was it just beginning? It's never easy to tell these days.

I placed the call through to Akron homicide and was not exactly flabbergasted to discover that the Internal Affairs people had been onto Saxton for sometime, building evidence against him, quietly waiting to catch him out.

Pittsburgh PD turned up first and kept watch on Saxton while they awaited their colleagues from Ohio. Lieutenant Boyd was the man who came to put the cuffs on Saxton. Saxton made some comments about Boyd's sexuality and questioned his loyalty, but Boyd seemed prepared for this and read him the riot act, telling him how it was important to get 'scum' like him off the streets, so that the public can trust the badge again.

It was all very exciting being a spectator for once and when they had finished taking statements and given their thanks for our help, Stevie and I found ourselves once more seated around the table in the kitchen. I had poured us both a large brandy. We'd earned it.

We clinked glasses, as we'd clinked bottlenecks when we'd first met. I looked him in the eye and saw the same look right back.

I knew that I was going to be friendly with Stevie till the day one of us shuffled off our mortal coil.

I filled him in on Saxton's confessions and it felt like a kind of closure. All the bad guys were dead or in cuffs. Boyd had told us that they'd picked Anthony Woolf up for conspiracy to defraud. We were warned that we may be needed for testimony if it went to court, but it may not come to that.

The important thing out of all of this was… we were rich!

No, that wasn't the important thing… but it seemed to be true! Unless Boyd was going to be showing up in the dead of night tomorrow (or make that tonight), then we seemed to be in the clear.

It was another late night/early morning. My body had no idea what continent we were on, or what day it was. I lay in bed wondering just how sleep would be possible. The clock read 3am. Which meant it was 8am in England. It was almost exactly a week since I had left Rachel a note and driven to Manchester airport. I had left home at about ten past eight.

But that wasn't home anymore.

Despite the tumultuous events of the past seven days I had come out the other side and things seemed much clearer for the first time in my life. I knew that this room wasn't going to be home, but I was certain that wherever home was going to be, it wouldn't be very far from here. I'd found my spiritual home and I'd fought very hard in the process. There was no way that I was going to give it up now, I felt very strongly about that.

As for Beth, well, only time would tell, but I felt very strongly about her too.

I hadn't known what I was looking for when I had begun this journey, but like all great journeys, one has to pass tests of courage and strength, to prove one's worth. Sometimes these tests appear greater than ones own capabilities and many a knight will fall by the wayside. I used to be like that, I thought. Backing out gracefully in the face of adversity.
I had gone through dramatic changes on my journey.

I fell asleep looking forward to the promise at the end of every legend… that the champion gets the girl and lives happily ever after.

www.ingramcontent.com/pod-product-compliance
Lightning Source LLC
Chambersburg PA
CBHW071856020726
47502CB00003B/780